Acephalous

/āˈsefələs/ A-ceph-a-lous
(adj.) Lacking a head; having no leader or chief.

Book 1

Amanda Marsico

Red Ink Enthusiast™

Published by Red Ink Enthusiast™
Murrells Inlet, South Carolina, U.S.A.

ISBN: 978-0-9984209-1-2

First Edition

DEDICATION

To everyone who has been on the receiving end of this phrase:
"I had the weirdest dream last night,"
And to all the dreamers, too.

ACKNOWLEDGEMENTS

A million "Thank You-s" to my husband would not be enough. Good thing I have a lifetime. Thank you for reading countless variations of this book when you could have been playing Zelda, for providing edits and insightful critiques after you had already worked a full day, and for filling in the gaps of my computer literacy while I attempted to create the cover on my own.

Thank you to my mom, who thought even the first draft was great, and to my generous friends: Dave, Kristina, Mark, Scott, Karen, Amy, Kelly, Sam, Chelsea, Missy, Mike, Rachel, Laura, and Frances, all who volunteered to read test versions of this story in the year leading up to publication. Before your feedback, this book did not exist.

Thank you to my "way-back-when" friends who sat with me around cafeteria tables, in bedrooms on inflatable furniture, in sticky booths at the skate rink, on beds with phones until the sun came up and listened while I turned the nightmare that inspired this book into a scene, and a scene into a story. Because of your friendship, bad dreams became perfect opportunities.

Prologue

"If we find ourselves with a desire that nothing in this world can satisfy, the most probable explanation is that we were made for another world."
C.S. Lewis

When Breena slept, her heart, mind, and soul sought places that held no memories or expectations. An all-encompassing presence of comfort guided her time spent wandering in the illusory worlds of sleep. Upon waking, she always felt thankful for the respite, never questioning the origin of that guiding presence. Every day, she stretched her arms from under the cover of dreams and woke with thanks to the gentle figure she'd seen in the distance of the fading images. Breena assumed it was God.

Chapter 1

Breena bumped her head getting out of the taxi. She swallowed a yelp and grimaced, red-faced, as the driver, who she'd nicknamed Lurch due to his stature, held the door open for her. She steadied herself on the cobbled sidewalk, and Lurch lumbered around to the back of the vehicle to unload the trunk of her large rolling suitcase, duffle bag, and cello. When she pulled her eyes away from the wisteria-covered walls of the old walk-up apartment building, Lurch was again at her side. Her bags waited on the ground beside his patent-leather feet, and he was waiting, hand outstretched.

Breena's face warmed. "Right, tip." She held her finger up and dug through her bottomless purse with her other hand, past tangled headphones, crumpled boarding passes, and empty gum wrappers for the wad of cash she had exchanged upon arriving at London Heathrow Airport. *I have no idea how much to give this guy.* She leafed past the slip of paper where her mom, Lexa, had written the deadbolt PIN to the rental flat, and seized a £20 note. She smiled tightly at him as she handed the money over, hoping to see some sort of reaction to the amount. Nothing passed across his stoic face. Instead, he nodded slightly, said thank you, and opened his door.

She called after him as the door swung shut. "Thanks again." Turning to the apartment, she smiled broadly. *Mom did good. Surprising.* Breena, determined to make it inside in one trip, grabbed all her luggage and waddled to the stoop, hauled her rolling bag up the two small steps behind her, and dropped everything at the door, including her cello which she accidentally let go of with the rest. She punched in the lock code after another search through her enormous purse.

The lock beeped and the bolt whirred inside the door. She tried the knob. *I hope it's as good on the inside as it is on the outside.* Breena pushed into the foyer of the spacious walk-up leaving the door open and her belongings outside. An urge to giggle welled up inside her and bubbled out as she explored. "This place!" *I could sleep on that couch forever. And the kitchen? Who am I going to cook for with all that space?* She moved down the hall and opened a door. *Bathroom.* "Marble everything." A cool breeze blew through the front door and down the hall. Breena glanced back to make sure her bags were still there then continued to the closed door at the end of the apartment.

This could be in a magazine. She flopped across the king-sized bed, careful not to kick the glass lamp on the nightstand. "Nnn, these sheets. Egyptian, maybe." Breena swayed her arms and legs like she was making a snow angel. Another moment passed and she sprang up, the excitement overpowering her exhaustion. She kicked off her shoes, crinkled her toes in the plush carpet a couple of times, and padded to the corner of the room. "Another bathroom!" She flipped the switch on the wall. "Two toilets?" She walked in. "Oh. Bidet." She inspected the components. It had a little drain stopper, like a tub, among other features. "Do you fill it then swish around in it? Eh, not like I'm going to use it anyway." Her attention shifted. "A walk-in shower." Breena peeked around the half-wall. "And double shower heads!"

Satisfied with her inspection, she brought her stuff inside the flat and closed the door. The lethargy of travel washed over her. After leaning her cello case in the corner, she hit the "ARM" button on the lock keypad. "Those can stay. I'll unpack tomorrow." Abandoning her largest baggage, she dragged her purse to the bedroom. Sitting on the edge of the bed, she poured the contents of the bag beside her. A tin can of breath mints landed on top, and she popped it open revealing her stash of prescription pills.

"One for groggy, two for slow, three for darkness, and four to go... to heaven." She had made up the rhyme two years ago when her friend Jet nearly died of an overdose of Ativan. She wasn't exactly sure how many he had taken, and she knew it had to have been more than four, but three was always enough for her purposes and the rhyme helped with the little bit of accountability she tried to maintain. Breena said it to herself every night before she used the sleep meds and pain pills she stole from her mom, her own little version of a cautionary bedtime story.

Before leaving Michigan, she had put in one of Lexa's refills and picked it up from the pharmacy "for her mom." The pharmacists in Grayling were great about handing over Lexa's medications. They were happy Lexa had such a helpful daughter that ran errands for her disabled mom. And, originally, that's exactly what Breena's involvement encompassed. Once the pleasant, recurring dreams she'd had since childhood started coming as nightmares, though, the weekly pharmacy runs presented themselves as easy access to a powerful solution, and Lexa rarely wanted to take the pills that weren't mandatory for her mobility, so she didn't notice their dwindling quantities.

In the apartment, Breena slugged back one pill and her guilt for stealing them with the water she'd kept in her purse on the plane. She usually went for three pills, or darkness, pushing her body to sleep like the dead and still wake up when it was over, but Breena knew she needed to stretch her supply if she was going to make it through the summer without a trusting pharmacist. There were enough for her to take one a day, but she was afraid to jump right in to taking less than she was accustomed to, both for the dreams that might start creeping back up, and the physical effects of withdrawal. A shiver raised bumps over her arms as she thought of the hallucinations she'd had last time around.

She stared at the ceiling, waiting for the slow relaxation to spread through her extremities and then her mind. It never came, and she was thankful she had a week in London before the symphony intensive, her whole reason for the trip, began. That was one week to fight through the headaches, nausea, nightmares, and restlessness of unfulfilled dependency. Sleep was slow to come, and it didn't help that the midday-sun of London's plus five time difference streamed through her bedroom window. Eventually, she drifted off.

The dream Breena took medication to avoid started again where it always did, in a grassy circle in the middle of a bright evergreen forest. In the distance, beside a hulking tree, a silhouetted figure stood looking back at her. Like a magnet, she wanted to go to him. The blades of grass rustled against her bare feet as she walked.

The closer she drew the more at ease she felt. In the midst of her walk, Breena gained lucidity in her dream world and thought to herself that this must be what dying felt like, that the figure calling to her with radiating warmth must be God. Breena shuffled to the edge of the grass and paused to scratch at the places where it tickled her ankles.

Looking down on herself, Breena noted that this is where the dream made its divergence into a nightmare. The reverie used to continue as a peaceful walk through the woods with the silhouette, who felt as familiar to her as air or water even though they never introduced themselves. Now, it proceeded in darkness. As her finger grazed the grass, its soft flexibility went rigid and sliced her fingers open. Breena jumped from her spot and looked around her. The sky was the black of an incoming storm. All of the plants had changed into blood-soaked spikes prying up from the ground at odd angles. Amidst them was the figure, not much more than a shadow, and his allure was just as powerful, even though it emanated danger. Despite the lucid pleas to her astral self, she could not wake up, and Breena watched her spirit weave through the field of spikes and fall into the tight embrace of the smoldering figure. When the pair looked at each other, the ground opened up and swallowed them down through a miasmic, twisting tunnel which delivered them onto a throne in the pit of hell.

Breena watched herself smile amidst the surroundings, but consciousness allowed the grotesque scenery, burning corpses and her own melting flesh, to shock the spirit back into her body. She startled awake at 11:00pm that evening, sweaty and shaking.

****

She scrubbed at her face. *It's like the insides of my eyelids are made of sandpaper.* "I guess one pill wasn't enough." Breena threw a hand out to her side, expecting it to land on a comforting pile of fur, but she remembered where she was as she sat up to look for her absent cat. "Right."

In Grayling, Michigan, Breena's two best friends, Jordan and Lilly, held a camera out in front of them and snapped three pictures in quick succession.

"One of them has to be good." Jordan hopped down from the boulder where they posed.

"Not if your hand was shaking. I told you we should have used my phone. It has an auto-stabilizer to keep the pictures from coming out blurry." Lilly sat down on the rock and rolled to her stomach. She slid off the perch feet first, then belly, then chest.

Jordan watched the awkward maneuver, mentally comparing Breena and Lilly. One graceful and unconcerned with the world around her, the other clumsy and overly attentive.

Breena moved through life with ease that masked her cynical outlook, resting on her talents to speak so she didn't have to. She got lost in her head so deeply and so often people had stopped trying to hang out with her by the end of middle school, although she was completely cool with that. Plus, it relieved her of some of the more shameless flirting from guys (and girls) whose existence she hardly noticed. Mostly self-absorbed, but adored.

Lilly, as evidenced by her ongoing dismount, always struggled at everything despite her laser-focus and insightful mind. She had what Jordan called "emotional intelligence." She saw what others didn't or simply couldn't relate to. Her wealth of knowledge instigated new fears and new compulsions all the time, though. Her feverish study of criminal events, for example, led to her ability to quote many of the Michigan State Penal Codes, including sections on Mayhem, Poisoning, and Fortune Telling which, she admitted, was useless since it had been repealed in 1993.

Jordan passed the camera over when Lilly returned to an upright position. She dusted herself and snatched the camera from him. "Ok, so these turned out nice, after all. Breena will like it."

"I hope she sends us some pictures of London. I wish I could be there and see it all myself. I can't believe she left without telling me."

"Jordan, you *know* why she left without telling you."

"Do I?"

"Oh, I think you do. Something about needing some space from your constant love confessions. Sound familiar?"

Jordan kicked a rock across the walking trail. "I was just trying to be supportive."

Lilly passed the camera back to Jordan and pulled a small bottle of hand sanitizer from her back pocket. She squeezed a drop of the pink berry liquid out and rubbed it in as she spoke. "How is it supporting *her* to tell her you're jealous, and of her music, no less? You're not even in competition with another human. You're competing against her *dream*. That made her feel very smothered, like her best friend was asking her to choose between him or her future."

Jordan stared at his shoes. "I didn't say I was jealous, and that's not what I wanted her to do. I just wanted her to know and to include me in that future. It doesn't have to be either-or. I've had years of being her friend to figure out that she's the girl I want. You should have heard her reasons for turning me down, though, like she was trying to convince me she isn't the one. She kept saying stuff like, 'I don't know why you'd want me,' and, 'I'm not worth the risk of hurting our friendship.' I love her, but she infuriates me as much as she owns me. Why doesn't she know how great she is?" Jordan shoved his hands in his pockets.

"Natural talent oozing out every pore, and she can't see what all the fuss is about. What she does is her 'normal.' She doesn't think she deserves praise for something that comes so easy to her. And she couldn't return your feelings. Letting you down made her feel like a failure. The way she sees it, it's just another thing in the list of ways she isn't what you think she is. She's caught in a vicious cycle of perceived inadequacies. She doesn't want to disappoint you, but being around you forces her to look her failure in the eyes. She didn't say bye because she couldn't face you."

Jordan sighed.

"Even so, you meant well, and she knows that."

"I feel like I need to explain myself to her, let her know I don't need or expect anything to change, but she won't answer any of my calls. I should go to London and tell her in person."

"What did I just tell you about her having to look you in the eyes?"

Chapter 2

Cool metal raised goosebumps on Breena's legs as she climbed onto a barstool at the kitchen island. She looked down at her phone. "Man, I was supposed to call Mom when I settled in." Breena played Lexa's voicemail.

"Hey, Honey. I bet you're having a great time exploring London. Just checking on you to make sure you got to your apartment Ok. Haven't heard from you in a while. I'm sure you're having a blast. But, it has been eighteen hours since you left. No, no, you're having a great time. Ok. Well, call me soon, Bug."

Breena rolled her eyes at the nickname. As a child, Lexa called her "Love Bug." By the end of middle school, it had been shortened to "Bug," to quell Breena's embarrassment.

"I'll never convince her to cut it completely." She shook her head at the thought and continued shaking it in disbelief as she scrolled through her unread text messages.

"Forty-two from Jordan alone? I don't have the energy for this." Breena dropped the phone on the glossy countertop and stared into the night outside the front window. The darkness shifted almost imperceptibly, and she rubbed at the new chill bumps tingling up her arms. *Probably just someone walking up to their apartment. I'll have to meet the neighbors.* In the background, the television murmured, but Breena didn't feel like it was enough noise to fill the empty apartment with life or to mask the crawling feeling that someone was watching her. *Or is that the crawl of withdrawal already?* The light outside shifted again.

"What the heck was that?" She seized her phone and stood from the stool. A pinching sensation made Breena glance down at her thumb. She had picked the skin away from her fingernail again, a nervous habit Jordan always fussed about. Pressing the bead of red to her mouth, she dialed her mom. No answer. She dialed Lilly. No answer. "Well, I'm not calling Jordan."

Breena tiptoed to the drawer beside the sink and slid it open. It squeaked like doors do in haunted house movies. "Shh!" She pulled out the longest knife and shushed the drawer once more as it cried about being closed. *I have a very special set of skills—* Breena approached the window, knife in hand, mentally reciting Liam Neeson's iconic lines from the movie *Taken,* and whose urgency and fear she felt she very clearly understood, now.

Leaning over the back of the couch with the knife behind her back, Breena discovered nothing. *Ok. Ok, yeah. Nothing there. Everything's fine. Fiiine. Now, the door.* In the corner, with her back to her cello, she swung the door open with haste and yelled, "Haa!" into the sleepy street. A cat meowed in the distance. After a few seconds waiting in the doorway, she stepped out and glanced around the corner of the apartment to the one beside hers, which was set back from the side walk. The flat was dark except for the blue flickering light through the gauzy curtains of their living room.

In the silence, the blaring ring of her cellphone triggered a shriek. She ran back inside, slamming the door behind her. She answered without looking at the number.

"Hey! You answered."

"Oh, Jordan. Hey."

"Why do you sound out of breath?"

"Huh? Oh. Nothing. It's stupid."

"Kay. So how's London?"

"Haven't really seen it yet. I took a nap when I got here. Now it's late, so I'll have to wait 'til morning to do anything."

"What time is it there?"

"Um, 12:30, I think." She pulled the phone away from her ear. "Yeah, 12:34."

"Cool. Well, I know we can't stay on all night, that would be expensive and with the time difference—"

"Yeah."

"Yeah. But if you don't have anything else going on, we could video chat."

Ew, glad he couldn't see that face I just made. "Maybe tomorrow. I'm still settling in."

"Right."

No one said anything for the most eternal second Breena ever experienced. "Well, I'll let you go, Jordan."

"But *I* called *you.*"

"Talk to you tomorrow. Night."

****

In his room, Jordan picked up the half-read book on his nightstand and flipped to a dog-eared page. "Screw it." He slapped it back down on the small table and threw himself out of bed. He caught up his running shoes on the way into the hall and called out into the vast house. "I'm going to the gym."

His mom poked her head into the hallway from the library where she had no doubt been smoking one of his dad's, Arthur's, Pro Maduro cigars in front of the open bay window. "Stop shouting. Your father's on a conference call." She disappeared back into the stuffy room and slammed the door. Jordan tromped down the stairs as loudly as he could.

He pounded across the treadmill willing his anxieties to leave through his feet and squash under his heels. *She shouldn't be alone in a new place. What if Breena meets someone while she's in London? I have to go see her.*

Beside him, a familiar voice broke into his sweaty wallowing. "Can't say I'm surprised to see you here."

Jordan looked over. "Hey, man." Breena's brother, Ari, started a slow jog.

"You talked to Breena, yet?"

"Once."

"And now you're here."

"As are you."

"You don't know what to do with yourself when she's gone, do you?"

"That obvious?"

"Man, stop pining and come out with me Friday night. "

"We can find you someone to pass the time."

"Thanks, but I think I'll pass."

"Whatever, man. Have fun getting frozen out all summer."

Jordan rolled his eyes and put his headphones back on. The treadmill had started its cool-down timer, and after five minutes, Jordan rode the belt to the end of the platform and stepped off. In the locker room, Jordan let his wet shirt hit the floor with a satisfying slap, the moisture like proof of another nagging thought evaded. But, he hadn't outrun anything this time, and another problem approached him as he unlaced his shoes.

"Hey, Jordan."

He looked up from his shoes. "Chet."

"You seen Breena around?"

"She's away for the summer." Jordan dropped his socks into his duffle.

"Damn. Well, if you talk to her, let her know I have something for her." Chet made a rude gesture closer to Jordan's face than anyone should have had to endure.

"I will not."

Chet laughed and sauntered out of the locker room.

****

Breena sat wide-eyed, but uninterested in front of the TV. "I really shouldn't have taken that nap. I should've gone to the grocery store." On her phone, she looked for nearby restaurants that were open at 2:00am. "Jackpot." Next, she looked up London's laws on carrying a knife.

"'It is illegal to carry a knife without good reason, unless it is a knife with a folding blade three inches long or less. A court will decide if you have a good reason for carrying the knife if you are charged with carrying it illegally.' Ok, then. No knife."

Breena reconsidered going out after her scare. "How am I supposed to protect myself?" Lilly's cautious voice popped in her head telling her not to go out at all. "But I'm so hungry." There hadn't been any creepy silhouettes or flickers of light in two hours, so

Breena swallowed her concern and got dressed for dinner. *Or is it breakfast, now?*

She wandered down the sidewalk, phone held in front of her to watch the navigation until she could see the café in the distance, the only place with lights still on. Inside, she stared at the menu and bakery cases for a few minutes. It wasn't the kind of place to go for a meal, so Breena ordered a variety of pastries to fill up on. A fleeting expression passed over the cashier's face. *She must think I'm high, out at this time ordering enough for a family.* Breena plopped in a wing chair by the window.

Cozy. Empty, but surprisingly not sketchy even at this hour. No reason to be afraid. This town feels safe enough. The food arrived and, with a lack of propriety she knew the English would condemn, Breena inhaled a cheese danish and a scone before her chamomile tea had finished steeping. She hated the stuff but ordered it because she'd heard it improved sleep. Holding the cup to her lips, she blew on the changing water and admired the black and white photos and old books on the shelves across from her. *This will be my little spot, I guess.*

The stoplight outside of the café window cycled through its colors though no one was driving. She absently watched it change and thought back to the last day of school.

****

"Why now, Jordan, if you've always felt this way?"

"Because I can't listen to you talk and talk and talk about how you can't wait to get on with your life, get out of this town, move somewhere far away where people don't know you."

"I didn't know it bothered you so much. I thought you'd be excited for me. I've always wanted to leave. I thought you knew."

"Yeah, I did, but how do you think it makes me feel that your biggest goal is to get away from me? I can't take it anymore. I don't want you to run off after graduation and never come back. Thinking I might only have another year with you is the worst."

"You're taking it too personally. My goal isn't to get away from *you*, but to go in general. You're not the cause, but it's selfish to think you're enough of a reason to stay, too. And I know that sounds harsh. I don't know what else to tell you. My dreams are pretty persistent, but I'd rather not have to choose. Won't you always be there?"

"Only if it feels like you want me to be there. And it doesn't."

Breena winced. "I'm sorry I come across that way."

"What a non-apology. You're not actually denying that you don't imagine me in your future. Look, I'm not asking you to choose, but I can't help but feel like you're going to anyway. I'm not in your dreams." He spun away and went toward his car.

"Jordan, I—"

He threw a hand up and kept walking. Breena slumped into her car and sat for a minute, resting her elbows on the steering wheel of her ruby junker, head in hands.

****

Still lost in the changing traffic lights, Breena went for another sip of her tea and came up dry, snapping out of her reverie. Breena glanced at her watch. "I've been here an hour? I better go back to the flat." The British slang felt wrong in her mouth. "Don't ever say that again."

A surge of dizziness overcame her when she stood, and her vision flashed. For a split second, the green clearing from her dreams appeared, this time with a shabby cottage in the middle. Someone was talking. "So I wait for you like a lonely house until you will see me again and live in me. Until then my windows ache."

As soon as the verse stopped, the images dissolved. Breena spun around at the touch on her elbow. The cashier was holding her. Breena snatched her arm away. "Why were you quoting Pablo Neruda at me?" The violation of feeling watched passed through her again. She shivered.

"Sorry, ma'am. I asked you if you were alright. You swayed, so I grabbed your arm."

"Oh. Really? I could have sworn I heard—" She finished the rest of her questioning inwardly and thanked the cashier, who had kind eyes and a worried grin. "I'll just wrap these donuts and get out of here."

"I can do that, if you'd like. I'll get some plastic from the kitchen."

"Kay."

The cashier made a face as she turned. "Who the hell is Pablo Neruda?"

Breena shredded the skin on her other thumb while she waited. *Hell of a withdrawal already.* The woman reappeared with Breena's food. Breena stuffed the parcel in her purse and slung it over her shoulder. "Thanks. Sorry I, well. I'm fine. Really. I am. Ok, have a nice night. Sorry, again." Finally out of the door, she gripped her phone like it was life. *Wish this was a can of mace. God, get me home in one piece.*

Breena crossed the street and stumbled over a loose manhole cover. A short chuckle sounded behind her, and she looked over both shoulders. "In your head. Just walk faster, Breena." From the shadows, a young man watched her disappear around the corner and grinned.

Chapter 3

"I saw her."

"Same dream as always?"

"No. Well, yes, she did sleep earlier, but that's not what I mean. I mean I *saw* her. In person." Atlas' heart raced under his ribs. Breena surpassed the expectations he had formed based on their shared dreams—her gold eyes, copper hair, the way she walked through the dark night with purpose, and the easy smile she wore when she didn't realize she had relaxed.

"I thought I told you it wasn't time for that, yet." Tabitha pressed her temples, her long black fingernails leaving rows of red lines the color of her hair.

Atlas crossed the shining wood floor away from Tabitha, rolling his eyes. "She didn't see me."

She trailed after Atlas, knowing her physical closeness would increase her sway over him. "As her chosen, you get no say. You are to be her mate. Nothing more. You'll do this my way." She tried to caress his cheek, to seal in her words with a touch, but he pulled away.

"I understand." Atlas cringed inwardly at the lack of control he had over his reactions, not wanting to give away his disgust and anger, but unable to fully play into her hands. He gave her a tight grin. "I have somewhere to be. You'll show yourself out when you're ready?" Atlas waited to close himself in the bedroom until her heels clicked out of the living room and the front door slammed.

He settled in the middle of his floor, crossing his legs into his lap and resting his hands, palms up, on his knees. After a few still seconds, the walls started to warp and a new scene replaced the décor.

A mother and a young boy played outside of a small cottage. Snow-capped mountains gleamed in the distance. Out of view, a screen door slapped shut. Atlas went rigid, shifting the scene to a more pleasant memory then relaxing again.

Sitting along the bank of a small stream, he dipped his hand into the icy water and focused on the burning sensation of the cold. He marveled at it, just as he had when he was young, pondering the way something cold enough could feel like fire. It had fascinated his young sensibilities, given him something definite to focus his anxious energies, and provided consistent input that proved his illusions could actually change the environment around him. In the background, his mother hummed while clipping flowers for the little window over the kitchen sink. He sighed, desperately missing those peaceful moments, and let the playback fade.

The room returned to normal and Atlas looked down at his hands, which had curled into tight fists. He moved to his bed and sprawled out. Staring at the ceiling, he seethed as the history lesson Tabitha had given him not long after he started working for her played through his head.

Atlas had been wandering France, searching for the spirit of his dead mother, Reine. He was convinced that she was still out there, that he could hold on to whatever might be left of her. After months of bumming a room, or sometimes just a pillow and floor-space, off of the underhanded employers financing his search, he met Tabitha on the metro.

She had watched from the sidelines his whole life, waiting for the right moment to introduce herself and teach him about his heritage. On the day they met, Tabitha approached him with a job offer.

"You ride this train every day. You never look happy. Going to a job you hate?"

"Pretty much."

"I'm sorry. What do you do?"

"I run books for The Artillery."

She waved her hand in the space between them like she was clearing the air of those words. "Terrible, terrible. A noble man like you shouldn't be working for those thugs." She reached out her hand. "I'm Tabitha."

Atlas didn't think anything about the "noble man" comment until a month had passed working as Tabitha's assistant in London.

One evening, she treated him to dinner at her house, part of his compensation she insisted.

"Atlas, now seems like the right time to discuss a serious issue."

Atlas ran cold. "Are you firing me?"

"No, no. Nothing like that. Atlas, I want to talk to you about your parents, about where you came from."

"I already told you. Born in France to a shit-show father and the best mother that ever lived. Then, he murdered her and dragged me to America. We traveled around while he looked for work, then one day he split. Haven't seen him since, and that's fine. I forged my way back into France, and then you found me."

"Actually, Atlas, Reine and Ameri weren't your parents."

Atlas dropped his fork.

"Oh, don't look so alarmed. This is good news. Here, I'll tell you the story. Your mother, her name is Edlyn, she is a noblewoman in the court of Gehenna. That's where you're from, too, but we'll get to that."

"Was there something in your wine? How do you know so much about me?"

"Hush."

"It sounds like you're making stuff up."

"I said *hush*." Something wild flared up behind her eyes.

The expression hit Atlas like a physical blow. He held his breath for a second then pushed back from the table. "Look, I appreciate what you've done for me—the job, the apartment—but I think I'd better go."

"You will not. Sit down." Tabitha waited to see if he'd choose to stay on his own.

Atlas stood, torn between the door and his chair.

"It is best if you obey."

Feeling the sway of her words again, like a hand on his shoulder pushing down, he sat.

"Now, then. Right. Edlyn. She is of noble, but not royal blood, as is, was, your father, Adalberto, long burn his soul. We all reside primarily in Gehenna—" She leaned in conspiratorially. "The humans call it Hell—and that is where you were born. You are part of the gentry class, which means you and all of the other gentry class children are sent to Earth as infants to grow up as humans and learn the harsh realities of this human life."

Atlas clutched at his stomach while Tabitha went on. Despite his immense desire to not believe her, all of the doubts he had about his nature started to make sense. He wanted to believe she was insane, but the origin of his blood resolved the questions of why Ameri had hated him so much, why the man always cursed him and "the wicked gleam in his eye." He always accused Atlas of bending reality. It was just the early appearance of Atlas' unmatured gift, a minor shimmering in the scenery that happened whenever Atlas lied. Ameri railed against Atlas like he sensed Atlas' darkness and hated it because it was a different darkness than his brand of blind rage.

"You've learned your lessons about the human capacity for cruelty and hate. Now, it's time to meet your mate and bring her home, to help fuel that cycle."

"So, you want me to go back with you to Hell so that I can help make the world a worse place. Why would I want to do that, especially after what I've lived through?"

"I've chosen you—well, really, she has chosen you—to assist her in ascension, to take my place as ruler. You're looking at your experiences all wrong. Don't see them as traumas; see them as inspiration for the way you will rule. I know your upbringing seems harsh from a human standpoint, but you are not human, and the existence of people like Ameri is what keeps the universe in balance with the good that's out there. Why do you think Reine was paired with him?"

"You let darkness take her!"

"As it sometimes does. The necessary balance." She practically spit out the last part, clearly resentful of the universe's checks on her power.

"Thanks, but no. Do I have any brothers? Ask one of them."

"You do not have siblings. No one in the gentry has siblings. It is to prevent disputes over who will marry the ascending queen. That will be you."

"Why me?"

"You're the only gentry child who connected with her in her dreams. You are her match."

The sun was rising when Atlas snapped out of his thoughts. "She wants me to fuel chaos? She has no idea what's waiting for her. May you live in interesting times, and may you find what you're looking for."

Breena woke late the next morning, her internal clock wrecked from the jet lag, naps, and early-morning pastry binge. She felt truly rested, though, for the first time in many nights. "No nightmares." She stretched her arms overhead and got in the shower. "I should've hung my wrinkled clothes in here with me." She tried to trap the steam in the bathroom when she was finished and ran down the hall in a towel to get her rolling suitcase. On her way back to the bedroom, she rolled through the kitchen to snatch up a leftover donut. She held it with her teeth until the icing and dough melted in her mouth and the rest of the donut dropped on the floor. Rather than dropping her suitcase behind her, she reached to catch it with the hand that held her towel. As her towel fell away, the sticky ring did too, bouncing off her belly and landing on her foot. She picked it up and blew on it. "That's not going to do anything; it's sticky." She popped it back in her mouth and hurried to the bedroom before it fell again. She ate it in a hurry and got back in the shower to wash the glaze off her stomach.

****

Jordan woke to the slamming of car doors below his window. He pulled the blackout blinds aside and watched his parents leaving the driveway. "What, now?" Downstairs, he found the note from his mother taped to the refrigerator door.

"Merger moved up. Flight to China this morning. Be back in two weeks."

He rolled his eyes. "So typical. 'Hey, Jordan, do you want to go to China during summer vacation?' 'Oh, no thanks, Mom. That wouldn't be a wonderful way to spend my break.'" Heat rose up his neck. "It's too early to be mad." He scrubbed his eyes and hurried back to his room to check his savings account. Landscaping, well, not so much designing the landscaping as doing the grunt work for the old company suits for the last two years, had paid off. "That's enough for a ticket." Three hours later, he was sitting in a terminal waiting for his 9:30am flight to London. He flipped through the boarding passes. "Let's see, so factoring in these layovers, I'll be at Breena's door by 8:00am tomorrow, London time." The call to board came over the speaker. He got in line. "Is this crazy? Eh, too late." While Breena organized her closet through the afternoon, Jordan was London-bound, laying over in Paris for the night before continuing to Heathrow.

****

Breena had a habit of forgetting to eat when she practiced the cello. She lost herself in the narration of her musical stories and the daydreams that took over her reality. As she played, the cottage she'd seen in the café the night before appeared in the living room, and its ring of flowers bloomed on a crescendo. A sweet breeze blew her hair away from her face, and she sung a verse of the previous night's Neruda poem into it.

"I needed the light of your energy, I looked around, devouring hope. I watched the void without you that is like a house, nothing left but tragic windows."

With the poetry, an entire countryside formed in her mind. She stopped playing to take it in. Around the back of the house, a rippling stream bubbled down the hillside and into the distance. She laid her instrument beside it then stepped in.

"Like ice."

On the other bank, a dove perched on a blossoming tree.

"Don't you guys usually live in pairs? Where's your wife?"

The bird looked steadily at her as she approached it.

"You're brave."

It sat, unblinking.

"Or scared stiff." She turned away from the creature and crossed back over the stream. Ignoring her cello, Breena ran around the side of the house where a flimsy screen door let the mountain air into the cottage. Sunlight filtered through the dust, creating a sparkling, ethereal haze in the room.

"No one's been in here in ages." Breena picked up a yellowed desk calendar from the modest kitchen table. "1996? I wasn't even born yet." A short hallway led her into a shabby bedroom, the only one in the house. An outfit hung over the foot of the bed. "What happened to the people who lived here? It's like they weren't planning to go."

A loud burble issued from her stomach, bringing her back to reality. "I have to go to the grocery store before it gets dark." Breena went back for her cello, and it dawned on her that she was just daydreaming. "Don't be stupid, Breena. That's not really your cello." She shook her head to snap out of the imagining, but it didn't budge. She strained her eyes to see through the mountains and trees to her living room. "Wake up!" The yell echoed across the valley. She tried closing her eyes for five seconds and opening them. Nothing changed.

In her chest, the hot flutter of panic set in. "Where am I? Why can't I wake up? No, Breena, you weren't asleep, so you can't wake up." She dunked her head into the icy stream, but the scenery was the same when she emerged. "Help! Anyone. Help me." Breena sat back on her heels and stared into the forest at the other bank. The dove was still there. Watching. Instinct kicked in. Breena knew the dove was there because of her. "Hey, bird!"

It lifted off the branch and flew into the woods.

"Wait." Breena bolted into the dense vegetation after it. Her footfalls crunched across a deep layer of dried leaves and broke through fallen sticks every few steps. *Sounds like a hail of those little, white snaps that pop on the sidewalk.* She would have smiled at one of her favorite memories if her breath wasn't so ragged.

The bird diverged, but the downhill momentum prevented Breena from following the sudden left. Straight ahead, a man appeared in her path. "No, no, no." Breena closed her eyes as she careened right into him. The wind knocked out of her was the strike of a poorly tuned bass drum, a sort of flat "guh" with no projection, the breath springing to life and dying the second it escaped her lungs.

"What a pretty cloud."

Atlas stood over Breena's sprawled body with a hand out. "Are you Ok?"

"Why didn't you move out of the way, stupid?" She took his hand.

Atlas blinked twice. "No thank you?"

"For what?"

"For coming to find you. I heard someone yelling for help."

"But you knocked me down."

"*You* ran in to *me.*"

"Only because you were standing in the middle of the path. Who are you, anyway?"

"First, there is no path. You're in the wilderness, not a campground—"

"You were in *my* path."

"Second, my name is Atlas. Still no thank you? Don't you recognize me?"

Breena squinted her eyes at him and pulled back a step. She sensed a familiarity she couldn't place and, while she absolutely found him attractive, she proceeded with cold caution. "Why would I?"

"Surely you've seen me here before. This is my illusion, after all. You wander into it sometimes."

Ok, Crazy. If this isn't real, why can't I see my kitchen or my sofa? She took another step back. "Right. Well. I should get going."

"What, down this nonexistent path you claim is yours? Aren't you going to let me help you?"

"Nope." Breena spun on her heels and started to walk back the way she'd come. She swished back through the leaves, which weren't nearly as noisy under her slowed footfalls. Her thoughts picked up the slack in volume.

Sure, Breena. You're stuck in a daydream. Sure, your subconscious probably sent him to you to help snap you out of this. But no, you don't stick around long enough for him to help you. No achievement is a success without a struggle, right, Breena? You can't just be happy you've accomplished something easy, and getting help would be too easy, wouldn't it? That's right. You crave the drama, don't you? It means you're not taking handouts and getting praise for stuff you didn't earn. When are you going to start allowing yourself little wins?

Breena exited the woods and sat by her cello. "I'm never going to."

Chapter 4

Jordan looked down on the Heathrow tarmac as it came to meet the plane. They bounced a few times before setting down and slowing to a steady taxi toward the terminal. He leaned over to the old man beside him. "I'm here to see a girl."

"Ye telt her anent it, ay?"

Jordan hoped he masked his startled expression. He hadn't expected the thick Scots accent. "Excuse me?"

"Ach. She ken?"

Jordan smiled as wide as he could without looking disingenuous. "Uh, it's a surprise. I kind of surprised myself, too. Just hopped on a plane yesterday morning. Spur of the moment."

The man nodded, so Jordan figured he responded appropriately.

****

Breena woke up in the corner of her living room on the floor between her couch and the lamp. She blinked away the sandpaper in her eyes, staring into the beams of light coming through the parted curtains. "It's morning. 11:00am? I don't even remember falling asleep." She raked through her hair with her fingers. "Why is my hair wet?" Breena shifted to stand. "Is that mud?" She picked at the dried clay on the side of her foot and it flaked to the floor. "What?"

Breena scrolled through her phone as she stood, playing investigative reporter to an empty room. "Sources suggest no signs of foul play. Unfortunately, sources are sparse and fail to explain just what happened here last night. Back to you, Lilly." A sad smile passed across her face at the thought of her friend. They often played reporters as children, reporting the day's events and even turning the game into a study tool by asking one another questions and reporting on their textbooks' intel.

"I could really use you right now, Lil. I'm sure you'd have some theory." She looked back at her phone. "Eh, still too early to call where you are. I need a shower. And a coffee. And I've *really* got to get some groceries."

Holding her growling stomach, Breena brought the cello back into the kitchen, the last place she remembered being, to store it. "It's been a solitary three days, hasn't it, Spud." She glanced over her shoulder to where her cat normally sat, an inch away from her heels. "Right. And you're not here, either." Breena stared into the well-appointed, but essentially empty room, overwhelmed by the solitude. "Ok. Shower, then interaction with humans."

A block away and heading toward Breena's stoop, Jordan struggled down the sidewalk carrying an immense flattened box and a ridiculous premade bow, the kind shown on top of cars in commercials. The wind gusts funneling down crossroads and alleys turned Jordan's box into a sail of sorts, and he was forced to turn sideways into the wind for aerodynamics. Walkers stared as he grapevined his way up the block and onto Breena's step.

Still fighting the wind, he popped the box into formation. Grumbling to himself, he devised the next step of his plan. "Ok, so I'll have to put this bow... on top first. Then I'll ring the bell and drop the box over my head real quick." He tried a practice round of getting into the box. It hung from the top of his head, leaving his shins and feet uncovered. "Not good." Jordan practiced kneeling from inside the box. The mantra of his landscaping career kicked in. "Bend with your legs, not with your back." His balance failed him during the clumsy plié, and the narrow confines prevented him from using his arms to recover. Jordan struggled back to standing after nearly face-planting against the door. "So I'll kneel and then put on the box."

Breena heard the bell as she stepped out of the shower. *They'll just have to wait. It's not like it's someone I know anyway. Just a salesman probably. Or girl scout cookies...* Her face fell. *They probably don't have that here.* Releasing the steam into the bedroom, Breena checked her phone before rummaging for clothes. *Surprised Jordan hasn't tried calling again. Maybe he finally got the picture.* She texted Lilly to plan a time they could get online to video chat and returned to her primping. By the time she finished, Breena had forgotten about the doorbell. Not wanting to struggle with the box again, and risk her seeing him mid-prep, Jordan sat in his box and waited for her to leave the house.

A couple hours later, after getting distracted with an email from the orchestra program and writing a grocery list, to which she was forced by the email to add skin-toned panty hose for the final showcase, Breena slipped on her purple flats and opened the door.

"Woah!" She stopped mid-stride. "Should've gotten dressed faster."

Jordan's heart skipped when she spoke. He fought back a chuckle at Breena talking to herself, which she swore to him she never did. He knew better.

She tiptoed to see the top of the box then looked back at the door. "Huh. No note. How am I going to get this inside?" She crouched low and threw her arms around the sides of the box, resting her chin on top. *Ok, up with it all at once.*

Jordan wiped his hands on his jeans, marveling at his new nervousness.

Breena inhaled. "One, two, three." Pushing up from her squat with unexpected ease, the box sailed up with her. Pulling back a couple inches to gauge her footing, she saw another set of feet and shrieked, dropping the box.

Jordan's dormant form sprang to life, pushing the box up and over his head as he stood. The empty container fell down the steps and onto the sidewalk. "Surprise!"

Breena stared blankly.

"Surprise!" Jordan made jazz hands beside his face to reiterate his greeting, but his excitement sunk. Rejection.

"Jordan! What the hell is this?" she hollered.

Rationalizing that he needed to power through the moment, right past the point where she could reject him, and into the part where she'd reluctantly welcome him and end up having a great time, he threw his arms around Breena and squeezed. "I'll explain. Let me pee first," and he bounded through the cracked door.

Breena nodded, still in shock, and called after him. "First door on your right." She went back inside with the box and leaned against the front door. *This isn't real. It's another one of those dreams. I'm awake, but I'm not.*

Jordan stumbled out of the bathroom and down the hall. The wrong way. Breena chased after him and entered the bedroom just as he flopped on the huge bed.

"What are you doing here?"

"You left without saying anything. I went over your house they day after school let out and no one was there. Lilly told me."

"Cell! Phone!" Breena interrupted. "Why show up on my doorstep?"

"Would you have answered? You haven't been. Well except for that once, but you didn't really want to talk then, either." Jordan lay still with an arm across his eyes. They were quiet for a tense minute. He sat up quickly. "Look, I missed you. We didn't end the school-year on a happy note. I feel like you misunderstood my intentions, and I wanted to clear that up."

"Does your mom know where you are?"

"No one's home as usual. They left a note. China this time."

Breena rolled her eyes. Humorless, she ordered, "Call your mom, and tell her you're in London."

"Geeze, *Mom.* I'm eighteen. Relax. I've got my phone if they call. It's fine." Pacing toward the window and throwing his hands up in exasperation, he challenged Breena. "You don't want me here, do you?"

No. Breena cringed inwardly for making him feel unwelcome. "I won't say it's not nice to have someone to talk to, and I do feel safer with you here, but you literally just presented yourself as a gift to women. Woman. *Me.* It's nuts."

"It was exciting."

"Yeah, I guess it was, but you know I wanted space."

Jordan shrugged. "I thought maybe once you got here you'd realize it's not as fun traveling alone as you thought. I figured you'd end up wanting company."

Breena got off the bed and walked to the foyer, still talking. "You're not totally wrong. It's been pretty quiet here, but coming here tells me you missed my point completely. I don't want to feel obligated to include you in my plans for the future, which is why I reacted the way I did to your whole, 'Don't you see me in your future?' question. Of course I see you in my future, but I don't see you in *every* aspect of it. Like coming here. This was something I did for me. Doing a summer intensive was a goal I had for a while, and I'm finally old enough to participate. It's a challenge I thought would help my goals and actually earn the praise that people usually just throw at me when I'm not even trying. Having you here makes it feel ordinary. You're just another person who sees me as so much more than I am. I thought I'd grow from some struggle, alone in a new place, work really hard, go back home at the end of the summer and maybe feel like I'm closer to what you all think I am."

Jordan followed Breena out. "You already are what we think you are. I know you. The only thing you're lacking is a proper self-image. It's not *our* interpretation of you that's wrong."

"See, that's exactly what I mean. You might be right, but I need this summer to learn that for myself."

"I'm sorry I ignored your wishes. I won't get in the way of your classes. Leave me here. I'll keep busy."

"You can stay until classes start, but then I want to really be able to focus on developing my talent." *And maybe meet someone.*

"Right." Jordan's heart flopped. It hurt that she didn't want him there. He knew when he left the U.S. that there was only a small chance he'd stay with her for the whole summer, but his hope bubble had gotten big enough to burst. "Well, we're going to make the most of these few days, then."

"I can't make the most of anything until I get *something* to eat. It's been, what, three days? I still haven't gotten groceries. Come on. Put your shoes back on."

They found a store four blocks in the opposite direction of the late-night café. Jordan pushed a shopping cart they had to pay to use, and Breena tossed a hodgepodge of ingredients into it.

"What are you going to make with that?"

Breena stopped mid-throw and looked at the big squash in her hand.

"Are you really going to cook? You'll have to buy every little thing you need to make it taste good. That kitchen isn't stocked with spices. Do you even have a knife big enough to cut through that?"

Breena grinned. "Oh yeah, there's a knife. The kitchen has everything but food in it. But you're right. I should get foods that are mostly ready to eat."

They strolled down the biscuits aisle expecting to find bread, and then they remembered that "biscuits" are "cookies." She grabbed a bag of ginger snaps and told Jordan to pick something out to take on the plane.

"Get something really English. An edible souvenir."

"I bought a souvenir cup, but I left it."

Breena rolled her eyes. Jordan had discovered Mitch Hedberg's comedy during the school year and constantly tried to insert quotes into the conversation, even when they weren't totally related. While Jordan scanned through the unfamiliar brand names, Breena wandered into the next aisle.

She picked up a box of dishwasher detergent and turned back around expecting to see Jordan standing beside her. She had felt someone approach. Instead, a lean guy not much older than her hovered at her shoulder. In most instances, this type of surprise made her jump, but upon seeing him, she got the sense that she had somehow been expecting him. He seemed familiar, not necessarily by looks, but by the feeling that emanated from him, or between them. She flipped through her mental face collection, wondering if he was someone she had seen in passing and whose face she banked for drawing later. The longer she looked at him without responding, the stronger the sensation of déjà vu grew. Breena realized she hadn't said anything out loud and said, "Excuse me," stepping out of his way.

"You're not in the way. I saw you there and I wanted to say hi."

She smiled and opened her mouth to speak when a flash of her dream came to mind. Breena closed her mouth and tilted her head, studying his face. His bronze skin and green eyes, and the wry grin he wore, were striking and familiar. "Have we met?"

"Not officially."

Breena stared openly.

"You feel it."

Her heart thrummed in her chest, and she wondered if he could hear it. Breena put a hand to her face. She knew she was blushing, and the embarrassment of blushing made it flame brighter. After a few more seconds of unabashed staring, she noticed he had been waiting for her to answer, again. All she could do was nod.

He stepped closer and extended his hand. "I'm Atlas."

"Breena."

When they grasped hands, they both swayed. For a split second, each of them saw a blaze of fire surround them.

Breena jerked her hand away from Atlas at the same time Jordan rounded the corner. He jogged over to them.

"Hey, Breena, I got some shortbread cookies from... Who's this?"

Breena couldn't pull her eyes away from Atlas. The adrenaline pumped through her, making her hands shake even though she wasn't nervous. Thrilled was more like it. *I know this guy. He's the guy from—*

"Breena, is everything Ok?" Jordan grabbed her shoulder.

"Oh, hey. Yeah. Jordan, this is Atlas. We met over detergent."

Atlas studied Breena. It was important to him that she wasn't scared away, but he couldn't read her expression.

Jordan extended his hand to Atlas and introduced himself. Atlas expected to have some sort of vision upon contact, but nothing happened.

"It was nice to meet you, Jordan. I've got to get going. Breena, would you like to have dinner sometime?"

Breena cut a quick look at Jordan. "Sure."

Atlas handed her a card with Tabitha's name in tall, red letters at the top. Under her information, the card said, "Atlas

Thorley, Assistant" in gold lettering half the size. "Number's on the back. Hope I hear from you." He turned away from them holding up a hand in a dismissive wave. As he left the store, Atlas considered whether he should tell Tabitha that he met Breena or not. Tabitha still hadn't approved official contact. He didn't care about the risk to himself, though. After holding Breena's hand, he understood what Tabitha meant by being a true match for Breena. Atlas replayed the moment countless times while he rode the tube back to his apartment, watching the flames burst up around him, feeling the sluggish beat of his heart as if he and Breena were moving through time faster than anyone else.

In the store, Jordan took his turn to gape and waited for a story from Breena.

"What?"

"You're going to go on a date with that guy? You don't even know him."

"That's what dates are for. Getting to know someone."

A twang of jealousy made Jordan's breath catch. Her easy acceptance to date someone else told him that she wasn't saying no just because she wanted to focus on herself, but because he was too familiar for her. He wasn't new or exciting enough. "Yeah, I guess you're right." Jordan prayed she waited until he was gone to give the guy a call.

At the apartment, Breena dug the key code from the bottom of her purse while Jordan waited, loaded down with grocery bags.

"So. What are we doing today?"

"What do you mean, 'What are we doing today?'" Breena snorted. "I should be practicing."

"Are you crazy? We're in London! Where's your sense of adventure?"

"In my suitcase with my unicorn and giant purple monkey." They pushed inside and Jordan dumped the bags on the island.

"Where's your computer? I'll find somewhere for us to go."

Breena pointed to the couch, and Jordan rushed over to turn on the laptop.

"I didn't plan for adventure. I planned for hard work." Breena thought about Atlas for the ten millionth time since they left the grocery store. *But maybe some adventure wouldn't hurt.*

"Here!" Jordan turned the laptop around so the screen faced Breena. "This is where we're going tonight."

Chapter 5

8:00pm rolled around, and Breena started to get ready to go out. He was taking her to a club. All she could imagine was a smoky bar with dim lights, bad food, and drunk guys with gross breath. In her bedroom, Breena counted her pills. *Let's see. I took one the first night here, two after I woke up on the floor, another when we came home from the grocery store... I'm going to have to find someone before the trip's over. I'm already short two pills and it hasn't even been a week.* The thought of going to a crowded club was more than she could stand. Breena threw back another pill. *No more today, Breena.*

She tore through her minimal wardrobe. Nothing looked posh enough for a London night club. *This will have to do.* She put on black leggings and a short black dress made of jersey knit cotton. The neckline in front plunged low, but the scooping cowl in the back hung even lower. She realized her bra straps showed in the opening across her back so she reached around and unhooked it. Just as she slid her arms through the straps and pulled the whole bra out from the arm-hole of her dress, Jordan walked in. At the sight of her bra dangling from her outstretched arm, he turned bright.

"Haven't you heard of knocking?"

Jordan stuttered some meaningless syllables and froze there.

"Well, get out!"

Jordan rushed through the door and closed it behind him. Breena heard a thump outside the door like Jordan was banging his head there. He was. The corners of her mouth began to quirk up and her hands fluttered to her face, now hot and flushed. *No, Breena. That was a bad thing. Bad Jordan.* Breena dug through her suitcase looking for her stick-on bra. After wiggling it into place, she slipped on her black gladiator heels and went into the bathroom for some makeup.

She entered the living room forty-five minutes after the dressing ordeal started, looking like a girl Jordan had never seen before.

"Alright, let's get this over with."

Jordan opened his eyes to find Breena standing over him. Jordan jumped, but tried to cover. She smelled sweet, like flowers and vanilla. His hands tingled the same way they had before his driver's license test. Jordan knew he wouldn't be able to keep the promise he made himself. With her so close, he discovered his will-power was pretty pathetic.

"Well?"

Jordan clambered up from the floor to stand in front of her. She looked on with a question. When he finally broke eye contact, he managed to speak, and the words whooshed out like he had been holding his breath. "Getyourpurse."

She snatched it up from the floor and Jordan made a strangled, gasping kind of sound as she did it. He prayed she didn't notice it or the way his hands shook. Despite the tension, or maybe because of it, he couldn't tell, Jordan was the perfect model of chivalry all the way to the club.

"Here, you stand in front of me. They'll let us in sooner if they see your pretty face instead of mine."

"Psh. You're so full of it." She stepped into the crowd ahead of him anyway.

The wind blew swiftly between the city buildings, all gray, all concrete. The thumping bass of the music pulsed into the alley.

"Hey, you need a coat?"

"I'm fine." Her stomach flipped—her first legitimate excitement of the whole trip. "Industrial music, huh?" she hollered.

"What?"

"Industrial," she yelled again closer to his ear.

A blank stare from her date.

"Never mind," Breena shouted, waving her arms around. They stood ten more minutes in companionable silence while the bouncer checked IDs. *I think I might actually have fun tonight. It's not like Jordan and I don't have fun together. Stop acting like you're not happy to see him. He made a big effort to do this for me. I guess he deserves some credit.* Her heart fluttered. *He would make a good boyfriend.* Breena snuck a look at him out of the corner of her eye, and they caught each other's stare. Her cheeks blazed.

"ID?" Jordan flashed his first and the bouncer waved them through without checking Breena's. "Ok."

"Should I be offended that I look old, or flattered that you were right about my face?"

Just inside the door where they stood, Breena saw two levels of the venue. On the bottom level, down two steps from where they were, was a large dance floor outlined by tiny white lights. It was packed with swaying, sweaty bodies. *Ok. It's crowded, but this is gonna be fun. It is.*

At the far end of the room, the DJ stood behind his equipment to the left of the bar. Bottles of blue, green, pink, brown, and clear liquids lined five shelves in front of a wall-sized mirror. A cluster of impatient-looking people lined the bar counter.

Jordan pushed past Breena, catching her hand as he went by. He tried not to think about her noticing how clammy his palm was and found a small space where they could dance. Breena trailed behind him, staring up at the second level, which ringed the entire club. *It's not as crowded up there.*

Jordan shouted something at her and started dancing. She bobbed side to side with the beat, arms pasted to her sides. *You're having fun. You're not missing out on practice. You needed this night out. Take advantage of the time he's here. Be a good friend.* He leaned in and snaked his arms around her lower back. *It's nothing we haven't done before.* They bounced together until the tempo slowed. Jordan rested his chin on top of her head. *But, this time, he loves me.* They rocked under the spiraling purple strobe lights. Breena fought the urge to relax into Jordan. *Although, he said he's always been into me. It's only new for me.* Their heartbeats buzzed between them. *It would be so easy to just accept him.* A small breeze tickled through her hair, interrupting her thoughts.

"Is he smelling me?" she whispered into the cacophony. Jordan pulled back from her and paused as if he was asking permission. She didn't pull away. Jordan neared her neck and hovered there for a second. He placed one soft kiss under her jaw-line. Breena swayed a bit, but her mind started racing before her body found its way back to Jordan's lips. *...but then I'd lose myself.*

Jordan pressed on. There was electric in his veins. For Breena, everything was too close, suffocating. *This isn't what I want. He's my best friend.* She said no, but it was too loud. He kissed her again. She said no again. He moved to kiss her shoulder, and she shoved him away, palms to chest. Jordan stumbled back, realizing what he'd done. He looked as miserable as Breena felt.

"Sorry. I'll go get drinks."

She let him go, digging into her bag for another pill to settle her nerves.

Jordan became one of those impatient people at the bar, waiting over fifteen minutes for two drinks. Breena was too short to be seen in the crowd, and he hoped she was Ok alone. He felt bad for leaving her, but he didn't feel right staying, either. He shook his head.

Breena tallied how many pills she'd taken. *I'm going to run out too soon. Dance. People are staring.* She resumed bouncing with the music. It couldn't be called dancing. *I should call that guy when we get back to the apartment. A date would be good. You can't ruin a friendship by getting involved if you're not friends first.* Behind her, a hand hovered over her shoulder, about to tap. A familiar surge of warmth spread over her shoulder and back. *He's here.* She spun around, and he caught her hand in his, bringing it to his mouth to deliver a delicate and old-fashioned kiss. With sly precision, he slipped a small, folded paper into her hand.

"Atlas?" Breena stared into his eyes. There was no explosion of flames this time as they touched, but her vision clouded around the edges in a halo of bright, swirling colors. "Small world."

"Not small enough."

"What?"

"Nothing. It's good to see you."

"I was just thinking about you."

"I know." Atlas scolded himself as soon as the words slipped. Breena gave him a quizzical look. "You know, the old 'if your ear is burning' saying."

"Right. Well, I'm glad to see you. I wanted to accept your offer for a date. How about tomorrow?"

"What about your friend?" Atlas nodded in Breena's direction, and she turned to see Jordan making his way toward them with two fancy green drinks. When she looked back to Atlas, he was gone. Breena quickly shoved the note in her uselessly small clutch and snapped the bag closed.

"Here! It's a—" Jordan said, handing her the drink.

Peace offering, she said to herself, the true title of the drink inaudible. She didn't really care.

Breena took it from him and sniffed it before slugging back the entire thing. Her face wrinkled and she smacked her lips. "Tart!"

"Who are you calling a tart?" shouted the scantily dressed lady next to them.

"No, the drink," Breena hollered, thrusting the glass forward so the woman could see it. The woman nodded in skeptical understanding and danced her way to another area on the floor.

"Hey, can we go see the second floor? Everything's too close." Breena's glass trembled in her hand.

Jordan led her out of the crowd to the stairs. As they climbed, Breena's pinched expression relaxed into a neutral one. The last pill worked its way through her bloodstream, though not as quickly as she would have liked, and dampened the overwhelming input of the club. But, even the drugs weren't enough to blot out certain intrusive thoughts, like how Jordan mindlessly rubbed across her knuckles with his thumb as he led her, and that she wished it was Atlas instead. *I need to read that note.*

"Umm, I'm going to go to the bathroom. Be right back. And get me a drink, please." Breena pulled away from Jordan. Their fingers intertwined for a moment as he released her from his grip. There was finality in it that made his chest ache. He ordered two more of the tangy drinks and flopped down on a small leather couch opposite the bar.

"Ahh, you're so lame." His head fell back against the cushion, and he closed his eyes. A minute later, the other side of the couch sunk under the weight of someone else sitting down. "That was fast.

Surprised there wasn't a—" Jordan opened his eyes. Atlas was beside him. "Oh, hey. I thought you were my girlfriend. You're that guy from the store. Atticus, right?"

"Atlas."

"Yeah, that. Some guy from a book."

Atlas feigned a smile.

"So where's your date, Atlas?"

"Where's yours?" Atlas angled his body toward Jordan and rested his elbows on his knees, steepling his fingers under his chin.

Jordan pointed to the lady's room.

"She's not your girlfriend."

"Who are you to analyze our relationship?"

"Did I offend you? So sorry. You're close. I get it. You've probably been pining after her since you were a child."

A flash of concealed hurt sparked in Jordan's eyes.

"Exactly. I just wanted you to know my intention with her. You know, since she's single."

"Oh, really? And what is that?"

"I am going to marry her."

A laugh burst from Jordan, and he immediately wished he could run away. Atlas' face clouded and his green eyes darkened to swamp. Jordan scooted back from Atlas, but Atlas grabbed Jordan's collar and brought their faces inches apart. "Give her up, or have her taken from you." Atlas shoved Jordan into the back of the couch and stormed off.

In a stall in the bathroom, Breena unfolded the note, heart pounding and then skipping a couple beats as she read.

Hello, Miss. I'm glad we've finally met. You're stunning when you sleep. I'll see you at the café.

Her hands tingled and sweat. She read it again. And again. Alarm faded into jittery excitement. *He was watching me. The other night. It must have been him moving around outside. That's creepy. Why do I feel so... so thrilled? He chose to watch me. He went through all that trouble for me. And he knew I'd say yes to a date.* Breena crumpled the note and shoved it into her tiny bag. *Get back to Jordan before he thinks you're taking a massive...* She rounded the exit of the restroom. *Are Jordan and Atlas talking?* She watched Atlas grab and then shove Jordan before stalking away. *Great.*

"What the hell was that about?"

Jordan handed her the cocktail. "That guy is crazy, Breena. I don't want you going on a date with him."

"Too bad."

"I'm just trying to protect you. You don't even know the guy."

"I know him better than you think I do." *I've been dreaming about him for years.*

"Breena, I don't trust him."

"Not your call."

"Do you know what he said to me?"

"Don't care."

"Breena, listen to me. He said he's going to marry you. How insane is that?

Breena narrowed her eyes. "He did not." She shoved Jordan playfully on the shoulder.

Jordan's eyes darkened. "He did."

Breena knew it was insane, and she tried her hardest to fight the stupid grin forming in front of Jordan, but there was no denying the nervous excitement fluttering in her stomach.

"No. No. Don't get that look. He's crazy."

He wants to marry me. He doesn't even know me. Or maybe he's been dreaming about me all this time, too.

"Doesn't my concern mean anything to you? I love you. I want to keep you safe. Breena, are you listening?"

"I don't need your protection. You're not my father! He couldn't protect me or himself, and neither can you."

"Breena, stop."

"No. I'm not going to stop. You always think you know what's best for me. Like this place." Breena flung her arms around. "What were you thinking? Do you know me at all? I hate going to crowded places. I can't dance. And I don't want to be here with you!"

Jordan recoiled. "Fine! If you hate it so much we'll just leave." Jordan raged, snatching the drink out of Breena's hand. It sloshed on a girl in a plastic skirt bopping beside the small end-table. Jordan noticed his error; he didn't care. He slammed the glass and what was left of the cocktail on the table beside them and stormed back down to the first floor. Breena followed, her cheeks hot enough to blaze a path through the strangers staring at them. Outside, they waited feet apart for a taxi to take them back to the apartment. In the silence, Jordan's teeth squeaked in his ears as he ground them together.

What an ass. I can't believe he made a scene like that. And that he thinks he should protect me? He couldn't if he tried. Although, I guess all this is the effort I always wished he'd put forth to get me. It's one thing to just say the same things everyone else says. 'I love you; I think you're beautiful; Oh, Breena, you're so talented. Be my girlfriend.'

They slid into the black taxi. *I haven't earned any of that affection. But now, he's got to fight for me. I don't know if I actually want him to fight for me. Atlas still seems like the more attractive option. Atlas has already put out a lot of effort to get to know me. Albeit creepy, but more intriguing than anything. Even so, Jordan gets to prove all those things he says are true. And if he still loves me in the end, well, I guess I earned it somehow.*

At the front door, rain pelted them while Breena fumbled through her purse for the lock code. *Why can't I remember the thing?*

"Give me that." Jordan snatched the bag from her and fished it out without a struggle. The lock clicked, and Breena shoved past Jordan into the foyer, safe from the worsening storm outside. Jordan followed at a distance. *I should tell him how unacceptable his behavior was tonight. I don't have the energy to fight.* She slammed the bedroom door behind her and dug the note out of her purse.

Atlas. It's like I know you, but I don't. You're a mirage, something I can see and desperately want, but haven't reached yet. I don't understand what I saw that day when we shook hands. Those flames. They weren't hot or scary. Not like they were when my dad died. I can still smell it, the house and all of my earliest memories burning. But I'm not afraid of you. Sitting on the edge of her plush bed, Breena smoothed the wrinkled paper over her knee.

Jordan wore a path into the carpet in the hallway. "Stupid, selfish, jealous." He chastised himself quietly as he worked up the courage to go settle things with Breena.

"I can hear you grumbling to yourself out there. Go to bed."

"Stupid, selfish, jealous. But right. That guy is dangerous." He paused in front of Breena's door. "Breena, let me in so we can talk about this."

"Go away."

Jordan went in anyway.

She shoved the note quickly under her thigh thankful he didn't notice her sleight of hand. Jordan sat down beside her. Breena rolled her eyes. "You know, there's a pattern of disrespecting my wishes emerging."

"Only because I think your wishes are dangerous and short-sighted. I thought you would like it there. I guess I should have asked before I planned it all out. I really did it all for you, though. You know that, right?"

"Yeah, I know. I just thought you knew me better than that."

"Well, I do know you that well. I thought it would be good for you to get out and do something different. Meet people, hear different music, get a little tipsy. You know. But, that kind of blew up when that guy showed."

Jordan's intentions are always good, even when he gets in his own way. Under different circumstances, I might be falling for him by now. It's not like he isn't trying.

"But we could have stayed in, played cards, watched bad movies all night. Even better would have been to stay in Michigan in the first place."

"I agree with you there. It would be so nice to have you home."

"And what about the kissing, Jordan? Was that in the plan, too? Did you think that would be good for me?"

He stumbled over his words. "Well, I wasn't really thinking much when I did that. I really am sorry."

I can't tell him what I really think about it. Not when it has to do with Atlas. Who do you talk to when your best friend is the one you need to complain about? There's no way to turn off that connection I felt with Atlas and choose the logical, safe option.

Breena reached discreetly under her thigh and crumpled the paper into her hand. She stood up and walked to her suitcase and dropped the note in while pulling out a set of pajamas. Silently, Breena took them to the bathroom and shut the door. She looked down at her shaking hands then struggled out of her clothes. Jordan waited while she changed.

"You have to go home tomorrow," Breena said from inside the bathroom. Somehow, standing one room removed from him made it easier to say.

"What? You said I could stay the rest of the week."

"Not now. It's too complicated having you here. There's all this stuff you want from me. Emotional stuff. I can't give it to you."

"Because of Atlas?"

"Yes, and also because I already told you before school ended that I couldn't."

Jordan scrubbed his hands over his face and left the room, pulling Breena's door behind him. "Why did I even bother coming?" He collapsed on the sofa and pulled a pillow on top of his face. His thoughts whirred until they ran together and he drifted to sleep. Breena stayed awake nearly all night fighting herself and justifying her choices.

The next morning, Jordan rolled off the couch early and made a mishmash of breakfast items. She woke to the overwhelming smell of bacon. She followed it to the kitchen to find sliced tomatoes, French bread, and a bowl of cereal with no milk on the island.

"Thanks, Jordan."

"Sorry it's a weird mix. Someone didn't buy eggs, or milk, or any other normal breakfast foods."

She swatted away the criticism. "Let's just eat."

They sat across the kitchen island from one another in silence and ate. When they finished, she volunteered to clean up and hurried Jordan to take a shower so they could go to the airport. Within the next hour, they were off. Jordan disguised his disappointment at leaving as poorly as Breena masked her relief.

They hugged like robots at security, and then she sent him through without hesitation. Before he had even cleared the corridor to the terminal, she had already turned to go back to her taxi. She didn't want to see Jordan looking back at her.

When Breena returned, she made straight for her suitcase and pulled out the balled paper. Again, she sat on the bed, smoothed it over her knee, and read it. Even in the privacy of her room, her cheeks flamed with embarrassment. *This should not excite you.* The air whooshed out of the fluffy pillows as she fell back on them. *Would I still be interested in this guy if I wasn't so mad at Jordan?* The dream Breena had before Jordan arrived prickled at her memory.

She and Atlas stood in the woods. He had come to help her when she called out. *Turns out he's just as good looking in real life as he was in that dream. But he doesn't* always *help me in my dreams. Sometimes he's the one after me, engulfed in flames and wearing my father's face. And then there was that fire I saw when we shook hands at the store. That fire was different, pleasant. I was drawn to him then, and I wasn't mad at Jordan yet, so that can't be the reason I keep thinking about Atlas.*

She held the letter in front of her face. *This really is a creepy letter. Was he watching me through a window while I slept, or was he watching me through my dreams? Maybe we've been having the same dreams all this time, sharing a subconscious or something. I don't know whether to go meet him or hide from him.*

It was only 2:00pm, but Breena fell asleep sprawled out on top of the covers. She dreamed of home and of Jordan. For a brief moment in the alternate reality, they were an incredibly happy couple. They stood at the end of a worn pier, holding hands under the sun and gazing out over the calm lake. In her lucid mind, Breena knew she had never been to that lake before, but her dream-self seemed to recognize the setting. Jordan looked over at her and said something, but there was no sound. His lips moved, faster and faster like he was yelling, and deep lines, fear, formed on his forehead. She screamed at Jordan to slow down and explain, to talk louder, but it was like he was behind an invisible wall, panic-stricken and alone.

Her dream shifted, and the lake turned to roiling ocean waves so tall they looked like they were touching the black sky. Jordan was nowhere. She ran down the pier and into the nearby woods, searching. She couldn't see anything through the tears clouding her eyes, and she ran too fast, as if she couldn't control her speed. All of a sudden, she slammed into something hard—a tree, she thought—and fell down. Breena wiped the tears out of her eyes and looked up. Atlas stood over her wearing a menacing grin.

His eyes glistened black and hungry; dripping hair, slicked back from sweat; sallow skin, feverish and dull. She backed away from him until she bumped against another tree. From this point, the dream replayed the same terror as all of the other nightmares she had about Atlas over the years. The only difference was that she had a name to put to the face of her tormenter.

He approached. She wanted to scream, and maybe she was, but the world was like the vacuum of space—no sound going out and no sound coming in. Breena thrashed her head side to side looking for a route of escape and hoping she would wake up from the horror. She knew she was dreaming, but her lucid body felt held in place. Even though the smell of salty sweat on his skin repelled her, even though the look in his eyes terrified her, she could still feel the magnetism between them. He took pleasure in her fear and discomfort. He grinned as he put his hands on either side of her head against the tree. Breena could feel her world closing in, and her screams broke through.

With a shriek, she sat up in her bed, sweating and gulping down air. She ran into the bathroom and sunk to the floor thinking she might vomit, but the nausea passed. When the room stopped swirling, Breena stood and stripped off her clothes. She stepped into the shower stall and turned the cold water all the way. *Hot water to help me think, cold water to stop it.* The water beat down on her head and she didn't think about Atlas at all. Even when she tried, the ideas were overruled by complaints about how miserably cold she was. *Which is exactly the point.*

Sufficiently numbed, Breena reached to shut off the water. Two loud knocks boomed through the apartment. She jumped at the sound and let out a gasp that felt way too loud. *There's only one person in this city who knows I live here.* Breena turned off the water and tiptoed into her bedroom worrying that Atlas was out there and could hear her moving around. Another knock rattled the walls. *God, don't let him bust down the door.* She waited in the corner where no one could possibly see her through any of the bedroom windows. It was silent for a while.

Breena, still damp, threw on some clothes and crawled down the hall. *This is stupid, Bree. It's been quiet a few minutes. No one's there anymore.* She stood halfway down the hall and did a sweep of the rooms. "See, no one outside the windows. No Atlas. Everything's fine." She walked to the door. Through the peep hole, Breena saw the back of a man's head right in front of her door. She jerked away and tripped over the runner. *Someone's still out there. Hide, hide!* Breena ducked down so he couldn't see her if he looked through the hole from the outside. *Peep holes don't work that way, dummy.* The man knocked once more and slipped something under the door. It hit her heel and she almost grabbed it, but she realized she should wait until he was gone. *Otherwise, he'll see me pull it inside and know that I'm here.*

His footsteps sounded hollow as he walked away from her door and down the steps. She pulled the envelope out. There was no return address. Her hands shook as she peeled the orange flap open. It looked like someone else had done the same. A loud laugh of embarrassment and relief escaped when she pulled out the contents to find a large 8x10 picture of Lilly and Jordan and a handwritten note which fluttered to the floor. The photo sported her friends in ludicrous poses on top of a rock at the park, both pointing to the space between them. Written on the back of the photo, dated before Jordan had arrived, was, "We wish you were here right between us."

"I wish that, too." Bree moved to stand up and noticed the small paper on the floor beside her.

"You've got great friends. I'm glad I got to meet Jordan. We had an interesting conversation. –Atlas"

Her stomach lurched. "That's it. No more hiding. Time to confront that psycho. Be firm, be direct, don't let him get too close." She repeated the mantra the whole way to café.

Chapter 6

Atlas paced in his room, fuming. "I should be there right now! I swear, one day, I'm going to get out of Tabitha's grasp."

He stomped to the kitchen and made a glass of ice water. "People like her are going to pay for the pain they cause. I don't care what she says to Breena. Tabitha's not the one who gets her in the end." Atlas gulped the water down and slammed the glass on the counter. The base cracked. Tearing himself from the urge to smash it, he stalked back to his room and slammed the door.

In the middle of the floor, Atlas piled up a circle of pillows then sat in the center. "I'll just have to show Breena I'm with her from a distance."

****

At the café, there was a line when Breena arrived. She sat at her usual table near the window to wait until the line dwindled down. The bell on the door jingled as more customers came in, but she didn't look at them. A headache was coming on, and the pitch of the bell plus the constant high-pressured air sound from the milk frother didn't help. She thought again about the photo and smiled. *I shouldn't have been so harsh on Jordan...*

As soon as the thought crossed into her consciousness, an intrusive vision of Atlas tore through. She rested her head on the table, her arms blocking out the light, and closed her eyes hoping the darkness would black out her thoughts. They intensified.

The dark shape of a man stood at a distance in a field under the stars. It was snow-covered, but he was barefoot. An old woman stood behind him, yelling, but there was silence. The silhouette turned, looked at the old lady, and raised his arm toward her. Immediately, the woman fell to her knees. Suddenly, Breena was in a clearing in the woods.

Atlas stood across the plush grass from Breena. It was cold and crisp outside, and the silence was louder than any noise could have been. He approached her. She backed away. He came closer. She backed into a tree. Unable to escape his presence or pull herself back into reality, she resigned herself to the dream, thinking some part of her would probably die in the clearing. Atlas wore an icy, calculating cool about him, the composure of a serial killer. Finally reaching Breena, he held his hand out for her. It hovered an inch away, yet he could not touch her.

A thin wall of energy separated them, safely shielding her in a world parallel to, but completely exclusive of, his. She stared into his stark expression and softened. It didn't look like he was trying to scare her. He needed her help. Breena put her fingers up to the barrier between them and focused her thoughts on cracking it apart. The invisible partition vibrated under her touch, the sound of the resonance growing from a low whir to a high-pitched hum. Then, it cracked. Her hands pushed through and met his.

As soon as they touched, the world around her was sucked, as if a painted canvas pulled into a vacuum cleaner, into blackness. Breena lifted her head from her arms and blinked a few times. The same people were still in line, as if the whole thing had happened instantaneously. Her mind felt like it had lived an extra day. Rubbing her throbbing temples, she shakily got up to stand in line.

****

In his room, Atlas came to in a heap on the floor. The effort to connect with Breena while she was awake turned his extremities to jello. He rolled to his back and stared at the ceiling. "She's incredible. That raw power. She shouldn't be able to do that, not without training. I see why Tabitha wants her. I want her."

Atlas shoved himself to a seated position and looked at his watch. "Screw Tabitha. I'm going to see her."

****

When Breena got back to her table, she found that a gentleman in his forties had taken it.

"Excuse me, sir. I'm sitting here. My things are right there." Breena moved to the opposite side of the table and rested her hand on top of her books of sheet music.

"There's no saving seats when it's this busy. Sorry." The man was clearly *not* sorry.

"Sir, I'm waiting on someone to join me. You don't need two seats. I do."

His cup of coffee entranced him.

Breena huffed and said, "Well at least let me get my stuff. How would you have known if I was saving my seat or if I was just in the bathroom, anyway? Rude."

He put his newspaper back in front of his nose rather than acknowledge her.

The two women that had been in line before Breena waved her over to a table across the room.

"Me?"

They nodded.

"Be right there. Let me just clear *my* table."

The man flapped his newspaper like he was shaking out the creases. *I know you heard me, old man.* She eyed his coffee. *I deserve award money for this level of restraint.*

"Some people can be such jerks, can't they?" the blonde girl said as Breena neared. She held out her hand. "Hi, I'm Linda."

Breena looked around for a place to set her things so she could shake Linda's hand. The girls scooted their coffees and laptops to the side, and Breena dropped her pile of stuff onto the table. "Thanks. I'm Breena. Do you know that guy?" she asked gesturing back toward him.

The brunette replied, "No, but he's a regular here."

"Yeah, a regular horse's rear," added Linda.

The brunette held out her hand. "I'm Tabitha, and you are more than welcome to sit with us. You seem interesting enough, and you've got to be nicer than him."

"Thank you so much. I appreciate it. I promise I won't be a bother. As soon as the person I'm waiting for gets here, we'll move to our own spot."

"No," the girls said in unison. "Not a bother at all," continued Tabitha. "We're in need of an addition to our café chatter."

"Yes, we could tell you're new around here. So, tell us. Why are you all alone in foggy London," prompted Linda.

"Well, I just got in earlier this week. I'm here for an orchestra intensive until September. I play the cello."

"Well that's lovely. You must be very talented. Linda used to play the flute."

Linda waved it off. "Not well."

"So, who are you meeting? One of your orchestra friends?"

"No, the course hasn't started yet. I don't really know anyone."

"Well, you know us, and you know your date."

"Oh, no, no. It's not like that. I'm not waiting for a date. It's a long story, really." Breena put a hand to her cheek.

"Oh, Breena, I made you blush. Sorry. But, are you sure it's not a date?"

"Certain. I'm actually here to tell him off."

Linda and Tabitha erupted in giggles. "I knew it was a boy. Linda, you thought so, too?"

"Mhm. No one blushes like that for no reason. You like this person."

Breena twisted in her seat.

"My goodness! A girl your age should be having the time of her life on a summer-long trip alone in London. What *mischief* we could get you and your beau into..." Tabitha mused.

Linda cut her eyes sideways at Tabitha like she was trying to signal her to stop talking.

"Well, not with this one. He started out kind of flattering, but he's a sad creep."

"And we'll get to meet this guy, right? He'll be here soon?"

"Ehh, I don't actually know if he's coming. We didn't set a meeting time. I had a feeling he'd just know." Breena rolled her eyes after she said it. *I sound like an idiot. What normal person would 'just know'?*

Tabitha smiled. "Why on earth would you think that?"

Yep. "I'm pretty sure he's a stalker, so there's that." Breena nodded like it made her statement more convincing. "And, well, maybe he's also psychic or something?"

"I want to hear all about this." Tabitha sat at the edge of her seat with her elbows on the table.

Breena couldn't tell if her interest in the account was born of concern or something else. She gave off a weird vibe that was almost like satisfaction. Linda seemed nice enough, nodding encouragement beside her, so Breena agreed.

By the end of her story, they were old friends. Breena invited them over for snacks and movies later in the week, and they hugged before leaving the café.

"Looks like your boy didn't show. See, I told you there's safety in numbers." Linda slung her huge purse over her shoulder.

"We'll just have to be everywhere you are this summer, won't we?" Tabitha held the door for the group as they filed out and parted ways.

From down the street, Atlas watched with a snarl on his face as Tabitha schmoozed with Breena and Linda. When the group dispersed and Breena started in his direction, Atlas stood from the bench at the bus stop and walked to meet her.

"I thought I'd find you here."

"I'm sure you did." Breena kept walking, and Atlas fell in beside her.

"What's that supposed to mean?"

"I'm sure you know."

Atlas wore a smug grin. Pride surged through him. "So you got my gift, then?"

"What, you mean the creepy note you left *inside* my package from my friends, or the creepy note you gave me at the bar?"

"You're mad."

"Stop playing dumb. Yes, I'm mad. You're stalking me. I don't like it."

"Breena, I was just trying to get to know you." Atlas almost made a comment about Tabitha's restrictions forcing him into such desperate measures, but he caught himself.

"Well, I think I know you enough. I don't want you around."
They stood at Breena's stoop. "It's a shame, too. It felt like there
could be something, at first, anyway." *Why did I say that to him?*

"Breena, there *is* something. You felt it when we met at the
grocery store. You can't just ignore it. Even if I stayed away, you'd
still see me. I know about the dreams."

She took a step back from him. "What dreams?"

"Now who's playing dumb?"

Breena blushed. People rarely called her out. She crossed her
arms.

"Look, I'm sorry. I did go overboard. I should have known all
that stuff would come across as creepy and invasive."

"Yes."

He took her hand. A jolt passed through them, but he kept
talking. "It's different to find this while I'm awake."

He's not wrong.

"It was hard to keep away."

"Don't you have any restraint?"

"You were across the ocean for so many years. That was my
restraint. Once I found out you were here, not thirty minutes from
my home, I was done."

I guess he was *having the same dreams as me. But how did
he know where I lived? I never got that much info about him from
my dreams.* Curiosity got the best of her. "If I agree to give you a
chance at a legit friendship, no stalking, no creepy stuff... like, you
come when invited, we go out as scheduled... you have to stop
sneaking around."

"Done."

"Way too eager."

"Can I ask you something?"

"You're going to anyway."

There was a glimmer in his eyes that mirrored the shine of
the wet road under the street lights. "Do you ever wish you could
change the way things turn out?"

Chapter 7

Jordan shoved his seat into what the airline claimed was a reclining position and tried to nap. It was a useless effort, though. He hadn't stopped berating himself since the taxi, and things with Breena seemed more unfinished the farther he got across the Atlantic.

When the attendant came by with drinks, he waved her away without taking out his earbuds. Jordan closed his eyes and tried to focus on the song playing, but the lyrics made him feel worse, so he flipped his iPod to shuffle.

"Please stay seated while the fasten seatbelt light is on."

He woke to the scratch of the announcement over the low-tech intercom system, and a rapid sinking sensation as the plane fell through a low-pressure pocket. Everyone sat white-knuckled and sweaty, just waiting for the pilot to announce that they were through the storm. It didn't bother him so much. "I don't mind the thought of disappearing," he grumbled into his free airplane blanket.

****

Atlas was still awake, determined to keep his promise to Breena that he wouldn't invade her privacy anymore. The only way he could think to do that was to stay up as long as he could, or at least to sleep only while she was not. It was inevitable that they would meet if they slept at the same time.

Coffee dripped into his mug little by little through the filter in his pour-over maker. Steeping it that way took longer, but he was convinced more of the caffeine came with it. He turned to the living room when the door clicked. Tabitha strutted in.

"I just got finished setting Linda up at my place. She was so happy. I had to get out of there. Can you believe the girl? Thinks we're in a relationship. Humans are so pliable. She makes a great pawn."

"It's 3:30 in the morning. I'm half asleep, and you don't live here. I don't care, Tabitha."

"We've been over this before, Atlas. If you want Breena, you'll care about my plans, and you'll respect them. We're in it for the same goal, you know."

"No, my goal is nothing like yours. I want to end chaos. You just want to feed it."

"How did Gehenna ever produce such a sensitive boy? And to be our king, no less. I'm starting to think I sent you to live with the wrong family. Your father must not have been as bad as you made him out to be."

Atlas tensed at the mention of his father, but managed to keep his thoughts to himself. He turned back to his coffee. It wasn't finished dripping, but he slugged it back anyway, shoving another cup under the filter to catch the rest.

"You know, if I had more energy, I'd just take you for myself, but you wear me out. And *not* in the fun way. I don't envy Breena."

"I wish you'd stay away from her. I saw you at the café."

"I know you did. It's not like you ever obey me and stay home when I'm trying to work. You know she thinks you're a stalker, right? Says you're pathetic."

"She did not say that."

"Did she not?"

Atlas paused and stared hard at Tabitha. Her face was stone. "Stop messing with my head! I talked to her. She agreed to be my friend."

"Out of pity?"

"Shut up! It's not like that."

"We'll see. I don't care if her feelings are genuine or not, as long as she comes home."

****

Breena shuffled down the hall in her slippers, rubbing her eyes so she could see. She had fallen asleep on the couch with sheet music scattered all around her. It was the first time she was really able to study it, no Atlas, no Jordan, no unexpected conversations in a café, but studying always knocked her out; no need for pills.

What time is it? There was a little clock on the counter in the hall bathroom. She squinted as she passed. *I don't know what that says.* Breena stumbled into her room, eyes already closed again. *Mmm, bed.* Cold air rushed out of the feather duvet as she flopped on top of it, falling back to sleep on the spot.

Not thirty minutes later, Breena sat up in the middle of the bed and pulled her knees to her chest. *I can't sleep like this. There's nothing there. Atlas. Where did you go?* She looked out into the darkness of her room. *I guess I got used to seeing him there.* The light seeped in from around the blinds, a royal blue. *Even if he was scary sometimes.*

Breena sighed. *The sun will be up soon.* She glanced at her phone and thought of Jordan. *We used to talk until the sun came up. Now, no one, not even in my head. Why'd you drive them away, Breena?* Another voice, the voice of her demons, answered. *Because you're selfish.* Breena nodded to herself in agreement and reached for her nightstand. *One pill. Just to get back to sleep.* Falling into her pillow, she forced her eyes shut.

"Atlas, you can come back." Breena walked down a long hallway with lots of doors. She saw him running away from her as she called out. Every door she passed opened, and reaching hands tried to grab her and pull her in. She pushed through them.

"Atlas, I'm sorry! Don't leave me with these people." Her voice didn't carry to the end of the hallway, she could tell. It came out tinny, muted. He walked out of sight. "Fine! Then go. I give up." Another hand reached for her, and she let it take her. The lights in the room brightened as she crossed the threshold. Jordan had her by the wrist and hauled her into his bedroom.

"Oh, it's just you."

"Who?"

"You, Jordan."

"I don't know who that is." He shoved her over to the bed. "Wait here."

The person wearing Jordan's face left the room. She waited, rifling through the familiar things in his room, clothes, books, CDs she'd seen thousands of times before. The strangeness of the dream told her to be on edge, but she felt at home. She waited for what felt like days. No one ever came.

She woke to her phone ringing. The room was bright with daylight.

"Hello?" Breena yawned into the phone.

"Hey, you answered! I just wanted to tell you I'm home."

"Good." *Am I still dreaming?*

"Yeah. I'm beat."

"I bet."

Jordan paused and stared at his shaking hand. Breena waited for him to say something, blinking to wake up. "Look, Breena, I don't want things to be weird when you come home."

"Then don't make it weird."

He snorted. "I guess I should've expected you to be like this."

"Like what, Jordan?"

"Walled-off, distant."

"I just woke up."

"That's not what I mean and you know it."

"I need to go get ready. I'm having people over later. I have to go to the store."

Jordan gritted his teeth then softened. "Ok. Be careful."

"Bye, Jordan." Breena lay in bed after they hung up. Her chest ached. "Why do I do this to him?"

****

Tabitha and Linda arrived at Breena's at 5:00pm, both with dishes they had made at home. The comforting smell of food wafted through the apartment.

"Let's just do a buffet. Less dirty dishes that way." Breena moved her neglected pile of sheet music off of the island.

Tabitha set three bottles of wine and a tray of finger sandwiches on the counter. "What did you make, Breena?"

"Macaroni and cheese, baked Ranch chicken, and Texas toast."

"American comfort foods?"

"Mhm."

"Isn't Texas toast just bread?"

"No way. It's huge, for one, and it's soaked with butter and garlic."

"Linda brought desserts! A gypsy tart and an arctic roll. You will absolutely love them."

"I don't know what those are, but I'm excited to try."

"You won't regret it. She won me over with her baking. You know what they say. The way to the heart is through the stomach."

Wait, are they a couple? Is that rude to ask? Breena passed on the prying and let their body language confirm the answer.

The group sat around the coffee table, Breena on the floor, cross-legged, and Linda and Tabitha on opposite ends of the couch, legs thrown about one another. They munched on their food and made congenial small-talk when Linda broke in and fired off the questions that she really cared about.

"So, have you heard from the stalker guy anymore?"

"We talked after the café yesterday."

"He called you? Had you given him your number?"

"No, no. In person. He was apparently waiting for me to leave. Caught me on the walk home."

"And you told him to bugger off, right?"

It was quiet for a moment.

"I think that silence means no," Tabitha interjected.

Linda shook her head. "Breena!"

"I couldn't do it. There's something about him."

"No, there's something about you. It's called Stockholm Syndrome."

"I'm serious, guys. I feel like I'm supposed to get to know him, even if he did creep me out. Who am I to judge? He promised he would stop invading my privacy and, so far, he's kept that promise. I didn't dream about him, I didn't see him on my way to or from the store, he wasn't at the store, and there haven't been any shadows lurking around outside."

"Wait, you said you haven't dreamed about him? That's hardly in his control. You must have just felt more at ease and so you didn't dream about him because you weren't worrying about him skulking around while you slept."

Nice one. "Right. Yeah, that's what I meant."

Tabitha chuckled.

"What?"

"Nothing. You're entertaining. Now then, let's talk about something else. No more of this night-creeper nonsense."

She's the entertaining one. Weird more like. What's with that laugh of hers? So fake.

After reaching for another slice of gypsy tart, Tabitha gestured at the TV with it. "Have you got any old movies we could watch?"

"Nope. This place might look great, but the only thing it came fully stocked with was furniture and boredom."

"Not true." Linda jumped out of her seat. "Time for some wine! Get some of this in us and we'll make this place fun."

Tabitha clapped and Breena laughed as Linda poured three glasses of Merlot and passed them around.

"To new friends," Linda toasted. They all took a drink.

"To making our own fun," Tabitha toasted. They all took another drink.

"To getting stalked!" Breena shouted last. They paused and looked at her. "To *not* getting stalked!" Breena corrected, and they all took yet another drink. Their glasses were almost empty by the end of their toasting round and Breena was already a bit tipsy. She hadn't told anyone that the night at the club was the first drink she had ever had, and she didn't mention to the girls that the smell of wine made her queasy. She held her breath, tossed it back, and enjoyed the buzz. *Besides, once I'm back home, it will be years before I can drink again. When in London.*

As the night went on and the bottle ran dry, the girls giggled about dating and sex, and the lack of dates and sex.

"I remember this one guy I tried to date," Tabitha launched into another dating horror story. "He was a lot younger than me. This guy was *the* worst listener. Not like he ignored me when I talked, but like he didn't want to do what I told him to do. I like obedient men, you know, but not weak men. He interfered with my work, he insisted on going out and about without me, and, get this, he used to wake up screaming in the night. He told me it was night terrors. I told him buh-bye. If a guy's too weak to handle a bad dream, he's too weak for me. My family was against it anyway. Said he was the right guy for someone else. They weren't wrong."

"I haven't heard this story before, Tabitha. I didn't realize you used to date guys."

And there's *my answer.*

"I thought I'd heard all your crazy stories. So what was his name?"

Tabitha looked at Breena for a flash of a second and then back at Linda. "His name was Atlas."

Breena coughed on her wine and the women looked at her. Tabitha tried to hide her smirk with a concerned raise of the eyebrows. Breena kept quiet as a sense of possessiveness washed over her. *But he's mine.* The gut response sounded foreign in her head. She hadn't noticed she felt that way about him. *And how many other Atlas' could there be? Why didn't she mention she knew him earlier? I never did call him by name, did I?*

Linda reached for her wine glass. "Oh, empty again. Aw, and our last bottle is as well."

"Well, I guess that's our cue. We only stay for the wine." Tabitha paused. "Just kidding!"

"We had a lovely time. We'll have to do it again."

"Sure, as long as my orchestra schedule allows. We start tomorrow." *Like hell we'll do it again...*

Breena escorted them to the sidewalk and waved them off. The rush from the wine faded and drowsiness from the alcohol mixing with her pills took over. Breena went straight back to her room, leaving the cold mac and cheese and other leftovers on the counter. She climbed onto the bed not even finishing her prayers before falling asleep, still wearing all the clothing she usually slept without.

Chapter 8

Breena kicked and turned more than usual. She woke up often, gasping for breath. The wine still left in her system intensified the dreams. In the hour just before waking, she dreamed of her stalker once again.

Her astral self materialized in a clearing among the trees. *Back here, again.* Before she had ever met Atlas, every dream looked like this one. Only since his physical presence in her life had the dreams taken on some variety.

I wonder why this place. Always this place.

Murmuring voices thrummed in her head, their cadence like audible longing. She spun around looking for a sign of him. Usually by this point in the dream, he had her pinned to a tree and screaming for help. *It never takes this long for him to find me.* Breena shuffled through the high grass to a birch tree at the edge of the open circle. Beyond the birch, the forest grew thick with underbrush. Finding footprints was impossible, so she watched for rustling branches. Her arms tingled and her hairs rose with the sense of being watched.

"Atlas? You out there?" She crossed to the other side of the opening and looked beyond the treed border. "Why did you bring me here? It's been a while."

A twig snapped in the distance, and Breena turned. A small chapel appeared nestled in the trees ahead. *Well this is new.* Breena crept toward it very aware that the dream was unlike her others. *New is unpredictable.* Beside the church hung a bench swing above a bed of daffodils, her favorite. The noise in her head increased in intensity, developing into words.

"Neruda again? It was you in the café, too?" She approached the swing. "I guess I shouldn't be surprised that you know my weaknesses, my favorite things. You've been here for years, just waiting for me. Haven't you?" She sat on the swing and pushed herself gently, her shoes stirring dust up around her ankles.

"Only do not forget, if I wake up crying it's only because in my dream I'm a lost child, hunting through the leaves of the night for your hands." As she swung and admired the glittering chapel beside her, he came out from the trees. "Pablo Neruda, Sonnet XXI."

Her breath hitched at the sight of him walking toward her. *Here it goes. The rest of the dream picking up like it usually does. Run.* She stood, ready to bolt, but suddenly he was in front of her, and he grabbed her wrist.

"Wait."

The jolt of fear she expected was more like the pull of a tide instead. *Those eyes. What is that look?*

"Do you like it? This place, I mean. I got you a bench swing." His excitable innocence was another departure from previous dreams. She opened her mouth to reply, but he put his finger to her chapped lips. Leaning to her ear he whispered, "I made it just for you."

The dream morphed back into the nightmare she had expected all along. Breena took a large step back and turned quickly to run. Searching for the path leading out, she stumbled over a root and staggered back up. There was no path. She ran as fast as her legs allowed, but the quicksand of drunken lethargy held her back. He chased after Breena gaining more ground every second, and she struggled to breathe through the cramps that stabbed her side. Breena abruptly turned to the left and found a large tree to use as cover so she could rest.

"Come back!" he roared at an earth-shattering decibel. Even the trees cringed at the outburst. They visibly shrank. "I'll find you; you know I'm everywhere."

Breena took to running again, this time even more restrained than the first. As the classic symptoms of nightmares wore on, complete with sweating, running without going anywhere, and screaming noiselessly, Breena eventually panicked her way out of her deep sleep. She woke for the fifth and final time panting, hair pasted to her chest, neck, and back by sweat. She shouted to her empty room. "Screw you, Atlas! I'm sure you can hear me."

Atlas wrenched himself out of sleep, gasping. "Dammit! Why can't I keep myself under control?" He threw his blankets and pillows to the floor, sitting up in the middle of his bed, hot and angry. "She's terrified of me." Atlas dialed Tabitha.

"Do you know what time it is?"

"Tabitha, when can I tell her?"

"It's no one, Linda. Go back to sleep." Tabitha left the bed and closed herself in the bathroom. "Why do you bother asking? You're not going to listen to me."

"She thinks I'm after her, that I'm doing this. She's never going to be with me like this. I have to talk to her, make sure she knows I'm just a guest in her effed-up nightmares, that her unhappiness is what causes them to take those dark turns." His volume escalated. "She needs to know it's not me. I'm not trying to scare her."

"Fine. Go talk to her. Tell her how you can't control your abilities or protect her, and that you need her to do your job. She'll love that."

Atlas disconnected the call. "One day I won't have to get your permission."

Breena swung her legs heavily out of the bed and stumbled into the bathroom. As the ice cold water flowed between her fingers, she grumbled under her breath.

"So stupid, Breena. This is what you get. Give him an inch... Of course he's going to try to worm his way in. He's psychotic. No one would try to win a girl over by scaring her for years and years. Even if he was nice, do you really deserve him? No. And you're not even here for that. Stay focused, do something important, get out of Michigan forever."

The red hue of overheated fear dissipated. She splashed her face with the water as it felt less and less icy. Breena looked up at her dripping face in the mirror in front of her. *Of all times to be alone. I shouldn't have sent Jordan home. No, but I did the right thing. He'll never stop having feelings for me if we're around each other all the time. And I have to show him we aren't an item. But I really wish he was here. I can't even tell him that because then he'll be mad I sent him back. He'd come if I asked him to, especially if he thought I was in danger. No. No, I'm not asking that of him. This is too much to think about.* Her thoughts trailed of as she straggled into the kitchen.

Back home, Lilly had taught her to emotionally eat when her cat Beebee died. Now seemed like another appropriate time to use her friend's advice. She heard Lilly's comforting voice.

"Full bellies leave no room for empty hearts." *Does a full belly fill up an empty apartment? I should call her soon. I know what she'd say.*

"You march yourself to that café and wait for him. Tell him to disappear, and then don't leave until after he does, that way he can't follow you."

The clock on the microwave blinked as it changed from 4:59am to 5:00am. *It's tomorrow. No way I'm going back to sleep, I guess.*

Breena brewed some coffee for the smell alone and flipped on the TV. In the entirety of her stay, it was the first time the TV had been turned on for the purpose of paying attention to it. *But what else am I going to do at 5 in the morning?* Breena settled into the corner of the couch with her blueberry coffee and flipped through the channels. News, news, news, infomercial, infomercial, news, old American western movie, infomercial, documentary: mating chimps, news... Breena turned the TV back off.

A familiar tune played in the back of her mind, but she couldn't place it. She plucked it out on her cello and, after a while, she realized it was the tune coming from inside the chapel in her dream. She developed the melody into a complete sonata before realizing it was already 8:00am. *Thank goodness. Some stores will be open by now.* Breena put on her ballet flats and jacket, gathered her messenger bag full of sheet music, and hoisted up her cello case. She stopped at a little store on the corner just to browse. Side-stepping through the aisles of artist's supplies and craft materials with her large load, a bright yellow box caught her eye. *Huh, Crayola in London. It really is an American world.* Breena grabbed a box of colored pencils and shuffled to the register.

After the art shop, she went to the café with her things to have some breakfast before orientation. As usual, she set her pile of stuff on the table and ordered her tea plus a blueberry scone. When she returned, she was thankful to see there was not a rude man sitting there. She decided to draw while she waited. Breena drew whenever her mind was too cluttered to think things through. All of her surroundings blurred away, and she became a part of the world on her page. She didn't notice the door chimes as more customers entered. She also didn't notice that one of them sat down across from her until he put a hand on top of her notebook in the way of her pencil.

Breena glared at Atlas sitting in front of her. He stared back with his green jewel eyes. Despite her hostile expression, he looked relieved to see her. *Don't fall for it, Breena. So what he's exactly your type? You don't want to touch his hair. You want to yell at him.*

Neither of them spoke. Breena was too busy fighting her attraction with anger, and he was too busy sizing her up. Sweat formed on her brow and she noticed how clammy her hands had gotten. Glancing down, she noted that she had steamed a handprint on the table. Finally, he broke the silence.

"Hello, Breena," he started coolly.

She shrunk back from the table.

Their conversation was awkward and slow. Despite all of the waiting and fear, now that he was in front of her again, he didn't seem very intimidating. *Don't forget the dreams. Don't forget the stalking.* She fought to maintain her negative opinion despite his magnetic presence.

"I should call the cops."

"No, please. I have to talk to you about something."

"You're still stalking me. You promised you'd only come around when invited. And what the hell was that dream last night?" The ambiance in the café consisted of a hushed thrum of voices, cappuccino machines, and keyboard clicks. She controlled her volume as best she could, but frustration boiled to the surface.

"I tried to stay awake as long as I could. I had to sleep last night, though. I'm so sorry."

"You were trying to stay awake? Do I only have those dreams if you're sleeping, too?"

"Yes. I knew if I stayed awake, you wouldn't be subjected to my nightmares."

"*Your* nightmares? I'm the one waking up screaming every night."

"It happens to me, too, you know. Our dreams. We share them."

"What are you? At first, I thought you were just a dream. You've been there for years. I even thought you might be God—"

"Ha! God?"

"—giving me direction in my sleep."

"That couldn't be farther from the truth," he mumbled as she continued.

"Then, the dreams turned. You got nasty, and I was afraid to sleep. Needed pills to get through the night. That turned in to needing them during the day. I come here thinking I'm going to escape everything that's happened to me in Michigan, work toward my goals, be at peace for once, and you show up in the grocery store. What was that vision I saw? The dreams got worse after that, and the stalking did, too. You haven't kept up your end of the deal."

"Stalking you? You still think that?" His tone was genuine shock.

"Of course that's what I think! You scare me. And what else am I supposed to think of a man I can't even escape in my sleep?"

"I really just wanted to know you. I saw you in *my* dreams first," he explained.

"No..."

"And then I found you while you slept. It was like your mind and soul were reaching out to me. We connected. Through your dreams I found out you were coming to London. Running into you at the grocery store was fate. I didn't plan that. But, then, I heard about your night out at the club. I'm sorry I scared you. I was crazy to think it wouldn't freak you out. I guess I've just been around for so long without anyone. I got over-eager."

"If you're looking for me to accept your weird pity-party apology, it's not going to happen that easily. How can you expect me to just be Ok with the way you've been terrorizing me?" Breena's voice escalated and her face got redder. "You act like all my dreams were fairy tales where we were just meant to meet and hang out. They were horrifying! What kind of explanation do you have for that? Huh? How do you justify the terror you put me through in those dreams?"

"I don't create your dreams. Your mind creates them."

"No, you just got finished saying they were *your* dreams."

"Well, they are in that I'm having the same dreams you're having. From my perspective, they're my dreams. From your perspective, they're yours. We appear to one another because we connect astrally when we sleep. Clearly, by your reaction, it's not intentional. Sometimes, my emotions get out of hand and influence the dreams. But, ultimately, all the power is in you."

"How do you know it's not you?"

"I know more about you from those dreams than you'd ever imagine."

"Like what?"

At this point, Breena had sweat through and removed her hoodie, her tea was empty, and all of the customers in the café were different than when she arrived hours earlier. She had missed her orientation, but hadn't realized it yet.

"I know you're immensely talented at things you haven't discovered yet. That you're secretly very unhappy with the path your life is taking. I know you want things you don't know how to get. I know that you feel different in ways that you can't explain to anyone. It makes you feel alone."

Breena raged, "Why should I trust anything you say or verify anything you ask of me? You've stalked me, scared me; I don't know you. I don't know your last name, your age, where you're from."

"My name is Atlas Thorley. You're Breena Scarlet. Now, tell me if my analysis is right."

She balked. "So you got my last name from the dreams, too? Or was that from the stalking?"

Atlas pointed at her cello case. "That."

She turned around. "Oh." Breena blushed.

"I didn't mean to embarrass you."

The obnoxious cuckoo clock on the back wall of the café, one of the many kitschy trinkets decorating the place, rang five times. "Crap. I'm missing my first day of orchestra. I've got to go." She stood up, shoving her chair back with her knees, and retrieved her purse. She scooped up her books and pencils and tried to shove them in her bag. "This is your fault. If I get kicked out, I'll never forgive you." It was a clumsy motion, and Atlas stood, reaching out, and closed his hands around hers. It wasn't a controlling gesture, but one aimed at comforting.

And there's that tide dragging me in, again. He's a lot like pills. Breena froze and looked up into Atlas' eyes. For the first moment in their entire encounter she wasn't afraid. She felt suddenly at ease with him, much like she used to when his appearance in her reveries had been kind, when she was younger and didn't use as much. *I'm so selfish, blaming everyone else for the trouble I'm having. And here's Atlas, just trying to be near me. Kind of sweet, I guess.*

Chapter 9

Breena set her bag back on the table. *No more pushing people away.* "Do you... do you want to come to my place so we can talk some more?"

"Are you sure? Normally people don't invite their hated enemies home."

"Then I'll pray you're not my enemy." Breena took her chances and left with her stalker in tow. Her desire to get answers outweighed her concern.

"Actually, would you rather come to my house?" Atlas asked as they exited the café. "I've seen that place of yours, you know, through your dreams—"

"You mean through my windows."

He acted like he didn't hear her. "It's pretty, but I've got movies and food, games..."

Breena thought for a second and nodded her head in agreement. They set off in the opposite direction. Butterflies tumbled around in her stomach. Half of them were there from the excitement and the thrill of wandering off with a stranger in a foreign country, the other half were there from the fear of it.

She followed him down the sidewalk unable to catch up until he rounded a corner and stopped at the crosswalk. Breena stood next to him, a good head shorter. They said nothing while waiting until the sign said cross. It was a straight shot from the intersection, an old apartment building with a gate at the front. The security guard buzzed them in. *At least now there's someone who has seen me come here with him.* He turned and looked at Breena. *He's giving me a chance to back out. Look how he's looking right through me. My guts might spill out onto the pavement, or at least my secrets. He wants me to follow him. I want to follow him. This is the most exciting thing I've ever done. Stop saying no to people. Go in.* She passed through the wrought iron gate and walked three steps. It clicked behind her. *That's the sound of the end. I'm not who I was when I woke up. And isn't that what I wanted?* It suddenly frightened her. *No, I've been scared this whole time.*

"It's Ok, Breena. We're going to have a good night," Atlas reassured.

"Oh, so now I'm staying the night?"

Breena and Atlas were in the apartment after climbing four flights of stairs and fighting the stubborn lock on his door. His words startled.

"You can sit over there. I'll be right back." Breena was certain he knew how fast her heart was racing; it was so loud in her ears. It seemed like he knew everything already. "And take some slow deep breaths. Wouldn't want you to pass out."

Atlas paced from corner to corner in his room, whispering to himself. "Ok, she's here. Get yourself together. Make her comfortable. Don't be a freak. Don't mention Tabitha." He paused at a mirror. "I don't think I would've gotten her here without this face." He shoved a hand through his chestnut hair. "You're an arrogant bastard."

Breena shot off a quick email to the director of the intensive, apologizing for her absence and asking for leniency, while she waited for Atlas in the brightly lit white living room. She picked at the skin around her fingernails—a nervous habit her mom called "unattractive."

Well, what if I don't care if I'm attractive or not? What if I feel like shaving off all my hair, wearing big baggy clothes for the rest of my life, and picking at the skin 'til it bleeds? As soon as the angry thoughts escaped Breena's subconscious, he returned.

"You look so beautiful sitting there in that stream of light." Atlas crossed the room and took a seat beside the fidgeting Breena. "I'm glad you came. I want to get to know you, for real, and to make up for all the trouble I've caused."

"You already know me. Down to the very last Neruda quote, it seems. Nothing good will come of our acquaintance. Unfortunately, you're hard to escape."

"They slipped briskly into an intimacy from which they never recovered. F. Scott Fitzgerald. There's more than Neruda, you know."

She made a thoughtful murmur of acknowledgement. The truth of the quote seemed to spell out their future. *It's already happening.*

"Why are you so unhappy? You obviously seek out alternatives to reality. It's how we met. We're the same." He looked at her with tenderness. "Start from the beginning. I want to know everything." It took Atlas no time to jump on the opportunity to comfort Breena by rubbing her back.

"Don't you already know?" As his strong hand passed slowly along her spine, Breena fought the urge to lean in to his touch.

"I want to hear it from you, Beautiful."

Breena cringed against the word and the expectation to open up. *I don't do that. I push. Just ask Jordan.*

He pushed the hair from her eyes, and wiped a tear she hadn't realized was rolling down her pale cheek.

"I can't believe I'm crying in front of you. How stupid." Her skin crawled and her soul wanted out. "And of course in front of the most gorgeous man that walks this earth," she mumbled quietly to herself.

Atlas heard the remark, and it filled him up, but he played at ignorance for her sake and held out his hand.

"Great, take advantage of the crying girl," she snarled.

"Someone sounds bitter," Atlas retorted. "I'm not going to hurt you. Don't you think if I was really all those things you thought I was, that I would have already done something evil by now? I want to make you feel better. It was our fate to meet, remember?" Atlas dropped his hand back to his side. Standing, he walked into the kitchen and pulled a tea pot out of the cabinet beside the stove. He filled it with water and set it on a burner.

"I know you like tea more than coffee," he mentioned as he fumbled around in the refrigerator, "but what do you like to snack on?"

"Anything, really. Surprise me?" Breena said through sniffles. She had quickly clamped down on the crying, but her nose was still drippy. She'd never felt less attractive in front of a man in her life. Breena got off the couch and walked over to the kitchen. She pulled out one of the barstools and settled herself atop it. "Whatcha makin'?"

"Anything. Surprising you," he answered as vaguely as she had moments earlier. "Your tea's ready."

Breena huffed in frustration, but smiled appreciating his humor and proof that he was listening to her. After about fifteen minutes, the various chopped ingredients in the pan began to resemble a meal. She still didn't know what to call it, and he still wasn't telling, but it smelled good enough that Breena didn't care.

When it was done, Atlas plated *it* and carried *it* to his table, which sat in front of the wall-sized window just outside of his kitchen. He went back, poured two glasses of wine, and finally settled in with her at the table.

"Tea *and* wine?" Breena wrinkled her nose at the combination.

"For a toast. You don't have to drink it." He lifted the glass and, between his smile and the strangely hypnotizing swirl of burgundy liquid, Breena found herself holding her breath. "To a journey from which we'll never recover."

Despite the ominous toast, Breena smiled broadly. They clinked glasses and took a sip. "To making friends with a stalker," Breena added. They laughed and drank again.

"This is the most pleasant dinner I've shared with a human in years."

The way he emphasized 'human' made Breena pause. She shook it off. "Me, too. I haven't been on many dates, not that I consider this a date, but I'm alone with a man that's not Jordan. It's weird to even think of Jordan as a man."

"Ouch. Poor guy."

"I'm not saying he's girly or anything. I just mean he's—"

"In the friend zone."

Breena grimaced. "That sounds so cruel, but, yes. I guess you're right. What did you say to him that night at the club, anyway? You really pissed him off."

"Eh, who remembers?" Atlas wore a contented smile as he listened to Breena gradually open up about her friends and her goals with the orchestra.

The wine smoothed over her nerves for a time.

"What are you giggling at?" Atlas broke in.

"That goofy little grin on your face. It's cute."

"Huh. Was I smiling? I didn't notice." Atlas drew in another breath like he was going to keep talking, but he held it in for a minute while he thought. "You know, I don't remember the last time I really smiled. Thank you, Breena. I'm really glad you decided to come back with me."

When the sun started to creep over the horizon, Breena rolled off of the couch and stood, pulling her hair into a ponytail. "I should go home and sleep. If I'm going to convince maestro Fussy Pants to let me be a part of the intensive, I should at least look like I have my stuff together."

"Did he ever email you back?"

"No."

"Well, you're welcome to sleep in the guest room if it would save you some hassle."

"Too much too soon. But, thanks."

Atlas walked her back in the soft morning light. He reached for her hand as they went. She let him take it. When they arrived at her apartment, they stood facing one another, silent, for a second.

"Well, I guess I should go in now," she sighed. Her heart tugged at the thought of leaving Atlas behind. *How odd that I would miss him so much after only one night...*

"Yes, I guess it is that time."

They stared at one another for a few more seconds. Atlas dropped Breena's hand and turned to walk away.

"Come in with me?" Breena called. She sounded like a little child afraid to be alone.

Atlas laughed to himself like he had expected her to ask and turned around, taking four cool strides back her way.

A look of relief washed over Breena's face and she punched the code in the lock, letting them both into the foyer. "I'm glad you're staying..." Breena had a lot she wanted to say to him, but didn't want to make herself sound any needier than she already knew she did by asking him to stay. "Maybe if you're here while I sleep, I won't have nightmares about you," she thought aloud. "And if I invite you in, I can't mistake your presence for stalking," Breena joked.

Atlas laughed, "Good, since I'm not. But I have a question. If it was too soon to sleep over at my house, why do you want me to stay here?"

"I guess there's a sense of security when it's my own place. Should I send you home, then?" she questioned playfully.

"No, no," Atlas answered too quickly. Breena gave him a suspicious look, but they continued into her apartment.

Breena kicked her shoes into the middle of the living room floor and continued into her bedroom. She hadn't realized how exhausted she was, but the cool embrace of her down comforter swallowed her body and sent her immediately to sleep. It had been almost two days since she had taken any pills.

Atlas was seconds behind her entering the room, but she was already out. He stopped in the doorway and looked around. He shrugged. "Now what?" He pulled off his socks and sat beside Breena on the bed. He fought with himself whether or not to touch her hair or leave her be. His urges were too strong to ignore. He brushed her hair away from her face. "She really is lovely."

Atlas mulled over what he learned about her over dinner. Breena was a straight A student at an American high school. She did many of the normal American things he imagined girls her age did. He also learned she had a darker, unhappy side—one that felt she didn't deserve her happy home, her talents, or her life. More than anything, Breena wanted new happiness. To her, a day was just another twenty-four-hour period the world used to judge her as all these things she felt she wasn't.

"What do you see when you look into the mirror, then, because I see so many wonderful things when I look at you," he'd asked.

Her reply: "I don't look in mirrors much." Breena had stared out the window. Her eyes sparkled from the tears she was stubbornly holding back. She whipped her head back around to Atlas and said, "I'm sick of giving myself to the day and having nothing left of myself by the night." Another wave of anger at him washed through. "And you! You caused all of those dreams that sucked the pleasure out of everything I love about the dark. I couldn't enjoy any of it."

"You live in your dreams."

"I used to. I'm so burnt out, though. I don't see what I'd like to anymore. It's all nightmarish." The second "because of you," was implied.

She had repeatedly asked him to tell her about himself, where he was from, how old he was, what his life was like. He refused each time. It was obvious that his dodging peeved her, but the thrill she found in taking such a risk overrode her nature to self-isolate. He was thankful.

Breena made a noise and kicked in her sleep, pulling him back into the present. He wanted so badly to show her more, prove how gorgeous she truly was; he burned to teach her how to realize her dream-worlds; and he had told her as much. But it was not yet time for that. "I'll continue gaining your trust," he'd promised. So, with much restraint, he stroked her hair and watched her sleep, imbuing her with beautiful dreams until she awoke midday in the same position in which she had fallen asleep. Atlas was still there, watching.

Breena cracked her eyes open in small slits. It was bright in her room from the afternoon sun. "Atlas, you're still here."

"Of course. I wouldn't just leave you," he asserted.

"That's sweet. Did you sleep, too?" *Most people*, she thought to herself, *would probably ask that question out of genuine concern for the guest's comfort. Here I am wanting to know if he slept so he wasn't awake to see my mouth hanging wide open, or drooling, or, heaven forbid, farting in my sleep.*

"No, I don't need much sleep. I'll be fine." Atlas brushed Breena's bed head away from her face.

Great, he was awake! "Are you sure?" She didn't see any exhaustion on his face at all.

"Mhm."

"I didn't have any nightmares. Was it because you were awake?"

"Yes."

"I'm sorry you're losing sleep because of me."

"Don't be so hard on yourself. I'm fine."

"Ok. What time is it?"

"2:15, actually. Still getting used to London time?"

She moaned. "I missed rehearsal. You are so bad for me."

"And so it begins. You're not that upset about it, are you?"

"Strangely, no. It's still your fault, though." She threw the covers aside. "Hey. I uh… I need to take a shower. I hate to kick you out of the room, but could you for just a minute? You're welcome to go watch TV if you want to stay. I understand if you have places to be, though."

"Don't be silly." Atlas got off the bed and went into the hall, pulling the door behind him. "Hell, she's great." In the living room, he pulled his phone out of his pocket and typed a quick text to a number that wasn't in his contacts:

"I'm holding up my end of the deal. Are you?"

Chapter 10

Breena grabbed what she needed from her suitcase, stripped down, and streaked into the bathroom. *I'm not crazy. This isn't crazy.* She started the shower and hung up her towel. *But if you're not here for the orchestra, why bother being here at all? You didn't come all this way to meet boys. Although you didn't come not to meet boys.* Atlas hummed in the living room, and the melodic sound dulled as she stepped into the warmth. Under the streams of water, her hair slicked down and stuck to her face. *How could I let a guy derail my plans like this? He really* is *no good for me. But maybe I wasn't supposed to have those plans. That's someone else's life. I shouldn't even be here. It was enough that I lived. I lived and Dad died. Being alive should be enough for me. It was selfish to go after something so big.*

I pushed and pushed until no one wanted to be around me because I cared more about getting out of Michigan and playing the cello than I did about any one of my friends. And here's Atlas, humming in my living room, willfully ignorant, despite our dreams, of the Breena that drives a distance between me and everyone else. He likes this me. Would he still like me if I chose the music? If I pushed back like I usually do?

As she soaped up her tresses, she played back the day before, watching her anger and frustration dissolve into comfortable companionship. *It isn't normal. He isn't normal. But, neither are you. I told him all that stuff about me and he hasn't shared anything in return. And now he's in my house. You should still be pushing.* At this realization, she sped up her showering and got out.

When Breena entered the living room, she found Atlas sprawled out, crucifixion style, in the middle of the floor. His belly rose and fell in a slow rhythm. *Did he fall asleep?* An old record player sat on the coffee table, vinyl whirring softly atop it. Crackling chamber music seeped through the speakers. *He looks more relaxed than I've ever been. Definitely more at ease.* The mood in the air made the hairs on her body stand up. *Creepy.* She cleared her throat. "Hey, Atlas?" No response. "Atlas? You Ok?"

He stirred and rolled onto his side to look at her. He stared into her eyes, but said nothing.

Breena took a few steps toward him and sat down, stretching her legs out and lowering herself onto her elbows. "Whatcha doin?"

"Listening."

"To this old music? It's kinda eerie. Where'd you find it anyway?"

"The top of your coffee table lifts off for storage. That's what I found inside." He gestured toward the record player.

Why would he think to take the top off my coffee table? "Huh." Breena shrugged. "So you like this music? You *wanted* to listen to it?"

"I didn't say I was listening to the music..." he replied. "I'm listening to everything."

"I don't understand." Breena sat up, suddenly uncomfortable with how vulnerable her recumbent position made her.

"In time. I can teach you some day." Atlas' heart skipped a beat and he sat up. He tried to play off the startled look he knew was in his eyes, but Breena was studying him like a specimen in a cage. "I guess I'm not used to being excited about anything."

She squinted. *Just push him away a little bit longer. Get some answers first.*

Suddenly, he jumped up and turned off the music, swiping his wallet off the coffee table. "Come on!" he shouted. "I've got somewhere to show you."

Breena laughed. "You seem different this morning."

"It's not morning. Remember, you slept in."

"Whatever. This afternoon. You're... giddy."

"Well, it takes a lot of pressure off a guy when he's sure the girl he loves doesn't think he's a stalker anymore."

"The what? What did you say?"

"When?"

"Just now. You said, 'The girl he loves.'"

"Don't be ridiculous."

Breena eyed him narrowly.

"You're making that face a lot today."

"You're making weird comments a lot today."

"Whatever. Sure. Now, come on!"

"Is this place going to answer some of my questions?"

"Come find out."

She grabbed her purse, and they were out the door. At the sidewalk, Atlas hailed a taxi. "You stayed overnight. I guess it's not too dangerous to get in a cab with you. Actually, I'm excited. I've never ridden in a cab before."

"Yes, you have. With Jordan."

"How did you... See, you *were* stalking me."

"I swear I did not watch you two go home from the club that night. Why would I want to see you guys together? I merely assumed since it's too far to walk."

"Well, you're right, but that night is better forgotten."

After some hushed instructions from Atlas to the cabbie, they drove away from the curb. The ride was long and bumpy as they entered the country. Atlas signaled the driver to stop, and they got out on the side of a partially paved road in the middle of a field scattered with small cottages. The pair was greeted by the fresh smell of nature. The crispness made Breena want to stretch and revel in the summertime. She lifted her hands to the cotton sky. For once it wasn't raining.

"We'll have to walk through the field to get over there." He pointed.

Hesitation is healthy. This is how you should *feel. Push him away just a little longer. If he doesn't fess up today, then no more.* He started walking, so she followed without questioning.

"Don't let your nerves keep you from enjoying this place. There's nowhere like it."

"Am I just an open book to you?"

"You think you're unemotional, but you wear your feelings all over your face." Atlas paused and reached for her wrist. "And your hands." He held her hand in front of her face, raw edges and picked fingernails on display as proof. "You watch someone for as long as I've watched you, and you learn to read them."

"Right."

After about five silent minutes of walking an uncut path across the field, Breena couldn't hold back the question she'd been chewing on all morning. "If you know me so well from the dreams, how come I don't know anything about you? I saw you there, but—"

"You were the one dreaming. Your mind made you an active participant in whatever events it conjured up. You weren't available to analyze anything objectively, including me. Plus, I was a guest, a passive viewer. Seeing what your mind created and how you reacted to it was very telling. You're rarely in the position to see what my mind is full of or how I deal with it."

"You *were* an active participant. *You* were the one I was always running from. You tried to kill me."

"That wasn't me. That was your anxiety. Your lucid mind probably felt my presence and reacted as if I was a threat. You saw whatever your panic told you to see."

The neared the tree-line. "And if I wanted to watch my dreams from the outside like you did? Or yours?"

"You just need practice. You won't *believe* what you can do."

Atlas allowed himself a wide grin out of Breena's view as he led her across the expanse. He was always so impressed with Breena, he couldn't help but feel a little pride in her and excitement for what she could become.

Breena let the subject drop. She was getting out of breath trying to keep up with Atlas' long gait across the rolling hills toward the woods. *The view from behind him is as good as the scenery.*

"See those woods over there?" He pointed to a small expanse of trees. "There's a little cottage right in the center of it all. No one has used it since..." he trailed off.

Breena saw the far-off look in his eyes. "Since when?"

He avoided the question and began humming a tune Breena recognized. *Another one from my, no, our dreams.* She picked at her fingers waiting for an answer, eventually accepting his unwillingness to divulge more information. She struggled along behind him across the field, which seemed to Breena like it expanded a foot with every stride; one of his was two of hers. When they finally reached the edge of the woods, they stopped to take a breather.

"See why I come here?" He interrupted Breena's appreciation.

Breena filled her lungs with rich air, fragrant with wet leaves and dirt. "It's perfect. Untouched." They were silent for another minute. "Hey, Atlas?" He was less talkative than he had been the night before. Breena pressed on. "Why were my thoughts and dreams the ones that stood out to you? Of all the people in the world, you found *my* dreams."

"Remember, you found me first, made yourself visible to those who felt familiar."

"There are others?"

"You tell me."

"You're the only one I've seen."

"Then, just me, but it's complicated. Just look at it like predestination. You and I aren't so different. You invited me and stood out because you're like me. We were bound to come together."

"What? I'm nothing like you. Your mind is calm. You're self-assured and unworried. I'm none of that."

He turned to face her and brushed a small wisp of hair out of her eyes. "Time will tell, dearest," he said, almost as if he was challenging her. *I hope she helps me.* Atlas stepped through the underbrush and into the forest.

Cold air hit Breena's face like a stone wall. She looked around, confused by the sudden chill, and noticed the white ground. The trees on the field-side of the small forest were fully adorned in their summer leaves. On the inside of the wooded area, it was barren, snowy winter. Breena turned and looked at the sunny, blooming summer behind her, then again at the crystalline fortress of trees in front of her.

"Atlas! It's winter. But, it's summer. What is this place?" Breena was dumbfounded. Waiting for an answer, she wiggled around in excitement and also for warmth.

"I'll explain when we get inside. It's cold; hurry up."

Breena nodded emphatically at his suggestion and power-walked beside his leisurely gate. The ground crunched as she hustled along. "You should have told me to dress better for this weather. My legs are popsicles, and I can feel every icy stick poking at the soles of my shoes. These things are not made for this."

"Would you have believed me? And did you even pack anything for weather like this?"

"Well, no."

Finally, they reached a cottage. It was petite, with mildewed white siding and a slate-blue tin roof. With a quick glance over both shoulders, Atlas approached the door and made fast work of the padlock on the latch. The door opened with a long creak. It made Breena shiver. She wanted to believe it was the cold, but she knew it was because Atlas had tensed as they got closer to the destination. *He seemed so happy a minute ago.*

As the pair walked through the doorway, Atlas noticeably relaxed. Stepping into hazy rays of light which poured through the three little windows on the front and side walls, his shoulders lowered, his back straightened, and his breath deepened.

"Ok, now spill. You say we're the same, that I've got power, that you can show me how to get the life I want. Time to prove it." Breena went to the built-in wooden desk and wiped a finger across one of the floor-to-ceiling shelves in the back of the room. "You haven't been here in a while."

"It's been years." Above the desk, a square hatch in the ceiling was partially open, the wooden door pushed slightly aside. "Well, here it is. Come on," he said, standing beside her. "I'll hoist you up." He stooped, holding his hands out, fingers laced.

"We're going up there? Why can't we stay in here?" *There can't be enough room up there for us.*

"It's just safer."

She sighed and complied. *Push a little, give in a little. Do what you need to get answers.* Breena put her left hand on his left shoulder. *Oh. Muscular. Nope. Doesn't influence me at all.* Stepping into his hands, she reached to grab the ledge. All of this nervous preparation was unneeded.

"Woo!" Breena squealed as he popped her right up into the little room above with no effort at all. "Ha. That was fun. I thought you were going to sail me right through the roof." Breena leaned forward to look down through the hatch. "How are you going to—"

He hopped into the attic gracefully and shoved the door into place. "Like that." He sat on top of it, cross legged, emotionless, and stared at Breena, who was staring at him. "Ok, Ok, I know I have a lot of explaining to do. I know you're worried and confused. I know you want answers. I won't say what *other*, more indecent, thoughts you're sending my way."

Breena noticed she was still leaning forward, inches away from his face. She blushed and pulled back. *What's that look? Like a hurricane on an ocean. Anxiety? That's new. Though, when would I have seen him look at me like this in the whole twenty-four hours I've known him in person?*

He cut his eyes to the little circular window in the V of the roof. She lifted a hand and rested it on his, a timid, senseless gesture she couldn't imagine was actually comforting coming from another nervous wreck like her.

He sighed.

Chapter 11

"When I was very young, my mother died. No one talked about how it happened, but I knew. I saw enough to know my dad killed her. By the time I was 12 or 13, I can't remember, no one ever celebrated my birthday, I was on my own. It's been a lonely life. My dad abandoned me in the states. I conned my way here." Atlas gestured around himself. "I wandered around town working for money under the table—just enough to eat and save up for a train ticket to the next place. I ended up staying, though." Atlas trailed off and scrubbed his face, thinking about the real nature of his parentage, and how he couldn't throw all of that onto Breena yet. It made his stomach hurt to lie to her.

"You were just a kid. How did you survive?"

"Managed to make a couple connections, not friends, but people that helped keep me alive." Atlas fiddled with his cell phone at the thought of Vos, the thug who took him in before Tabitha came around. Atlas' gaze trailed Breena's features, landing intensely on her eyes.

Breena twisted her hands. *Oh, my gosh can he hear my heart thumping? What am I supposed to do with this information? You can't just say 'It's Ok,' or 'It'll be alright,' to something like that. Why is he looking at me like that? Oh, crap, did I miss something he said?*

"I'm sorry I'm not very good at this. I've never told anyone about myself. There was no one to listen before you." Atlas pulled his knees up to his chest and rested his chin on the right one.

Breena sighed and brushed a few strands of hair out of Atlas' eyes. "It's alright. I want to know. I have all summer." *Stupid! I told you not to say, 'It's alright.'*

"I run. I hide. I don't let people get to know me. I don't want to be like that with you, though. You're special. Equal. I can feel your soul and it feels like something to hold on to. You'll bring me happiness."

Breena straightened. "That's a lot to live up to."

"You can do it."

She pursed her lips, unconvinced.

"Before Mom died, things were far from perfect. My dad was a monster. But, Mom made her own happiness. Her name was Reine. She was beautiful and kind. All the men in our little town wanted her, and maybe that's why Dad was so violent, like it was her fault the other men looked and his show of dominance would keep them away. I don't know. But, despite his rage, she had strength. It was otherworldly, in a way, how she projected her calm onto the chaos around us. In France, where I was born, there were rolling valleys and a ridge of mountains that you could see from our house. She and I had a special place on one of the lower crests that we used to visit. We always went there together." Atlas looked up at Breena. He was beaming with pride in his mother, but the sorrow seeped out of him like a toxin.

He went on, absently picking at his lip. "One day, I came out of the house, and I saw my father beating on her out in the field beside the house. I wanted to run, or scream, or kill him, but I was too scared, and too young, and too weak. Instead, I hid inside until it got quiet. I knew. Her soul came to me; she wanted me to run as hard as I could to the spot we used to share. I'd never been up there alone."

"You don't have to tell the whole story at once. We can go outside and get some fresh air."

"No. It's Ok. My father burst into the house, so I did run. Right past him and out the door. I wouldn't have had the guts to get near him like that if Mom hadn't been there beside me. As I ran, he hollered that it was all my fault, that if I had obeyed them, he wouldn't have had to punish her for raising a disobedient, evil son. Dad didn't follow me far. I guess he wore himself out beating Mom. That, and he just didn't care if I got lost in the woods or not. When I got to the top of the ridge, I sat down and crossed my legs. I just sat. I didn't even cry. It was like I was waiting for her. But, night came and I still sat alone on the ridge. Nighttime noises began at sundown, and they startled me. Finally, I cried."

Breena scooted closer to Atlas. *I feel so bad for him. There's nothing I can do to fix his past. I guess if he thinks I can make his future happier, I should stick around for him and try.* He tugged at his hair. Breena thought he might not go on.

After a heaving breath, he said, "Morning came and I woke up under a tree. I still, to this moment, don't remember walking to that tree deep in the woods or falling asleep there. So, after I woke up I wandered around until I found myself back on the trail down to my house. When I got back, people were everywhere. Apparently, he hadn't bothered to hide what he'd done to Mom, and after the first person spotted her slumped in the yard, the neighbors flocked to our house. You know how small towns are."

"Wait, so why didn't they take him away? Punish him?"

He gave a wry smile and a shrug. "*He* was the law. So, I shoved through the crowd. My dad was slouched against the door jamb looking out at all the people with a hollow expression I'd never seen. At least when he was in a rage, there was some obvious emotion there. But, he just stared at me: cold, absent, hateful."

Atlas shivered. "In that moment, I felt his soul. That man was evil down to the frame of his being, and not like the demon versus angel, balances the good in the world with the bad, type of evil. Human evil. Vicious, senseless. And then he grinned at me. I didn't realize at the time that that's when my gift made itself known. Awareness of it came in my teens, but that's how I was able to feel him like that. My dad, he was grinning, and he said, 'Your mom left.' Of course, she never came back. For years I searched for her soul, but I didn't know what I was doing. I came to the conclusion that my gifts were inadequate, that *I* was the reason I couldn't feel her. Maybe I was evil like my father said I was, like he thought my mother had been; maybe we deserved it. If we hadn't been different, maybe he wouldn't have hated us. I know he was the malicious one, but as a kid it's easy to believe what a parent tells you."

Atlas' recount of his childhood frayed Breena's nerves so entirely that she could no longer sit still. *I should've brought some pills.* She was acutely aware that the sun was dimming outside, that her feet were falling asleep from sitting, and that Atlas was nowhere near finished talking. *Just let him finish. I'm getting to know him. This is what I wanted, right?*

"And that's why we met in our dreams. I was out searching. The only way to find a dead woman is to scour the spiritual world. Maybe one day her soul will reach out like yours did. I need that happiness."

By this time, Atlas had reclined to his side, but he didn't look any more relaxed. If anything, he had paled from recalling those memories and lied down from faintness. "For years after she was gone, Dad moved us from town to town trying to keep people from getting to know us. Eventually, we went to the U.S., but I never liked it there. He hit me often for no reason. He was always drunk. Then, one day, he wasn't there at all. I never saw him again. That's when I started drifting." He paused. "Talk to me."

"I'm just so sad for you." Breena leaned across the small space and reached her arms around him. She rested her head in the curve of Atlas' neck. They both sighed deeply. Her embrace was warm and soft against his cold body. Atlas inhaled her sweetness and shuddered at the way she swept her nails across his back.

He reached up to her shoulders to pull her off of him so he could look into her eyes. They were misty. "Why are you teary? I haven't even gotten to the sad parts yet."

"Haven't gotten to the sad parts? It's *all* sad!"

"Well, we'll see what you think when I'm done." Atlas started back into his burden. "The first few towns I wandered through after Dad left were the worst. I was about 12, so it was almost impossible to find a job, even with the crooked bastards that paid below minimum wage under the table. By the time I looked like a man, finding a job was no big deal. Finding places to stay, well, let's just say I had to sacrifice a lot for a room. The last person I stayed with lived in a town called Hell. I don't remember what state it was in, but the irony wasn't lost on me. It wasn't even irony, really. It felt so true."

Breena's eyes widened when he said, "Hell," but he sped through his story too quickly for her to interject that the town was in Michigan where she lived.

"Anyway, I stayed with this old lady in a pretty crappy house. She paid me to keep up with the few animals she had and the land that she owned..." Atlas trailed off, remembering.

"You Ok?" This particular scenario didn't seem so bad to Breena, so she started to believe Atlas' "I haven't even gotten to the sad part yet."

"Yeah, I'm fine... just getting to the parts that I'm not so proud of, but I want you to know this stuff. I want you to trust me, no secrets."

Do you still want to know? No backing out, now.

"When I wasn't ignoring these visions, because that's what I thought they were at first, I was trying to pray it away. I started to resent God for making me into such a person, and for leaving me after countless pleas to be relieved of my so-called talent. One night, I was out in the little shed where the old lady kept her gardening tools. It was so cold and clear. All the stars blinked and the air smelled like chimneys and frosted grass. I'll never forget how deeply I breathed that air, thinking the freezing sensation was the feeling of the purity burning away the blackness I felt inside of me. She had asked me to put away the rake I'd left on the porch before dinner. I didn't want to go back into the cold. I had finally begun to warm up during dinner. But, she gave me shelter; it was only fair to do what she asked of me. Anyway, while I was in the shed, I started thinking about this fantasy I had in my head. It was a recurring daydream I'd had since I'd gone on my own."

"What was it?"

"My version of perfection. I envisioned myself on top of a mountain, the very top, standing in awe of everything below me— the valley, the rays of sunlight streaming across all the trees, little streams. I tried to notice everything, to take it all in, so that when my daydreaming was over I would feel as if I'd been there and life wouldn't be so empty." Atlas stopped like he was calculating how to broach his next statement. His eyes lit up and he asked, "You ever have those dreams that feel so real you can't tell if it happened or not when you wake up?"

"All the time."

"Well, I thought that was happening to me. Part of me thought I'd lost myself in this beautiful place inside my head, but somehow I knew it was different than a daydream. I spun around in circles on top of the mountain; I could smell the pine trees and the wind; I could hear the little stream nearby that trickled down the mountain. It all felt too real. Suddenly, Ms. Peters walked into my daydream. I was taken aback. Certainly I wasn't dreaming of her. In reality, she had found her way through the dark to the shed, worried something had happened. Apparently, I'd been out there a while. She wandered right into what I had thought was my daydream. It was more of an illusion. The vision in my head became a sort of reality. I was still in the shed, but the scenery had changed."

That's what happened to me in the apartment. Breena stared on, rapt.

"As soon as Ms. Peters entered the shed, she panicked. She acted like she'd been abducted by aliens or something, first quiet, stunned, and then full-on tantrum, screaming at me for kidnapping her to that place. Her reaction proved it was real. Or, some sort of real. I didn't understand it all yet. All I knew was this wasn't just in my head. It was around me. I knew others could see my hallucinations."

Atlas shook his head, correcting himself. "They *weren't* hallucinations. So, I just stood there in the little shed, surrounded by nature while she yelled, looking this way and that. It's not like she could escape down the mountain. She was no match for the terrain. I closed my eyes and tried to focus on something that would make the scene go away, but I didn't know what I was doing. It had seemed like my longing brought on the illusion, and there was no sense of longing to draw from to get me back to the shed. It wasn't where I wanted to be."

If longing brings this on, what does that say about my nightmares?

"Fortunately, if you could ever call making a granny scream fortunate, her panic, plus the realization that my daydreams were materializing, rattled me enough that the image fell apart on its own. I eventually learned that strong shifts in emotion were the quickest way to interrupt the visions. Anyway, that was the last day she let me stay with her. As soon as the image fell, she grabbed a rake by the door and chased me out saying not to ever come back, that I was the son of Satan and a user of black magic." Atlas chuckled bitterly to himself at the Satan comment. "If she only knew."

"Wait, this thing you do is magic?"

"No. She sounded like my father. So far, I've done a great job living up to his low standards. After that, I started to put together all the strange moments I'd had 'til that point—starting with the day I felt my father's soul after he killed Mom."

Atlas stopped and stared out of the little window in the eve of the roof. Breena leaned in to look with him, and a strand of her hair brushed past his cheek. He turned to look at her; she didn't notice.

I wonder what he calls that gift of his, the dream and illusion stuff. Was he influencing me this whole time? Even when I was awake? That's the only way to explain that scene in my apartment.

Atlas studied Breena, his hand hovering above her back. Her hair smelled like warm sugar. The light streamed through the window, rippling through the swaying trees outside, and cast a faint yellow glow around her, an angel's aura. They were as far from "angel" as creation allowed, and he couldn't believe Breena came from the underworld. He could feel his own darkness, always had; it was something that made sense given Tabitha's little history lesson. But, Breena seemed like light. Not burning and blinding like the sun. She was the moon, a soft glow in the darkness. She turned toward Atlas then, and caught him staring.

"What? You don't have to talk about it anymore if you don't want to."

Atlas blinked a few times. "No, it's fine."

"Uh huh…" she nodded skeptically. "It's Ok, 'ya know."

"What is?"

She wiped the wetness from the corner of his eye. "That."

"Ignore me. You'd think as many times as I relived this stuff in my head I would've gotten over it by now."

"Don't beat yourself up. You went through something traumatic—"

"I *am* something traumatic."

"No. It's Ok to think about it. I know what that's like." She leaned across the small space between him and rested her forehead against his, willing some relief into him.

"You're beautiful." She leaned back putting space between them again. Atlas continued before Breena could protest further. "I know, I know, you hate that. But, maybe you won't mind hearing it from me?"

"Well, it's still not my favorite, but..." she trailed off as if she could convince herself that she could deal with it.

"If it helps, it's not just because of your looks. Not that you're looks are bad or anything." She turned to stare out of the window some more, and Atlas immediately regretted bringing any of it up.

"Look, I'm sorry. Really. I think it's sweet of you to say, and I guess it's true. Enough people say it, so it must be, right? But you know how tired I am of people trying to woo me with no real effort, without getting to know me. Not that I like to open up to people, anyway. It's just never going to stop bothering me. I don't deserve that kind of unearned attention."

"Obviously, I think your wrong, but I understand the struggle. It's hard to be happy, satisfied, when you feel like you're someone different than everyone assumes. Sometimes I wonder if it's even worth the trouble. Who am I trying to convince? Mainly myself, I guess."

"We really are alike. When people are constantly telling you you're one thing, and it doesn't fit what you see in the mirror or feel in your gut, it makes life feel like a constant fight. I'm tired of fighting. It's like I'm not really supposed to be here. Not that I'm supposed to be dead, although maybe that's true, too—" the night of the fire loomed over her "—but that I'm not supposed to be *here*. Like I'm something else entirely." Breena gestured around herself.

Atlas could barely resist the urge to let her in on her full history.

"Ugh. Enough of me. Finish your story."

"Ok, then. Where was I?"

"The old lady, Ms… Peters? She wouldn't let you stay with her anymore."

"Right. Needless to say, she was terrified of me and the whole situation in the shed. I was more astounded than scared, myself, but she wouldn't even let me explain, not that I really knew what to say that could explain *that* anyway."

"Can you explain it now? Does what you do have a name?"

He shrugged. "Call it what you like. So, I left in my long johns, a jacket, and my boots without the few things I owned. Worst of all was the journal I had to leave behind. Thinking of her reading it still makes me cringe."

"How long ago was this?"

"Um, six years ago?"

"And you were around 14. So, you're 20?

"Something like that."

"I can't believe you were in the same state as me. You could've been any guy I saw on the street. What if we met once way back then?"

"I guess it's possible, but I feel like I would remember that. There would have been a sense of familiarity when I came across you in my sleep."

"So you weren't dreaming about me back then?" *That would be a little bit flattering if he'd been searching for me all this time.*

"I was dreaming about someone, but I didn't know who it was back then. I suppose it could have been you. Children don't really show up as clear souls in dreams. They are constantly changing, so their dream personalities vary from dream to dream. If I dreamt of you then, you're too different now for me to know that you're the same person. But it's not impossible."

"Huh…" She picked at her fingers. "Yeah, you wouldn't have wanted anything with a little kid like me, anyway. I was eleven when you were working on that farm. And how did you get into London? Your dad had already split by then, right, so who brought you here?"

"I forged my way back in—fake documents. It wasn't easy."

Ok. Pry just a little more. You can't go along with whatever he says and not ask questions.

Chapter 12

"You said you hadn't gotten to the sad part yet. That was a while ago. So, why are you so ashamed of that story? You didn't mean to scare the old lady."

Atlas laid back and stared at the ceiling. Little clusters of cobwebs shook as he exhaled a deep sigh. The reluctance to do what was required to gain her trust was a powerful barrier, like a muzzle on his memories, but he needed her trust. "Well, after I was a state away from that lady's farm, I holed up in an abandoned hunting cabin in the woods. It was a lot like this one, actually. I lived there for a few months doing nothing but exploring my daydreaming and the images that formed. As I got better, I realized that I was creating illusions rather than day-dreaming things to life. I could do it at will without getting trapped in the dream."

"That's amazing."

"It didn't feel amazing. It was a burden. It *still* is. I was very bitter about my childhood, my father leaving, having to wander the states, and about having to leave that lady's house without my belongings. I vacillated between loving the potential power my talent gave me and hating it for the destruction it caused in my life. I wanted my journal. So, I went back there. I broke in; I threatened the old woman with a knife, tied her up, and tried to find my journal. It wasn't under the mattress. I was furious. All of my actions and implements were illusions, but she didn't know that. In my anger, I played around with the illusion to scare her some more. I enjoyed her terror. It made up for losing my journal. It was the last piece of my mom. She had written a note on the first page when she gave it to me. So, I left the old lady in her fake bonds until I was out of the state again, then I shattered the illusion."

"Did she send the cops after you?"

"She died of a heart attack from the fear before I had even left her cottage."

"Atlas!" Breena cried.

"So, no, I did not flee to England because she sent the law for me. I was just fleeing the memories my father had stained the U.S. with."

"You can't blame her death on your father. *You* did that."

Atlas bolted upright and gaped at her. "You're defending him?"

"No, but—"

His volume increased. "You don't know what you're talking about. He was a murderer who hated his own family. You have no idea what you're talking about."

"So are you! You killed. Do you see that? You have to take responsibility, too."

"You think I don't replay that day until I can't see anything else? I do. I force myself to relive it. It's the only penance I get."

Breena had scooted away from Atlas until her back was against the wall.

Atlas cursed under his breath. "Great. Look, Breena, I'm not mad at you. I'm angry at myself. I don't like to have my weaknesses on display, much less shoved back at me by someone who barely knows me." He closed his eyes and held his breath. When he opened them again, the emotion had gone from his face. His eyes were blank.

Just like his dad.

"When I first came to England, I was still wandering. I lived in this cottage for a few months before I made a permanent home in London. Every day, I walked to the city to search for a job. I finally got one, and my apartment, through the good will of a lady I met at the café. The shelter of the woods gave me good cover for practicing, too." He hated lying to Breena about his living situation, but it wasn't the right time to introduce Tabitha as his benefactor or her mother.

Breena tried hard to stifle her gut instinct to run. *Change the subject.* "See, so there are good people some places." *Like me. Don't hurt me.* "What do you do?"

"I'm the woman's personal assistant. She did me a favor and got me a job. Now, I do her favors. I owe her. We have a good arrangement." He mentally rolled his eyes.

Breena nodded. "I'm glad someone's looking out for you. So, now, tell me why it's winter in these woods in the middle of summer."

Atlas scooted over, lifted the lid off of the hatch, and jumped down to the room below. "Just a little illusion for you. Proof, if you want to think of it like that. Come on, time to go. There's somewhere else I want to show you."

Lilly's voice swam through Breena's memory. *"Never let him get you to the second location!"* Lilly always gave words of caution after watching too much CNN. Now, it didn't seem so unreasonable. Her own voice of rebellion piped up next. *But you've already been to the second location, and look, you're fine.* To stall their departure, Breena decided to take close study of the craftsmanship of the little attic's interior. *Last chance to back out of whatever it is this is becoming.*

"Come on!"

Breena wiggled over to the hatch and dangled her legs through the hole. "How am I supposed to get down from here?" Atlas made a grunting noise. *Guess I'm on my own.* She rolled over onto her belly and slid down through the hole.

Atlas wrapped his arms around her thighs so she could let go of the ledge.

"Oh, hey, you're close." *Don't be a freak.* She dropped into his arms. He spun around with her. Breena felt the edge of the large desk press into the backs of her legs. Atlas sat her down. His arms were still around her waist. *He's still holding me. Why does he have to be so pretty?* His eyes lingered on her lips, then eyes, neck, back to the lips. Breena knew where this was headed.

She fought the attraction with her lingering disgust and fear. *Ugh, Breena, don't act like you don't want him just a little. Or a lot.* Atlas placed his hand at the base of Breena's head and curled his fingers into her hair. She sucked in a breath and tilted her head slightly back, knowing which side of her conscience was about to lose. Atlas brought his face close to Breena's neck and inhaled deeply.

"Thank you for not freaking out." His lips grazed her neck. Breena shivered and Atlas gripped tighter, the hand still around her waist pushing into her flesh.

"You're not that person anymore." The whole scene moved in slow motion, tentativeness mixed with appreciation.

"No."

Breena let go of Atlas' earlier admissions entangling her hands in his hair. "I'm holding you to that." She slid them down the sides of his face and guided his mouth to hers.

Atlas grabbed Breena's legs and pushed them aside. She spun around on the desk, and he climbed up beside her. They kissed a few more times reclining further with each advance. Breena shut up the last of her inner critic and relaxed under his cocooning weight. Atlas smiled a devious grin against Breena's lips, and she let go of her doubts.

"Teach me how to make an illusion. I want to see it myself," Breena whispered.

"No, you're not ready for that," he protested between kisses placed roughly along her collar bones.

"Please, Atlas? Come on. I want to know first-hand what it's like. I want to know I'm not crazy for believing you." *And I'm starting to withdraw. Give me a distraction.*

He knew Tabitha wanted to train Breena herself. Tabitha would be furious if she knew. Atlas knew, though, that the quicker he had Breena fully on his side, the quicker he and Vos could do away with Tabitha, and the quicker he and Breena could create a new reality for the world. "Look in my eyes," he commanded.

Hell yes. The scenery around them wavered and she could feel tingly heat brushing against her skin. The air looked blurry and tangible. Then, it settled. Breena sat up and looked around. She and Atlas were sitting beside a waterfall on a patch of lush green grass. There were trees on the opposite bank of the river fed by the falls. Atlas rolled back on top of Breena and they continued kissing—legs, arms, and hair twisted together. Sealed in a tight embrace, they romped in the grass for what seemed like hours. In reality, it had only been ten minutes when they returned to the cottage as it normally appeared. The illusion faded, and Atlas rolled off of Breena. Standing up, she glanced at Atlas and mumbled something lewd under her breath as she walked to the window.

Running her finger across the sill to check if it was all real she said, "That was amazing. Thank you for showing me." She cracked her knuckles. "Until now, I've only been able to find peace with sleep and dreams. I thought you were going to teach me how to create it, though."

"Told you. Not ready."

"Well, I guess I'll just have to stick around, then. You've given me something to look forward to. Maybe we can both find some happiness."

"Thank *you*. Without you there, my illusions feel more like curses. Can you imagine how empty a world that beautiful feels when you have no one to share it with? When all it did in the past was hurt people?"

"As corny as that sounds, I guess that's a good point. I'm sorry you're lonely." Breena stared at the ground. Her temporary high was quickly vanishing. The more she got to know him, the sorrier she felt, and the longer they stayed out, the worse her shakes got.

"Oh, no, no, no. Smile. Don't be sad. I'm not trying to make you feel bad. Please, don't be sad," he begged.

"I'll cheer up." *As soon as I get some medication in me.* "But only if we stay friends when I leave London."

"I guess I can put up with that."

Atlas dropped Breena at her door late that night. "I can't stay tonight. I've got a meeting with someone."

"In the middle of the night?"

"He likes to keep a low profile."

Breena raised an eyebrow. "Just don't do anything stupid, Ok? I finally decided you're not dangerous to me, so don't go proving me wrong."

"Yes, ma'am." He saluted then gave her a quick peck on the cheek before leaving.

Breena hustled inside too desperate for a pill to watch him go. She plugged the sink and held the baggie over it as she fumbled with the plastic zipper. *If they spill, they spill.* With a clumsy yank, the bag popped open and about half of the pills rained down into the sink, bouncing around in the porcelain basin like jumping beans. *Told ya.* She grabbed one wishing it was two and swallowed it without a drink. Breena waited for it to take hold, but she was still buzzing with energy hours later. *What an amazing day. I have to talk to someone about it. What time is it at home? Let's see... 3:00am minus five hours... 10:00pm. Lilly's definitely awake.*

"Lilly, you'll never guess what I did today."

"Hello to you, too." Lilly stretched over the end of her bed, hanging upside down with the phone in her hand.

"I went to a cabin in the woods with a guy!"

"What? Who is he? Are you going to tell Jordan?"

"Hell no. Besides, we really haven't spoken since he went home."

Lilly swayed back and forth, admiring her wall posters from a new angle. "No kidding. Now I'm the one who has to hear all his thoughts you must have listened to all these years."

"Oh, so he's shamelessly coming on to you, too?"

She shook her head and the fountain of red hair spilling down to the floor swayed with the motion. "I didn't mean that. I just mean the family problems and the you problems and in-depth discussions about bands I have no idea about. But enough about him. Tell me about your adventure!"

"Ok, so I met a guy at this café I've been going to."

"Name?"

"Atlas. I was hesitant at first. He's very... intense. But, he's also got this thing, I don't know what it is. It's like a magnet. I couldn't help but be into him, even when I was intimidated. He invited me back to his place and, like a crazy person, I accepted."

"Breena, that's so dangerous!"

"I knew you'd say that. We ended up talking all night, and he stayed over my place when I went back home." She heard Lilly gasp on the other end, but kept going. "Nothing happened. So, today, we went to the country and he showed me this amazing little cabin in the woods. We hung out and talked until late this evening. And that's it."

"He didn't make a move on you? He just wanted to talk?"

"I didn't say that..."

"So he did?"

"There was no hunter and prey situation. It was mutual, and it was amazing. I mean, I don't have a lot of people to compare him to, but let's just say he topped the ones so far."

Lilly sat up from her hanging position. "You slept with him?" The rush of blood leaving her head made the room spin.

"No, Lilly, jeez. I'm not *that* rash. My first time with a stranger? Please."

"Good. Sleeping with a stranger might *give* you a rash. Gross."

Breena cringed into the phone then sighed. "I miss you. Up until today, I've just wanted to come home. I'm starting to think it might be worth it to be here, but I still miss hanging out. Thank you for the picture by the way. It cheered me up."

"So how's orchestra? How'd you find all this time to spend with boy toy? I thought it was an intensive schedule."

"Yeah, it is, but I'm not a part of it."

"What do you mean?"

"I missed my first day. They wouldn't let me come after my absence."

"Your mom is going to kill you!"

"No, because *no one is going to tell her.* Right?"

"I wish I didn't even know."

"You *don't* know."

Lilly groaned. "Don't know what?"

"There ya go! Thanks, Lil. Hey, so, it's really late here. I'm gonna go try to get some sleep. It was really good to talk. I'll call again in a few days?"

"You better. Sleep good."

"Night."

****

Atlas met Vos across town behind the pub where Vos tended bar. It was a cheery, raucous kind of place, and Atlas always found it amusing to see Vos in there, huge and sober, with all the cackling drunks around him.

"So did you get her on our side?"

"She's on my side. She doesn't know about you yet, and I haven't told her who she really is, what she can do, or what we plan to do. It's only been a day. But I told you I was keeping my end of the deal. I'll get her to help us. Don't worry."

"I'll worry if I damned-well please. Atlas, I told you before. I am not doing this for you. It is not a favor. I want Tabitha gone, too, and for my own reasons, so don't cock it up. You'll have to hide from Tabitha *and* me."

"I don't think *you* realize who you're dealing with. You have no clue what I'm capable of. My influence over Breena is strong, and the only reason I need her is to maintain my image with Tabitha. I don't need Breena to do my job." Atlas resisted the urge to pace. He knew it would make his show of power less convincing. It killed him that he wasn't strong enough on his own to get rid of Tabitha. He didn't want to use Breena, and he definitely didn't want Vos' help, but Vos had lost his son to the family Tabitha sent him to grow up with. It could have just as easily been Atlas dying at the hands of his father. Atlas understood Vos' motives.

"Well, the next time we meet, you better give me some proof she's been trained. Otherwise, I might have to report to Tabitha that her daughter's destined mate has met an unsightly, accidental death. You are, after all, far easier to replace than the girl."

A cop car with its lights on slowly rolled by the men, startling away a large dove from the roof across the street. Atlas turned on his heels and walked in the direction of his apartment. Over his shoulder, he told Vos, "I'll text you when she's ready."

Atlas woke up to a text from Breena.

"Atlas, I thought the nightmares would end after I got to know you. If we're going to see each other in person, why do you have to keep visiting my dreams?"

He pinched his nose. *I've lost control.* He wrote back. "I wasn't doing it on purpose. We're linked, now. It's like muscle memory. I just keep coming back to you."

"Well come over here, then."

They spent the day in bed, Atlas projecting image after image on the room around them like they were taking a world tour. He taught Breena lucid dreaming methods that might help curb her nightmares. Guilt sat heavy in his chest. All her fears and anxieties wore his face when she slept. He wasn't trying to embody those characters.

They went on like that for weeks—eating, sleeping and canoodling, practicing. They went back to the cabin one day so Atlas could teach her how to create illusions using his soul as a template, but his guard was still up about her true nature and Tabitha's involvement. Breena hadn't contacted Tabitha since the awkward end to their dinner party. He knew Breena wouldn't take it well. Instead, Atlas presented the training as another method for coping with her unhappiness.

"Maybe it will help your anxiety. If you can escape while you're awake, maybe once you sleep there won't be as many fears running around in there." He tapped Breena's temple.

"My biggest fear now is going back home." She threw an image of the place up on the cabin wall in front of them. Atlas clapped. She'd gotten good in a short time. "One month left. I don't want to go. I have more in common with you than anyone else I know. I'm going to be completely alone when I get back. I've changed too much. Everything will feel foreign."

"Did you feel that way when you got here?"

"Yes."

"Do you still feel like that about London?"

"No."

"Ok, then. I think that means you'll acclimate. Try not to worry away the rest of your time here."

"Give me something to remember. Please?"

Atlas stared at her. "I haven't given anything memorable yet?"

"No, I didn't mean it like that. I will always remember this, but—" she looked into his eyes.

"You want more, don't you?"

"Yes."

"Don't lose yourself in this lifestyle. You can't live in your fantasies all the time." *And after we're done with Tabitha, you won't have to.*

"Just do this for me!"

"Fine. But, if I give you this little trip, you have to promise to keep practicing to do it for yourself. You're almost there."

"I still don't know why you're so convinced I can get as good as you," she argued.

"I'm not convinced. I'm certain. I *need* you to be."

Breena huffed and agreed. Her needs in the moment were stronger than her lack of confidence in her capabilities.

"Why don't you start this one," Atlas suggested.

"Fine. Look in my eyes." Breena stared into his eyes as a way to focus on the vibrations around her. He had taught her to do this until she could better grasp the concept of creating the images solo. She didn't need the crutch anymore, but it provided a great excuse to stare. Their eyes were locked for a minute, but nothing happened. Frustrated, she threw herself back on the bed and slammed her fists down beside her.

"I can't focus. You make me all... Come on. Just do it for me tonight. Why do you insist on making me work for it?"

"Breena, hush." Atlas lay beside her and grabbed her hand. "Come on, let's go."

She turned her head and sighed with relief. Atlas brought to life a fantasy world so fantastic that Breena gasped loudly when it appeared. Breena took a few steps down the long pebbled walk, the smooth stones cold under her bare feet. She paused for a second and spun around. *The forest is so dark, almost like it's not even green. Looks dangerous.* They resumed walking. At the trail's end, the white stone of a gothic citadel kissed the endlessly grey sky with large arches and buttresses. "Can we go in?"

Atlas nodded.

Breena followed the white marble corridor until a large cherry wood door blocked her path. She tried the knob. "It's open." She shouldered the door open. "Woah, that smell. Oleander?" Fully inside, she gasped. "Atlas, look at all the flowers! The walls are made of flowers! Orchids, lilies, hydrangeas... How did you do this?" Breena dove across the bed in the center of the room, a white four-poster bed with a mattress so thick she nearly needed a step-stool to mount it. "The ceilings are way up there, aren't they?"

"So your sky light is closer to the heavens."

She stared up through the one large window in the top of the room. The clear, shining night sky hung above it. *I could fall asleep. Oh, a butterfly.*

Atlas stood in the doorway with a self-satisfied grin and watched her admire the tiny red butterfly that had landed on her outstretch hand.

"Red to match your lips," Atlas said into the silence, then turned and left the room.

"Wait, where are you going? I'm coming!" Eluded by his quick exit, Breena launched herself off the bed and hurried after him down another hallway and out an intricate stained glass door into a garden. *I don't understand how he made such a huge illusion. How are we walking around in it without leaving the bed? Don't worry about that now. Look at what you're missing!*

Small waterfalls surrounded by soft beds of flowers contradicted sharp statues. "You thought of everything."

Atlas reclined against an angel statue, giving Breena a smug smile.

"You're not very talkative."

"This time is for you." Atlas rested his head against the grey marble. He loved watching Breena discover all that an illusion could include, but maintaining one so thorough sapped his energy. He closed his eyes.

Oh, that water's cold. Breena pulled her hand out of the cascade and followed a short path around the angel statue and under an ivy-covered pergola. A damp breeze crossed her, and she noticed clouds gathering. *He even got the weather right.* In the distance, rain fell on the forest around their fortress. *Actual rain. It's getting closer. And there it is. Immediately soaked.* Breena's drenched dress clung. *I don't even care.* She danced in the rain like a child. Lightning crashed around the garden, missing them barely. *Everything seems so real. The lightning is hot. Feels the same as when we first met, that fire I saw. Maybe that was an illusion, too. I guess if this is all a part of him, then it would have a similar composition.* Breena spun until dizzy, her thoughts spinning, too. When she sat, her surroundings still whirring past her, she caught Atlas' expression in the passing images, a smile that reached his eyes. *That's new.*

Atlas knew he couldn't maintain the illusion for much longer, so he seized the opportunity to take Breena's hand while she was finally still. He pulled her off the ground and wrapped his free arm around her waist.

He smells so good. Goose bumps rose on her arms as his hand settled on the small of her back.

Still holding Breena's hand, he raised her arm into a proper waltzing form.

I don't know how to dance.

Atlas glided around in a smooth waltz with Breena aptly in tow. He did all the work, and her insecurities eased. *Apparently he does.* They whipped around the garden patio at an increasing gait; Atlas made sure Breena never missed a step. *I shouldn't have done all that spinning. And, there go the knees.* She hung from Atlas by her wrists where he caught her.

Atlas howled with laughter. He lifted her chin.

"Don't laugh at me just 'cause I don't know how to dance. You didn't know how to eat corn on the cob last night." When Breena met his eyes, he was alight with joyfulness she never saw outside of his illusions.

"I'm not laughing at you. I'm having *fun*! As for the corn..." Atlas paused for a moment to really look at Breena. She had an impish grin on her face, and her dripping dress clung to her down to the ankles. "Forget the corn. Let's go find more clothes." It was the perfect time to head back inside. He needed to drop all of the detailed components of the illusion and funnel the rest of his energy into her flowered room.

They changed and sat on the edge of the large bed to admire the flowers one last time. Atlas leaned over to Breena and whispered, "In a perfect world, you could have this every day." With that, he broke the illusion apart. The dusty attic room of the cottage came into focus.

During their taxi ride back to Breena's flat, she stared out the window into the dark night. *In a perfect world? Why can't it be like that, now?* Breena closed her eyes and imagined her version of a perfect world. *Adventure, freedom from expectations, my biological family...*

Atlas waved a hand in front of her face. "Where'd you go, Bree?"

"Oh. Ha. Just thinking. So, where'd you come up with that place you showed me?"

"It's everything you ever wanted. I've seen enough of your dreams to know. I know you never thought your dreams could live outside your mind, but they can. We can make a new world together, one where everyone's happy." There was genuine promise in his tone, but something sinister flashed in his expression. Breena drew back. *What was that look?* Breena smiled as convincingly as she could at his offer. "As good as world peace or whatever sounds, if wishes were fishes... you know how that goes. There's no real way to make a perfect world. Let's just start with a good night's sleep."

When they arrived, Bree raided the fridge before heading to her bedroom. Atlas stood behind her while she piled two bottles of soda and a jar of pickles into her arms, wondering how he could convince her without giving too much information. "You underestimate the effect you could have on this world."

She gave him a skeptical look walked off.

The next morning, they awoke in a bed with no blankets or sheets. *Oh man. What was I doing in my sleep this time?* Atlas cooked breakfast while Breena showered. She practiced creating the illusion of a steamy tropical rainforest in her bathroom, but she didn't succeed. *I'm too distracted. If I could just stop thinking about what Atlas said last night, maybe I could do it. 'You underestimate the effect you could have on this world.' Sounds like a warning more than encouragement.*

Frustrated, Breena choked down her breakfast.

"There's something I've been meaning to ask you. Since you don't have much time left here, I think I should out with it. The woman who gave me a job and my apartment, she's not a good lady. I was desperate when she found me, and I didn't know what she was when I got involved. She wants to use people like us to put chaos into the world. Not good chaos, not excitement, but full-on anarchy and destruction. I've got a friend helping me to get rid of her, the one I met with the other night, but you're our best defense. I know you don't see it yet, but you will be stronger than all of us. Help us get rid of her."

"Um, what?"

"Help me and my friend depose a tyrant."

"You're hilarious."

"I'm serious."

"Yeah, and I'm a llama. Come on. We're going to the café for tea to take to the cabin. I *am* going to pull an illusion together today, so stop distracting me with creepy jokes."

Atlas worried at the coins in his pocket as they walked. He didn't want to go to Vos with bad news, but in the time left, Atlas didn't see a way to get Breena on board without telling her everything. Atlas preferred to chance Vos' anger than put Breena at risk of knowing too much. She couldn't be associated with his plans to oust Tabitha. He needed Breena to have connections with her mother to help plan the best way to attack, sabotage her from the least-expected source. Atlas settled on the idea that he would have to keep playing along with Tabitha until Breena could learn the truth and make her own choice.

When they arrived at the cottage, she threw her stuff down on the desk, climbed on top of it, and hoisted her weight nimbly into the hatch. Atlas followed her up and sat next to her. She was already in the meditation position Atlas recommended: legs crossed, eyes closed, hands in lap.

"Now, focus on what you want most right now," Atlas guided. "Reach out with your soul and feel all the life in the world. Ok, good. Now, feel for the vibrations in the universe that we all cre—."

Breena opened one eye. "Shh! You're distracting me."

"—ate." Atlas put his hands up then scooted away from her.

Bright flowers exploded into the grey of the room.

"Open your eyes, love."

Breena crinkled her nose and shook her head. Atlas had taken to giving her various pet names until he found one that really fit. Love wasn't the one, but it was appropriate for the moment.

Breena clapped once. "Finally. This," she gestured around her, "is what you get when you're quiet." She did a small victory dance in place, and as her concentration waned, so did her illusion. The smile on her face faded with the flowers around her.

"It's Ok, hun. You'll get it. Practice, practice. Here, give me your hand." He created another lush field around them. They cuddled up under a large tree and the warm sun and took a nap.

Atlas pretended to sleep, but stayed awake to maintain the illusion. He wanted Breena to wake in the same place she'd fallen asleep. Picking a wild onion growing beside him, he mumbled to himself. "I've gotten less sleep since I've met her than I did when I was bumming beds off of people."

Breena jerked in her sleep, waking herself. She surveyed the blowing grasses through blurry eyes. "How are we still here? I didn't know you could keep this up while you slept. I want to learn to do that."

"No, I didn't sleep." He dissolved the field and then hopped down from the hatch.

"Oh." Breena pulled her phone out from her purse. "7:00! We should go get dinner." She dropped down to the floor below.

"Yes, a goodbye dinner." He brushed a hair from in front of her eyes.

Backing away from Atlas towards the door, Breena gave him her best "Oh, puh-lease" face. "Please don't remind me about going home."

On her last full day in London, Breena couldn't get in touch with Atlas. She listened to his voicemail again.

"Hey, Hun. I know it's late. Just got home from work. My boss had me putting out her fires all day. I'm beat. Let me get some sleep, and then I'll call you later on. I missed you."

I guess he's still asleep. She looked at the clock. *It's 1:30 in the afternoon, though. Maybe I'll just drop by and surprise him.*

Breena pressed her ear against his door after knocking for a solid two minutes. "Absolutely silent in there." She knocked again then rubbed her hand. "Ok, no more knocking. Hey, Atlas? It's me. Are you sleeping? Do you want to go get some lunch? It's my last day here. I thought we'd spend it together." *I hope he's Ok.* Breena leaned against the door, sliding down it to sit for a while. After ten more minutes, she gave up and went back to her apartment.

She called every hour after that hoping for an answer. *I can't just waste my day waiting on him. But what else am I supposed to do? He's the only one I know. I always thought an adventure like this would include more people. I guess he doesn't have any connections outside of work.* Lilly's voice chimed in. *Red flag.* Breena answered her thought. *Or just sad.*

****

Atlas fazed back into consciousness. The metal still bit into his wrists as he hung. The floor, which he could barely see under the blindfold bridging his nose, was grey and spattered with blood. The tickling drips he felt down his chest and back meant the red was his own. He strained to stay lucid this time, stressed duly by the pressure on his diaphragm caused by having his arms overhead for so long. In the echoing space of his unknown prison, the claps of high heels grew louder. Atlas flinched. "I hope you've had a change of heart." Two red patent pumps peeked into his view, one on either side of his feet. "Do you still hate me?" the female voice purred into his ear.

"No," Atlas struggled out through gritted teeth.

"And why not?" She stepped away.

Atlas roared. "Because I hate the world more."

The woman released Atlas from his bonds and he dropped to the floor. She peeled off his mask.

Blinking a few times, Atlas noticed a blurry figure beside him and looked over. It was Vos. Atlas remembered, then, that there had been someone else screaming last night. He looked dead.

Tabitha took Atlas by the chin and redirected his gaze at her. She kissed his forehead. "Now that there are fewer distractions for you, go get your happiness. Go take back what your father ripped from you."

****

At 8:00, Breena resigned herself to her pajamas, the last of her clothing left unpacked aside from her travel outfit. She sat on the edge of her bed in the silence, tearing her fingernails raw. Breena's heart lurched as she thought about all the time and effort she had devoted to Atlas over the summer. *I could have just as easily, no, more easily, rejected him from the start.* Her cheeks started to burn and her hands shook.

A full-on rage cascaded over her. *Used. Forgotten. How stupid am I?* She chucked a pillow to the ground. The pillow made a dissatisfying "plff" sound as the feathery mass hit the carpet, and that angered her, too. She looked at her suitcase. Breena shouted into the room. "And if I hadn't packed yet, I'd have something else to throw!"

She went into the bathroom, fists balled and ready to take out the mirror when the baggie of pills caught her eye. It had been weeks since she'd taken more than one at a time, some days going without any, making up for the overuse at the beginning of the trip.

He helped me off of them, and now he can help me back on. Breena punched the mirror anyway, not taking her eyes off the medicine.

They spoke to her louder than the thrumming of blood in her ears, louder than the throbbing in her knuckles, so Bree snatched the bag from the counter and poured the contents into her hand. She swallowed all of them with water straight from the faucet. Breena left the pieces of shattered mirror and tiptoed around the sharp mess back to her bedside. She turned off every light in the apartment, set her alarm for four hours before take-off, and got in bed still seething.

Chapter 13

Lexa, Lilly, and Jordan surrounded Breena's hospital bed, their faces worn with worry and sallow by the poor light of the room. They looked as ghostly as Breena did. She lay there in the bed, eyes closed, hands resting on her belly. She was completely unresponsive and had been for the three weeks since she'd missed her flight back to the U.S. The doctors came in to question Lexa for any clues about Breena's catatonic state. All she could do was shake her head.

Linda and Tabitha walked into the tense silence.

"Hi, I'm Lexa, Breena's mom. I'm the one who called you. We found your numbers on Breena's kitchen counter. Thought maybe you guys would know something."

"Sorry, we only hung out once. Had a good time, but Breena said her orchestra schedule was hard to work around, and we didn't do anything else for the rest of the summer."

"But she didn't go to orchestra. They kicked her out for missing orientation."

"That's news to us. Guess she was trying to avoid us. Sorry, Lexa, but we don't know anything."

"Well, if she wasn't spending time with you, what was she doing all summer?"

Jordan thought of Atlas and cringed. He stepped into the group of ladies. "Look, we already know she overdosed, and I don't think it matters much who she was with or when. If the doctors don't know why she hasn't woken up yet, why would they?" He turned to Tabitha and Linda to catch them up. "The doctor said the drugs are out of her system, that most people would have come to within a couple days max. She hasn't. It's been three weeks."

Tabitha turned back to Lexa. "Well, what do you want us to do about it? I don't know why you asked us here."

Lilly shot off the bed. "Look, lady, you don't seem to care much, and we already know you guys weren't very good friends if Breena spent the whole summer avoiding you, so why don't you just leave if you're going to be such a bitch." Lilly shook. She was not the confrontational type and it showed.

They're fighting because of me. They're worried because of me. But, I haven't found him yet. I'm a terrible person. Breena's consciousness drifted away as she withdrew back into her dreams.

****

Atlas tried to roll over in his sleep, but was jerked awake by the cuffs holding his wrists and ankles to the plywood bed. Silence filled the warehouse. He took a chance at opening his swollen eyes, but the effort of scanning the room for Tabitha and Vos made his vision swim. Atlas' lips were crusted with blood. His mouth stung as flesh split back open when he moved to speak. "Where is my mistress?" He coughed through the words, his mouth and throat so dry they seemed to stick closed.

Tabitha's voice pierced his thoughts. "Go find your bride and put her in her place."

"You left me alone, Mistress."

"You'll be Ok for a little while longer. Now go."

Reeling, he fell back into the blackness.

****

"Atlas." *Why can't I see anything? This is my dream, right? I should be able to make it beautiful. What do I get instead? A damp forest and a few stars.* Breena looked down at her feet as she walked. *You're making too much noise. They might find you.* She paused. *Wait, who's going to find me? Stop it; you're being irrational. And you want him to find you. It's just a dream. Keep walking.* The darkness started to lift revealing an unfamiliar setting. "I didn't make any of this. How did I get here?" She hoped Atlas was somewhere in the illusory bubble of night. Breena called his name again, still with no reply. "Atlas, come on. If you're here, just come to me. I've called you so many times your name doesn't even sound like a word anymore. Please. I need answers."

Fatigued from searching, she sat down at the base of a tree to rest. "What happens if I fall asleep here? Do I go back to my body, or does my spirit stay here? Not that you'll answer me."

A stick cracked to her right. Breena jumped to her feet, a sense of hope filling her heart. *Is this a "find out" dream or a "run away" dream?* She walked slowly toward the crackling noises. *Guess I'm going to find out.* "Atlas? I need you... are you there?"

Breena reached the cluster of trees where the noise issued and glanced in all directions. She dropped her head. *No one. Do not cry.*

"Breena." She heard a whisper. "Breena, I'm over here."

Lifting her head from her hands, she stared into the inky night. Breena still couldn't see much, but she got up and followed the whispers. For every few steps she took, the voice led her a few steps further. Eventually, the calls stopped, so she stood still. A stiff gust of wind barreled through the forest and the clouds above moved from in front of the moon. The light revealed the clearing of her recurring nightmare. *Soon, Atlas is going to come out of the trees and chase me. Don't stand still! Stop waiting.*

"I'm so glad you found me, little one," he cooed as he came out of the woods a moment later.

Too late. "Where were you? We were supposed to spend the day together. You didn't care."

"How wrong you are." Soft, patronizing, he was too calm. Breena twitched—nerves and fury. "I've had a wake-up call. I'm doing this because I want you to have one, too. We care about you too much—"

"We?"

"—to let you waste your life away in your fantasies like I have. It's time to face reality, time to actually *do* something with these dreams of yours. I thought you could help me."

"I thought you could help *me!*"

Atlas approached her slowly, hands dropped to his sides, eyes locked on hers. As hard as Breena tried, she couldn't break the connection. It was as if his eyes held her there. Just as in all the other dreams, he backed her toward a tree. She didn't scream this time. *It's an illusion. He can't hurt me. He can't hurt me. Our bodies aren't really here. He can't.* Her back hit the spiked tree bark and she stopped. *He looks like an animal.*

"You stupid girl," he crooned. "You thought you could follow me into this world and bring me back? Thought we could really have some type of earthly love? Part of me can't believe how easily you fell for all my stories. The other part of me is so grateful you did."

"Stories? They were all lies?"

"As real as this place we're in."

"I don't know what's real anymore." Breena could hear her teeth squeaking in her ears she clenched them so tightly.

"Look at those wild eyes. So pretty when you're angry, stupid girl."

"Tell me who you are."

"I'm Atlas. You know that."

"I trusted you," she admitted in a tone much too soft and sweet for the situation. "You came to me when I was hurting and alone. I wanted to know more about the world. You showed me beautiful places. You taught me how to get *here*..."

"Indeed."

"And then you hijacked my dream. Let me leave. I never should have come back for you."

Atlas paced in front of her. He could feel their previous connection, his love for Breena, straining the conditioning Tabitha had so brutally instilled. "I love you, Breena. Obey me!" His brow wrinkled between his eyes, his lips pursed into thin lines, and he wrung his golden hands into whiteness. Tabitha's agenda warred inside with his. He stopped pacing and threw his head back, yelling into the night. "What do I do with her?"

This is my chance to run. I never outrun him. He will catch me. But he's hurting and I'll be just like him if I abandon— "Atlas! Look at me."

His gaze frantically fell back on Breena.

"If you don't want me wasting away in my dreams, why are you holding me here? What do you want from me?"

He tugged at his hair as if he could pull Tabitha out of his mind. With a ragged sigh, he pushed down the harping long enough to say something true. "I remember how you scared me. I was utterly entranced by it, by the way my chest got tighter at the thought of who you might be, the flutter I would work myself into as I debated whether to get help from someone for my visions or keep it, keep you, to myself. It was so exciting. Too exciting to run the risk of anyone putting an end to it."

He paced. "The first time we met, I had to coax my soul back into my body. You stopped time and I floated out to watch myself encounter you. You moved into my world like a superhero. Inhuman. The day you smashed into me in the woods while you dreamt, later when I shook your hand at the store, you brought me back to life. There's life in me, again. Fire. Even after what has happened to me." His thoughts snapped back to Tabitha, although Breena thought he meant the death of his mother and his harsh adolescence.

Atlas' energy waned as he struggled against the new thought processes Tabitha had programed in. He put his hands on his knees and hung his head for a moment. "She tells me I'm wrong, that it's not supposed to be like this between us, and yet I feel like I have to be near you. You burn me up, and it hurts and it's raw and I feel empty when it's gone. When you're gone." He looked back up at Breena.

She swayed then moved toward him wanting to examine his injuries closer, anger melting away. *I really shouldn't fall for this.* Standing, he pulled away from her reach.

"Don't bother. It's already healing." Atlas shrugged and stared in Breena's direction, his gaze passing her face and over her shoulder to a tree where a bird was preening. Under his breath, he grumbled, "You did to me exactly what she said you'd do."

"Huh? What who said?"

"You made me weak." The air tingled around his outpouring of emotion, and the bird flew off as if disturbed by the breeze of feelings.

Breena traced a scratch on his jawline so lightly she couldn't actually feel his skin under hers. But, she could feel the heat; they were both burning up. He shuddered.

"Sorry, did I hurt you?"

"No. It was nice." Atlas covered her hand with his and flattened it against his cheek. He winced, but the catch in his breath eased into a deep inhale. His eyes fluttered shut. Atlas pushed harder into her palm, nuzzling like a cat.

Breena stood frozen, a gap still between them. *This has to hurt him.*

His other hand, dangling at his side, tremored.

Breena noticed. "See, I *am* hurting you." She started to pull away.

Tabitha was screaming in his head, and his thoughts scrambled and screeched like an emergency alert test signal breaking into a TV show. "Dammit, Breena, just touch me. Please." The last word tore out of him, ragged and full of loosely restrained longing to have her quiet his thoughts. After another second of inaction on Breena's part, his eyes flew open. He seized Breena with a firm hand spanning the back of her neck and pulled her into him.

Their lips crashed together, teeth knocking like some fresh adolescent's first kiss, and he smiled into her lips briefly before the raging firestorm of conditioning consumed him in a blinding oblivion. As if the alert was no longer a test, a switch flipped in his brain, and Tabitha took hold of him once again. He shoved Breena, sending her tumbling to her back. She hit her head on a tree trunk.

"Why can't you just do what you're told?" Atlas screamed into the still forest, unsure whether he was questioning Breena or himself. They were Tabitha's words. He pressed the heels of his palms into his eyes and took a deep breath.

Breena sat against the tree holding her head, tears silently rolling down her cheeks.

As if nothing had happened, Atlas snapped back into his stoic state, lost to his controller. "Little one, calm. All of this is because I know your favorite place is lost in your dreams, since it lets you escape from reality. But you just don't get it. We can make all of this a reality. We can change the world. *You* can change the world. It's what you were born for. The only thing keeping you from knowledge is time. I have so much to teach you. We're supposed to be a team."

"If you wanted me by your side, if you wanted to be a team, why did you abandon me that day? Why are you treating me like this? I don't understand."

Atlas smirked. "I know you don't. For my absence, I apologize. I was detained. And that's my whole point, my pet. You were distraught without me. You will always come back here, searching, yearning, *needing* me because you can't get the answers you're looking for without me."

"That's not true."

"Oh, but it is, Breena. Why did you come here, then, if not for an answer? Why did you keep me around in the first place, if not for answers? I *know* you were scared of me."

"Because I missed you!" Breena stood, hushed and dejected. *He's right.* "But I wish I couldn't even remember you. You're not the Atlas I love."

His heart throbbed, and his behavior made him want to throw himself off a cliff, but he had no energy left to stop his mouth. "Well make sure you remember this. Your friend Tabitha is the one who did this to me. She's the woman I work for, and she's also your mother. You are heir to her kingdom, Gehenna. The source of your talent, of your discontent, is your birth. *You* are what's wrong with the world."

****

In the hospital room, alarms and beepers shrieked. Doctors corralled Breena's friends and family out of the room and into the hallway. From the clearing, Breena felt a tug on her body.

As her astral figure shimmered in and out of focus, Atlas lunged toward her, grabbing her by the throat. "You're not going anywhere. I *said* we're supposed to be a team."

I know what's happening. Breena went limp in Atlas' hands, giving in to the pull of her physical body.

Atlas roared in frustration, but was helpless to keep her there. A hole in the sky opened up and sucked the trees through and away, one by one. The little chapel nearby flew past their heads and out of the hole. Atlas' fingers went through Breena's image. There was nothing left to hold on to. Before the ground crumbled from beneath him, he walked slowly back into the woods mumbling. "Mistress will be displeased."

Doctors rubbed the paddles together once again and shocked Breena's limp body. And again. A third time. Her pulse finally started. *I'm back. I don't want to be.*

The nurses bustled around her, calming as the electronic beeping of her heart settled back into a normal rhythm. "Should I go get the family, now?"

"She's stable. Go ahead."

Everyone is waiting for me. I don't have the heart to come to.

****

Atlas' eyes shot open when the dream fully dissolved. Tabitha was peering down at him from the edge of the bed. He gasped. "Tabi— Mistress. You're back."

"As are you."

Curling his hands into fists, the cuffs dug into his skin. Tabitha wore no expression, and he found that more frightening than her out-right anger.

"Can you handle her?" She brushed her fingers over his bruised cheek.

He winced but didn't dare pull away. "Yes, of course."

"Can you handle yourself?"

"Yes. Yes, Mistress."

"Saying it twice doesn't make it true. You have one more chance to get her on our side, Atlas, and then I'm going to give her an attitude adjustment."

"No."

"Excuse me?"

"Time. I just need another chance. She's hurt and confused. She doesn't want to be near me."

"And whose fault is that? You got her thinking she's supposed to be in a kind and loving relationship with you. If you had done this my way from the start, and not fallen in love with her, she might have already come home with us. You are a business arrangement, not a love match. You are not her partner. You are a means to an end. A tool. And I'm going to have to make sure you remember that." Tabitha summoned a hulking man from the shadows to drag Atlas across the room and string him up by his wrists again. She followed with a glass of water, which she left at Atlas' feet.

****

For four days, Breena continued to sleep, trying to relocate Atlas. *Why am I asking for this kind of punishment? What he said was right... I guess I always knew. He never seemed real.* She searched on anyway. On the fifth day, she found herself in the clearing once again. It was wrecked from her resuscitation—the damage to her body manifested in the worlds her mind created. *I destroyed such a beautiful place. The chapel Atlas built for me is in shambles.* She stood beside the rubble and waited. Atlas never came. *I give up.*

Lilly was the first to notice Breena's eyelids fluttering as light filtered onto her face from the window. Breena groaned and the others looked up. The group rushed to her side. *All this attention, but I feel so lonely.* She looked over Jordan's shoulder as they hugged, hoping to find someone else waiting to hold her. *Of course he's not here.*

"She's fine to go home at this point, Ms. Scarlet."

Breena glanced at Lexa. She'd aged since May. *That's not my mom...* She pulled the heated hospital blanket up to her chin.

"But she's only been awake a day. What if she goes back under?"

"Her bloodwork is completely normal. I have no reason to believe she will have another episode. The drugs are out of her system already. Her beauty sleep took care of that."

"You're sure?"

"I'm sorry I don't have a better explanation for her comatose state other than withdrawals affecting each body differently. Call me if you have any questions in the coming weeks. And make sure you find and destroy any remaining pills she may have hidden around the house."

"Thank you, doctor."

As the family walked in their house, grimy and groggy from a red-eye flight back from London, Lexa started in on her five-hundredth spiel of forced excitement. "Breena! Honey! I'm so glad you're back." Lexa wrapped her arms around Breena from behind and waddled them into the kitchen. "Sit, sit. You should have something better than hospital food."

"Mom, I told you I'm not hungry."

"Oh, but the best celebrations call for food. I've got my girl back."

Smile, nod, eat the food. Then, you can go to bed. "Hey, Mom?" *What are you trying to say to her? It's not like you didn't know you were adopted.*

"Glad to be home? I'm glad to have you home."

Not that. "Yeah." She clenched and unclenched her fists under the table.

Lexa prattled on about jet lag and exhaustion, and Breena was relieved her mom took her silence as agreement. *She hasn't mentioned the pills yet. Wonder when I'm going to get that earful. Maybe when the excitement of having me back wears off.* "Mom, I want to go to bed."

"I know, but you need to stay awake, get back on home time."

She went to her room with the steaming cup of coffee Lexa thrust into her hands. *This is insufferable.*

Lexa's voice drifted up the staircase as she paced in front of it while on the phone.

"Look, Ms. Vale, you assured me that the apartment was insured by you and that it covered any potential damages caused by a guest renting the space."

Breena stood in the door to her room.

"No, I am *not* paying for the broken mirror. You've already kept my deposit. *That* is your payment."

Ari came out of his room and noticed Breena standing in the hall. "You shouldn't be out of bed, Bree."

"I'm fine."

"I used to believe you when you said that." Hurt flashed across his face and he turned to go downstairs. Looking back once more before leaving her to her moping, he added, "Oh, yeah. I made first string for football. Not that you care about other people's lives."

Breena lunged to grab his shoulder. "What is that supposed to mean? This is the most you've talked to me since I woke up, and you're acting like I did something to you."

"Acting? This isn't acting. You're the one acting, telling everyone you're fine, using pills to get you through the day, hiding what you did in London instead of the orchestra."

"Symphony."

"Whatever. Just, why don't you try looking at how you hurt the people you love because you were too proud or stubborn or stupid to get some help. It's not like any of us would have been surprised. You've had an effed up life."

Breena struck Ari across the face. "Don't talk about me like I'm some wounded animal." She spun on her heel and slammed her bedroom door so hard the family picture in the hallway fell to the floor.

Breena lie in bed, miserable. *I have to get out of here. I have someone to find.*

Chapter 14

Breena flipped over her phone as soon as she woke to see if her call with Jordan had dropped. *Right, Jordan and I aren't talking. Guess sleeping with him on the line is another habit I need to get used to living without. 6:23 in the morning...*

She crept out of her bedroom and down the hall. In the bathroom, she started the hot water, straightened the bath mat, got a new roll of toilet paper out for the back of the commode. *Please let the mirror fog over before I turn back around. Already know I slept bad; don't need to see the proof on my face.* Breena tested the water and stepped in. She let the warmth run over her face. *I could go to sleep right here.* She had a brief moment of silence, a rare empty space of consciousness, and then she snapped out of it. *Ok, Ok, wash something.* Breena finished and wrapped herself in a blanket-sized towel. She opened the bathroom door a crack and scanned the hallway. *Everyone's still sleeping. Good. I don't even want to look at Ari. He can take the bus to school for all I care.* She threw the bathroom door open, dashed to her bedroom, then shut the door behind her, catching it just before it slammed.

What to wear, what to wear... First day of school, Breena. Make it good. But, it's only the first day of school for you. Everyone has been back for weeks. Screw cute. No one's going to notice me anyway. Breena pulled open her bottom drawer and slipped into her favorite pair of jeans. They were soft and worn, the dark wash faded into a light blue, and the fabric on the rear thinning. *Need to find some fabric to patch that.* She opened her creaky closet and pulled down the same ratty hoodie she always wore. Breena dug through the basket on her dresser for a hair tie and slipped it around her wrist.

She heard pans rattling downstairs in the kitchen and went to get some breakfast.

"You're up early," Lexa said in shock.

"Yeah, I couldn't stay asleep."

"So... you didn't take anything for it?"

She instinctively shoved a hand into her hoodie pocket, but it was empty. "I was wondering when you'd ask."

"You don't have to talk about it. Just making sure you didn't use some secret stash."

"They're all gone. Everything I had went with me to London. Whatcha making?"

"Whatever you want?"

"In lieu of an unending sleep, I guess I'll have eggs. And toast."

"Bree, don't joke like that. I know you're tired, but don't worry. The doctor said you won't sleep right for a while. Between the jet lag, withdrawals, and the coma..." Lexa had stopped pushing the eggs around in the pan. She held her hands to stop their shaking. "Hey, go wake your brother up while I cook these," Lexa gestured with the pan.

"I don't want to talk to him."

"Just go do it, Breena."

She stomped up the steps hoping her noise would wake him before she got to the door. "Get up," Breena shouted with little kindness, her mouth to the door.

When Breena got to school, Jordan was waiting for her in his usual parking spot. He leaned against his car like nothing bothered him, but Breena knew better. They hadn't talked since she got out of the hospital. She had avoided Lilly, too, out of embarrassment and exhaustion, but that was easy. Lilly didn't push like Jordan did.

As Breena cut the ignition, Jordan let his foot fall down from the tire he had it propped on. He moved to open her door, but was too slow. Breena stepped out and grinned at Jordan sheepishly. She knew what was coming.

Jordan wasted no time getting to the meat of the subject. "Breena, if it makes you *that* uncomfortable, which clearly it does, then you don't have to think another second about it. You should be with me because you want to, not because you feel like you have to. And clearly you're still not ready to deal with this or you would have answered my calls."

"Woah, take a breath, man. I was going to say most of those things, but let me get all the way out of my car first. Goodness..." *Is it too mean to ask him to go away? Yes, it is, Breena. What is wrong with you?* "Top Gun's my favorite movie."

"What?" Jordan choked out.

"Just wanted to clear the air of all the awkwardness." Breena gestured around her with both arms like she was sweeping away negative energy. "Thought I'd throw something new out there. I see I've just made this a significantly worse conversation." Turning away from Jordan, she leaned back into her car to get her bag from the passenger's seat.

"Are you Ok?"

Of course not! "Yeah, I'm fine. I'm sorry if I seem kind of twitchy or anything. I haven't been sleeping well."

"Yeah I figured. You woke me up a few times last night."

"I woke you up? We didn't talk..."

"Well, I guess I mean *not* hearing you there woke me up. I can't get used to this no contact thing. Can we just go back to normal?"

"I can try." *The right answer is 'yes.' You need someone on your side. Jordan will always be on your side.* "Yes."

The pair walked into the building together.

"Hey, where's Lilly?"

"Home. Why?"

"Is she sick?"

"Oh, right. She doesn't have class until 10:30 this year, but you wouldn't know that yet. I keep forgetting it's your first day back." Aside from the curious stares and a missing Lilly, their morning routine picked up like it had never been interrupted: drink machine-Orange Juice for Jordan, Water for Breena; bathrooms; lockers; class.

"Well, this is where I leave you. I got stuck with history first thing. Super hard to stay awake. You know where you're headed?"

She pulled out her schedule. "Uh, art."

"Cool. Well, see ya at lunch, maybe."

Breena backtracked down the hall they had taken from the parking lot. *My face is hot. It's because everyone's looking. Don't stare back. Just go to class like you've always done. You used to own this school.*

A hand thumped on her shoulder. She jumped. "Hey, Bree, it's just me. I'm glad to see you out and about."

"Hey, Jet. Thanks. Though, I hardly call school 'out and about.'"

"Well, if you need anything," he patted the pocket on the breast of his jacket, "hit me up." Without waiting for a response, he walked away.

He's never tried to sell to me before. I guess everyone knows about the pills now, too. The bell rang.

Breena pulled a large sheet of paper out from the storage rack and got three willows of charcoal from the drawer beside it. *Jordan was right. I would have said the same in his position. Sounded so harsh coming from him, though.*

Kelly cleared her throat from across the table.

Maybe I should tell Jordan about Atlas' training. If he knew what was really going on, maybe he wouldn't want me so much. He'd finally realize I'm nothing like him.

Kelly repeated the signal.

Breena looked up, "Hey Kel."

"So do you know what you're wearing to the debate tomorrow night?"

"What debate?"

"Don't be silly. *The* debate. I know you haven't been around, but maybe it would be good to get involved in your senior year. Maybe it would help you adjust to being back."

"Kelly, I'm not going to the debate. I'm not on the debate team; I don't want to be on the debate team; I am no more interested in it than I was last year."

"Oh, someone's snappy today, aren't we? You should be excited to be back! Let me just fix that frown around!" Kelly reached for Breena's face.

Breena reared back and smacked Kelly's hands away with black, dusty fingers. "Seriously, Kelly? Don't touch my face."

"You're right. You haven't changed from last year. What's wrong this time? You're never in a good mood."

"It's a long story." Breena shrugged the questions off and kept to her work. *She hasn't changed either.* Breena yawned.

"Oh. That's why you're cranky. You didn't sleep well."

"You could say that." Breena swept the page off of the table like a table cloth from under china. A vague black dust swirled around her. In the courtyard outside of the art room, Breena absently applied the fixative to her charcoal drawing. *I miss him. Wish I was standing on that pier with him again.* The air around her started to shimmer and the hazy image of a lake formed across the courtyard. She stared into the scene as the can of spray emptied. *Did we really even go there? Was anything we did real? Is he?* "I'm not crazy!"

Kelly bolted into the courtyard on the teacher's heels.

"Are you Ok, Breena?"

Kelly pushed past the teacher and was at Breena's side in an instant.

"Yeah. Just, uh, got lost in my thoughts and didn't notice the wind shift. Got some spray in my eyes. Lame, right? I know." *They seem convinced.* Mrs. Martin offered to send Breena to the nurse to rinse her eyes. Breena waved her off and went back inside.

Chemistry's next. And Jordan. I shouldn't dread seeing him like this. I am a selfish friend.

"Hey, Breena!"

Why does he have to look so happy to see me? She pulled out the lab stool next to Jordan.

"So, about earlier..."

Breena put a hand up to silence him. "Not now, please. Please..."

"Ok."

"Thanks. I'm exhausted."

"Yeah. I know." Jordan's shoulders slumped like the goal of a lifetime was slipping away.

Breena leaned over and rested her head on Jordan's shoulder. "I wouldn't trade you for anything," she whispered. Jordan briefly tilted his head to the side and let it rest against the top of Breena's, then he straightened on his stool as the teacher entered the lab.

Class started with their teacher handing back old tests, which made Breena groan—absences equal zeros. "Let me guess. An A?"

"Yeah," he answered hesitantly. "But a zero isn't so bad! Look at it this way. The lower your grade is now, the more of a difference you'll see when she curves the grades at the end of the year. With mine, I won't really be able to tell because..."

"Because your grade can't get any higher," Breena huffed, frustrated.

"Well, yeah, but I wasn't going to say it like *that*."

"Thanks for trying to spare my feelings."

By the end of class Breena was nearly in tears from aggravation with the Chemistry they learned. Jordan helped her pack up her books, and they headed to lunch.

"Oh, meant to tell you. I got a text from Lilly. She's not coming today. Something about the full moon being proven to increase risks for violent acts. You know her."

"I'll call her after work tonight and see what's up."

Sitting down at their table, Breena picked at her fingers. "Well, this is either extremely convenient or extremely awkward."

"What is?"

"Us alone at this table." Breena commented through a mouthful of baked chips.

"Why is that awkward?" Jordan was smart, leading her into further conversation about their predicament by feigning obliviousness.

"Well... we still really haven't talked about what happened in London. And either having the table to ourselves is convenient because we *can* talk now, without Lilly's listening ears, or it's awkward for the same reason." Breena laughed through a tense smile.

"Breena, what's with you? Since when do I make you nervous?"

"Since you professed your undying love for me."

"Is that really how you see it? Undying and begging and all that? You make me sound so desperate."

"You must be to want me..." she mumbled, eyes cast down to the table.

"Stop that. You know, most the kids in this school would kiss the ground you walk on. You don't know them, but they know you. They watch their prodigy musician do things they could never hope to do. They are in awe of you. I'm not the only one."

Breena stared at Jordan for a few seconds. *I'm not who any of them want me to be.* She stood up with her purse and lunch tray and walked off. *Where are you going to eat lunch now, Stupid?*

Jordan let her go, pushing at the limp lettuce in his salad. "I think she made my lunch wilt."

Breena dumped her tray and waited outside of her next class for the last fifteen minutes of lunch. *In movies, everyone dreams about being popular. People make themselves into new beings to get attention. But, my life isn't a movie, and somehow Jordon and all those other people have built me into this new thing that I'm not. I wish they'd all stop watching. If a popular girl plays cello in the woods and there's no one around to hear it, can she still make a sound? Does she still exist?*

Breena went to work that evening as scheduled, even though she was exhausted. *At least I still have a job after a summer away. Might as well jump headlong into the routine.* Through yawns, she scanned fruits and vegetables at the grocery store like she did every night, fighting with herself about Atlas and Jordan the whole time. When she got home, she dropped her bag right inside the door. No one was in the front of the house. "Mom, I'm back. Making a sandwich then going to bed." *Don't want to get caught in Mom's 'first day back to school' questionnaire.* She made herself a jelly-only sandwich then went to her room. *Screw homework.* Breena flopped on her bed. *Screw school, screw Atlas, screw my sense of adventure*

and the day I met him. Screw all the times he was right about me. I
don't need him to help me escape. I've been doing it on my own for
years apparently. I can do it again.

A loud text alert interrupted Breena's seething. "Now what does Jordan want?"

"Don't forget to call Lilly."

"K."

Breena sighed. "I'm tired of being mad at him." She gave Lilly a quick call to check on her.

"Everything is fine, now, but I was right to stay home, Bree. That thing I saw about the full moon and violence was true. Not two hours after it was on TV, the news station broke in to say some guy had robbed a gas station near my house. They caught him a couple hours ago."

"Your crime watch hobby is more like its own form of imprisonment sometimes. Come to school tomorrow, Ok? I need a buffer from Jordan."

"Still not speaking?"

"No, we're talking, but it's just not the same any more. He's being really understanding, but I still feel guilty. I'm not who he paints me out to be, I can't return his feelings, and, based on today, I can't even get through a lunch with him anymore."

"Like you said. He *is* understanding. He's bad at giving you space, I agree, but his constant closeness isn't because he doesn't understand. He wants to prove he's there for you even if it's not to his benefit."

After the phone call, Breena curled up with *The Selected Poems of Pablo Neruda,* but couldn't concentrate. *There's too much Atlas in this book, now.* She tossed it across the room. Breena drifted to sleep during her contemplation and slept through the night. It was full of darkness, not as if she did not dream, but as if the dream itself was nothing and Breena was lucid in the emptiness. *You're alone. No one's watching. Isn't this what you wanted?*

The following weeks passed in much the same manner. Hollow dreams continued, and Breena attempted to control them, trying to paint a setting over the nothingness, to relive her summer with Atlas and discover exactly where things had gone wrong. She never found it.

Chapter 15

By their return from Christmas break, Breena and Jordan were back to normal, and her classmates had stopped staring like they were surprised to see her alive or like they were secretly embarrassed for her. She was no longer part of the latest gossip about who had fallen off the wagon, although she had, and people didn't offer intrusive help anymore.

She made her way to math class, shivering in the school's inadequately heated cinderblock halls. *I've done all of this before. It's like last school year never ended, like I never changed. Same classroom, same desk, same overly enthusiastic math teacher.*

Jordan scooted his desk up to Breena and put his hand over hers. Through her artificially relaxed state, she hadn't noticed him walk in. Breena sighed.

"You look tired."

She nodded. *Same Jordan.* Breena's mind drifted to Jordan's confession of emotion at the end of their junior year. He was and always had been the most stable thing in her life. Listening to the teacher lecture gave her an opportunity to consider for the thousandth time all the ways she had taken Jordan for granted. Breena slowly reached for his hand under the desk. He returned her grasp without hesitation or question. As the last bell rang for the day, they left class and went to her locker, then his, hand-in-hand. When they headed to the parking lot, Jordan stopped half way and turned to look at her.

"What?" she barked. The meds were wearing off, and his intense gaze made her edgy.

He opened his mouth like he was about to say something, then closed it. Then, opened it again. And closed it. He cast his eyes down for one quick second. When he looked back up, Jordan took Breena's face with his free hand and kissed her with passion and desperation she had only felt one other time.

Breena dropped his hand and snaked hers up the side of his neck and around to the back, letting her fingers comb through his toffee hair. She kissed him back like her life would end when the seal of their lips broke. *What am I doing?*

"Do you mind?" An angry shout broke apart their kiss, reminding the pair that they were standing in the middle of the parking lot, and currently blocking traffic.

Breena jumped back from Jordan, pulling him with her so the guy could pass. She set off walking hurriedly to her car without saying anything to Jordan.

"Breena."

No response.

"Breena, wait!"

No response. Breena had reached her car and already had the door open.

"Breena, I'm sorry. I should have asked first, or told you I still—" he put a hand on his chest, "—or warned you..."

"*Don't.*" She was nearly shouting. Trying again, she softened, "Don't. You don't need to apologize. I kissed you, too. I could have pushed you away. I... liked it."

"One would hope."

"Stop." Breena stomped her foot. "Please, with the self-deprecating humor. You're the only one who has paid any real attention to me since I got back. I mean, *everyone* has paid attention. A lot of attention. But, I mean real focus on what's going on with me. So don't act like you aren't enjoyable, or that no one would want to kiss you." *Huh, I sound like him.*

"But, Breena, you're the one who said, and I think these were your exact words, 'I just can't be with you right now.' That was six months ago. You also told me that day that you didn't know if you ever could. Then there was the whole London club thing... So, knowing that, I had no right to force a kiss on you like that."

Well he's right about that. "Jordan, stop!"

"I'm sorry."

"Enough with the apologies, Jordan. It's Ok. I liked it. I haven't felt that alive since I was with—"

Jordan grimaced.

"Never mind."

"I can see it in your eyes. There is no 'never mind' about him. You still miss him."

Breena leaned in and kissed Jordan again. "I said 'never mind.' Now, I have to go, but in case you still aren't convinced that I liked it, call me when you get home."

Jordan stared as she drove away. "She's always hiding something."

Shortly after Breena arrived home, her phone rang with Jordan's face displayed on the screen.

"Come outside." He said as soon as she answered.

"Huh?"

"Just do it."

"Ok, be right there."

Jordan was sitting in his car when she stepped off her front porch. He had his windows down and called for her to get in.

"Where to?"

"Somewhere we can talk."

Images of London flashed through her head, of running off to hidden places with *him* so they could talk and practice. Her palms started to sweat. More thoughts assaulted her—the dreams, the fields he showed her, Atlas' violent change in personality. "Ok."

Breena struggled to keep afloat in the wash of memories and sudden lethargy that came over her. *We do need to talk. I need to talk. I can't keep on like this. He's going to turn the music off when we get there. Wherever. He's going to expect a story. I can't do it.*

Jordan took roads she wasn't familiar with and, after twenty minutes, they arrived at a state park she'd never visited. By the looks of it, no one visited. The painted letters had worn off the sign, the gravel entrance was bumpy, and the flowers lining the road were overgrown with weeds and running vines. *Looks too much like places Atlas used to take me.* The picnic shelter was in shambles. She gritted her teeth.

Jordan pulled his red Neon over beside the shelter and parked. The engine popped as it cooled, the leaves rustled every now and then, and the occasional bird circled for prey. She felt Jordan staring and looked over. *This is nothing like the dreams.*

"I think it's been at least five minutes since we spoke."

Jordan laughed and shrugged his shoulders. "There's never uncomfortable silence with you in my opinion, but, for the record, I'm waiting for you to spill about, '...since I was with...'" he said, feigning Breena's voice and using air quotes.

Breena groaned and Jordan shook his head.

"You can't possibly want to hear about him. Don't you hate him?"

"Correct on both accounts. But, whether I want to hear it or not, you need to talk about it to someone, and I'm not convinced you're going to tell anyone else, so I might as well listen."

Can I do this without crying? Or vomiting? I'll make something up. No, Jordan deserves more than that. She balled her fists until the nails cut into her palms and began to tell her story about London—the real story this time.

"—and that's why I can't seem to get past this agonizing sense of loss." Jordan gaped. It was his signature look of the day, apparently. He hadn't said a word to her during the whole recount. "Please, Jordan, say something."

"You're kidding me. So you're saying you are destined to marry that creep; have super powers; and this is the one I'm the most pissed off about, faked that whole sleeping episode in the hospital."

"Not faked, prolonged."

"I need proof."

She crossed her arms over her chest. "I knew you wouldn't believe me. I guess I owe you, though." Breena hesitated, then took a deep breath and closed her eyes. She looked deep inside her soul and mind to try to find one thing she wanted most of all that didn't include Atlas. He seemed to be the basis of all of her desires, though, so she let go of her fears and allowed herself to connect with the need to find him. Maybe this time would be the time she'd succeed. Managing the "travel" was much more difficult while awake. She decided to create an illusion of the cottage she and Atlas used to train in. She had just told Jordan about it. *If I can show him the place, he'll have to believe me.* Just like Atlas instructed her to do months before, she focused on the vibrations of the universe, and she wove the image in her mind into those vibrations.

"Holy shit."

"You don't have to whisper. You won't break it." She was exhausted now. This was the first complete and successful illusion she had created while awake since being in the states. Bree wondered if her brief sobriety during the prior two months had been keeping her from succeeding while awake. *The pills definitely take the edge off. It's not so overwhelming to be back here again. But now...* She reached out of the car window and snapped a leaf off of the bush she'd placed beside them. "Here. Proof?"

Jordan took the leaf and studied it. "Yeah."

The familiar sights should have comforted her, but the memories there felt so false after Atlas' betrayal. "Can I close it now?"

"Can't we look around?"

"I feel sick. It's too much. Plus, I don't think it's a good idea for you to be here. As much as I'd like to find him, I don't want you involved in whatever is going on. If he happened to be here, the one time you're with me, I think it would be pretty awful."

"So, this isn't just your invention? It's, like... a real location? He can come here, too?"

"No, it's not a real location. I don't teleport people; I connect the astral world to the physical location we occupy. It's only because of our connection that he can go where I go without my invitation."

"Oh, Ok. Well, thanks for showing me. I didn't doubt that you could do it because you never lie to me. It's just a hard thing to believe in *at all.*"

"I know. So, about earlier at school..."

"I figured you'd bring it up."

"Yeah." A nervous laugh. "Well, now that you know everything, you can understand why I had such a hard time starting school again. It never had anything to do with my coma or being sick. It's emotional. And in the parking lot today, you made me feel wanted like he did before it fell apart."

"I'm glad I can make you feel better, but don't try to replace him with me. You didn't want me like that before him. I'm nothing like him, and you'll only end up more hurt if you try to fill that gap with a rebound."

"Always with the wise advice even at your own expense. This afternoon changed things for me. I didn't think I could see you in any new way. I didn't think I could feel better, either, but I'm starting to. What were you going to say to me before you kissed me?"

Jordan ignored the question and put his hand on hers like he had earlier that day. Breena leaned over to rest her head on his shoulder.

"We've always been this close. That won't change. But I promise I will try to protect you from all of this."

"Jordan, it's you that needs protection from him. If he comes around, I feel like it's going to be bad for you *and* me."

"We'll be fine."

For the first time in weeks, Breena truly relaxed. After half an hour of cuddling, they decided to drive back home. Breena dropped the illusion, realizing that she was so relaxed it had stayed up without maintenance or incident.

****

Jordan drove home in silence. As he rounded the curve into his neighborhood, he realized how tightly he'd been gripping the wheel. His knuckles hurt. The picture that he kept on his dashboard of his dog, Raisin, who had recently passed away, flicked in the breeze of the heater. "Is that why you always barked at her? Could you smell her magic or whatever?" He shook his head. "Is she a demon, devil, witch? None of it's real. Yet, she showed me." Gravel skittered under the tires as he careened into his driveway.

"I'm back. Anyone home?"

A door slammed. "Jordan, I told you to stop spraying gravel into the yard like that. So help me if you keep driving that way I'm going to take my putter to your windshield." Arthur stormed back into his office.

"Good to see you, too, Dad." Jordan shuffled into the kitchen and read the note taped to the refrigerator as he filled his water bottle.

"Gone to Chicago. –Mom"

"Surprise, surprise. Another city, another 'spa weekend.'" From upstairs, angry voices filtered out of Arthur's office. It was no cause for concern, just another heated conference call from "those indecisive bastards" his dad always complained about. "Those 'indecisive bastards' pay your bills, *Dad*."

He climbed the stairs in his socks, tiptoeing around the famously creaky places. Jordan dumped his bag and coat on top of a pile of magazines he didn't know why he kept. "Hey, Fishpants." The pungent scent of beta flakes filled the air. "Have some dinner." Watching the orange and green shavings drift to the bottom of the tank was the most tranquil thing he'd done all day. "Way more relaxing than kissing Breena." A shiver traveled down his back.

"I kissed her. Again. Damn, that was stupid. After London? But this time she kissed me back. She *really* kissed back." He made a fish face at Fish. "I don't even care if she's using me."

****

Dinner was on the table when Breena came through the door. The family ate immediately and without ceremony. Ari jabbered away about soccer practice, although the commentary wasn't needed. He hadn't showered yet, and the grass stains all over his knees, elbows, and uniform spoke for themselves. Lexa tried to chime in intermittently, but failed to lure Bree into the discussion.

"You've been so distant, Breena. Are you using again?"

"Mom!"

"I know. Sorry, I have to ask."

"Everything's fine. Just tired." Peas still on plate, Breena excused herself to her room for the night. It was difficult enough to tune out Ari while fielding her mom's questions as vaguely as she could, but to do so while another layer of anxiety, source unknown, settled on her chest was insufferable.

Breena excused herself from dinner and attempted to think herself out of the state she was in, using logic to convince her body to call off the guards. Working fruitlessly to calm down, she shuffled through drawers, bags, and clothes pockets for her pill stash. There was nothing left. *Mom.* Panic made her cold but sweaty, so she stripped and got into bed under extra blankets. Rational thought was no weapon, though; impossible scenarios mated with standard fears and old memories to create a foul bedmate. She stared at the corner of the room as shade changed to shadow, and then the shadows moved across her wall until it was pitch black.

The phone rang, and for the first time since being back from London, she was glad to see Jordan's number.

"Hey."

"Hey."

"Can't sleep."

"Me either."

At some point, she did.

Chapter 16

"So explain to me when and how you and Jordan became a thing, and remind me where I was, because I so didn't see this coming." Lilly had a habit of demanding personal details, and remained consistent over her breakfast pizza in the parking lot the next morning.

"Well, it just happened yesterday, and I don't know if we're a thing. Besides, how have you already found out and had time to get offended for being the last to know? You're not the last to know. There's nothing to know."

"Jordan called last night about some homework and mentioned that you two went and parked last night."

"Wow, he really said we parked? He's from the 70s now?"

"I guess. So what changed? I thought you were still mad about London."

Breena chewed at her lip. *What am I supposed to say? 'Yeah, I'm just using him to forget Atlas.' Then she'll want to know the details. Nah, let's keep Lil in the dark a little longer.* "Jordan kissed me after school yesterday. It was random, and scary, and surprisingly wonderful. *That* is the how and when and where it all started."

"And you kissed him back?"

Breena nodded, grinning widely. *Feels weird to smile.*

"So are you going to date him or..."

"I don't know. For now he's just being a great friend to me."

"A great friend with great benefits," Lilly interrupted.

Breena ignored her and went on. "He makes me happy. I'm not as afraid as I was to be more involved with him. I have a feeling we can handle whatever—" *given that he stuck around after everything I told him last night.*

Breena went to Jordan's after work. Her boss was giving her two hour shifts because he didn't believe she could handle more. *In his defense, I do still look really terrible. Tired.* When she pulled into

Jordan's driveway, she could hear his music thumping from outside. It was no surprise he was home alone, so she let herself in. She went straight up to his room as was customary for them both since childhood. Jordan sat on his bed with a textbook, wearing jeans with a hole in the knee. Breena stopped in the doorway. Normally, this wouldn't have fazed her. Jordan used to be just any boy. Now, this seemed to imply other things. *Should I be embarrassed for walking in on him? No, he was just studying. Should I toss him that shirt? No, that would imply that he was showing too much. Do I hug him like usual? That's the big question.*

All of these hesitations flew through her mind in a short time, though it felt like ages that she stood there staring. He hadn't noticed her deer-in-headlights approach, but by the time she decided to just go sit beside him and not hug him, the song ended and he snapped out of his music trance. *Oh, shit. Do something. Arms out? Hug it is.*

He talked into her hair as they hugged. "I'm so glad you're here."

"Me too."

"I was doing some homework, but it can wait. What's up?"

Breena was still stunned at his bare chest. Jordan had bulked up over the summer it seemed. There was defined muscle where there used to be flat stomach and chest.

"Breena. You alright?"

"Yep. Fine. You, uh... yeah. Hi." She sat down on the bed.

"Hmm. Not fine, I don't think, but I'll give you the benefit."

"Thanks." *What is this feeling? I need something to drink. My ears are ringing. Has that clock always been so loud? Oh, Lord, I didn't get that ketchup off of my shirt. He's looking at me!* Her gaze quickly dropped down to his chest and flashed back up to his eyes, but his stare was locked on her face and he noticed her moment of weakness.

"Breena, I'm the same me I've always been: your best friend that loves you and wants you to be happy."

She stared at him.

He took her hand, slowly, and flattened it over his heart—over his bare chest. Breena sucked in a breath. "I hate that I suddenly make you nervous after all these years. I kind of love it, too."

He let go of her hand, but she didn't move away from him. Her face flamed, but she fought it, sweeping her hand across his chest to the other side, then down to his stomach and quickly back up to his shoulder where she gave him a tight squeeze. She traced over his collar bones, and his eyes fluttered shut. Now very aware that she was doing this strictly for pleasure rather than curiosity, she moved her flattened palm down his torso. She stopped when she got to the waist of his jeans, and he snapped his head back up, eyes wide.

This is so different. Safe. It was always about control with Atlas. His, mine. This is innocent. She could see that, now. Even so, when Jordan grabbed her hands to move them away, she grasped the waistband of his jeans.

Jordan stared at Breena with caution in his eyes. "Baby steps, Breena. You can't replace him with me."

Always with the advice. "I know. I'm not trying to. You're nothing like him, and that's exactly what I need and what I want. Only if you want it, too, though."

"Hell, Breena. Do you know how many nights I've dreamt of this exact scenario? Too many nights to admit. It's unhealthy how much I... No. I care about you more. What you told me last night is proof that you're not over everything that happened in London. This will not fix you."

Breena recalled her confession of summer love and the previous night's fitful sleep. The desperation crawled through her. It was cold unlike the passion she had felt with Atlas, but it burned inside her all the same. With Atlas, it had reduced her to begging. She would not beg Jordan, too. "Jordan, I think you *can* fix me. I don't *need* to find him when I'm with you. I don't *need* those answers when we're together. And you want this."

"Breena, I'd feel like I was taking advantage."

"Don't feel that way. I'm consenting. I'm asking, telling you. I want more." A sick flood of memories rushed back at the last phrase. Atlas had pried the very same from her the first time he taught her.

She could feel the next whispered question from months earlier forming on her lips. Bree bit down on the pleading words. She would not allow it. Instead, she said only his name, barely louder than a whisper.

He cupped her face with both hands and kissed her without restraint. Breena took it as a yes and began to unbutton his pants. He moved his hand around and pulled her hair tie out, letting the tresses fall down her back. She paused with his pants to fling her shirt to the floor.

In the midst of throwing clothes into various piles, Jordan stopped. "Breena, we've known each other forever, but I have loved you every minute of every day since I realized you were a girl, and that it was a good thing. That's why we're not doing this yet."

"I know you can't replace him. I want you to erase him."

"Only you can do that."

Jordan drew Breena close in the corner of his bed against the wall and put on a movie. Two hours later, Breena was yawning away the remnants of the dull plot when a severe migraine came on.

"Jordan, I can't see."

"Huh?"

"Jordan, do something! I can't feel the bed under me. Am I falling?"

"Lie down!"

"Ow. Jordan, it hurts! Do something."

"I'm calling an ambulance."

"No! I don't want to go back to the hospital. Don't. Just... just get me a cold rag. I'll be fine."

"I don't want to leave you."

"Then don't."

He looked down on Breena, who held the back of her head and kept her face buried in her arms, stricken.

"It's Ok. It's passing. Can I sleep here?" *Atlas is trying to find me. It's going to hurt until I'm asleep. Like he's in my head picking locks.*

"Always."

****

"You've been cheating on me."

Breena looked around, not recognizing the place. Atlas hadn't brought her to the clearing this time, or to any place he'd ever shown her.

"What are you talking about? You've been gone, and the last time I saw you seemed a whole lot like grounds for breaking up."

"You little whore. Back in school three months and you're already in bed with him. Did you forget about me?"

"We watched a movie. And yes, that was actually the purpose of the exercise. I want nothing to do with you. Screw you, screw your answers, your teachings, your past, your present, and any hopes you had of our future."

"Acerbic little bitch, aren't we?"

"Go to hell."

"Already there, but it's missing its finest female." At that he projected flames and heat and evil flying creatures that screamed at Breena from above. "You do *not* turn your back on me."

It's just an illusion, just a dream. He's in my head. "I will turn my back whichever way I please. And may I also remind you that you turned your back on *me* first? You try to act all kind and unthreatening, and then you flip like a switch into *this.*" Breena stepped forward and jabbed him in the chest to accent her anger.

He softened, as if one touch quelled the rage Tabitha had trained into him. "Everything I told you was true. I just omitted a bit. Now, it is time for you to know the rest. Since you have chosen to replace me with *him,*" Atlas formed an image of Jordan and Breena together just a few hours earlier, "I am going to make sure your loyalties still lie with me. You will continue to train with me, on my terms, or your new toy will be thrown out."

"Jordan has nothing to do with you."

"Come train with me every night. We're a team and I missed you. You're supposed to lead us. But, first, you have to let me lead you."

"And if I don't?"

"I haven't decided yet. That would be blackmail, and I don't want to hurt anyone. But, you *will* come. You love him. And you still love me."

"No I don't."

"Sick isn't it?"

"Yes."

For all his vibrato, the intent to intimidate didn't reach his face. Atlas fought the urge to tell Breena exactly what Tabitha had told him. He knew Tabitha couldn't kill him since he was the only one matched to Breena, but he still wasn't completely convinced that he could survive another round of Tabitha's conditioning.

Breena waited for Atlas to say something else with her arms wrapped around herself, but he was far away. The illusion shattered and Breena sat up in Jordan's bed, soaked with sweat, unwilling to sleep. Her response to Atlas hung in the air. She couldn't decide if she had been admitting that she was in love with both boys, or acknowledging how wrong the situation was. *How could I love him? He's* changed.

Breena glanced at the clock: 4:35am. She elbowed Jordan then climbed over him. She pulled on her jeans and a t-shirt and shook Jordan again.

"Hmm? What's it, Breena?"

"Jordan, get up."

"No. Why?" He rolled over to face the wall.

"I'm going for a walk. Come with me."

Jordan groaned. "'Kay."

Breena tugged on Jordan's arm until he was upright, reluctant and mumbling something about the sunrise.

"I need to get some air."

"I'm coming."

Outside in the glowing dawn, Breena and Jordan walked deeper into his neighborhood shoulder to shoulder. The crisp wind blew between them, and Breena put her arm around Jordan for warmth.

"I'm worried about you. When are you going to tell me what happened last night?"

"Nothing happened. I got a migraine."

"That was no migraine."

Breena stared up into the pink sky to avoid the drawn expression on his face. *He wears all of his feelings in his eyes. I hate that look. I don't want to be the person that always puts it there. That means I can't tell him anything else about Atlas; I can't keep doing this to Jordan.* She stopped in the road and came chest-to-chest with Jordan, wrapping her arms around his waist loosely. She rested her cheek on his chest, not bothering to look up to his eyes when she spoke. "How many mornings have we done this?"

"Too many to remember or count. Why?"

"And how many nights have you been the only reason I felt safe?"

"You tell me."

"Too many to remember or count. And how many years have you loved me?"

"All of them."

"So what you're saying is that one thing we've always had is time?"

"I guess you could put it that way..." Jordan fidgeted in Breena's grasp. He leaned back to try to see her face.

"We're going to keep having time. I promise. That means I don't need to explain last night right away. It also means I can make things right." *I couldn't begin to explain right now.* "Let's head back."

Breena stood in Jordan's mirror, her face scrunched in dissatisfaction. "Hey, you got any clothes I can wear? I don't have time to go back home, and I can't wear this two days in a row."

"Look around. Whatever fits." Jordan studied Breena.

"What?"

Jordan stared. "Damn. You are more confusing than you are beautiful."

"I can't tell if I'm supposed to say thank you or be offended." She pulled a sweatshirt over yesterday's top and went to the door.

"Well, you've said nothing that makes me worry less about you, and I know you're keeping something from me. I know it's because of *him*—" disgust flared in Jordan's eyes, "—but I don't understand why you feel like you can't tell me. After the last secret you shared, I'd think it couldn't get any bigger than that."

She shrugged.

"All you're gonna do is shrug? You have nothing at all to say? What about yesterday? You want me to help you get over him, not that I'm going to let you use me like that, but if I were, don't you think I'd need a little more input in order to know how to help?"

Breena had been standing with her hand on the doorknob waiting for Jordan to drop the issue. *I know my silence comes across as secretive, and I guess it is, but...* "I don't know what to say. I'm sorry." She left the room and plodded down the stairs. Jordan followed.

"Breena, are you sure you're alright to go to school today? No one will think anything of it if you miss. You've got plenty of doctors' notes. Mom's still in Chicago and Dad flew to Paris on Monday. We can stay here and work things out. You can show me some new places, too, you know, to take your mind off it." Hope mixed with concern made Jordan's eyebrows sit high on his head and his mouth quirk up at one side.

"I'm Ok. Talking it out won't make it go away. Plus, I can hardly stand to say his name and it's *my* brain. Hearing it out loud, it... Get dressed; we have to go in five minutes."

****

School was the same Wednesday as it was every other day. After dismissal, Jordan said his goodbyes at the car and left. *I'm kind of glad he has a project. I need some time apart to get my thoughts straight. I'll go to that park Jordan took me to Monday night.* She waved Jet over after Jordan was out of sight. "I only want one."

Jet winked and took her five-dollar bill.

Pulling up beside the ransacked shelter, she rolled her windows down and turned off the engine, leaving the radio playing. It was frigid outside, but the cutting air cleared her head. Pill in hand, she studied the ceiling of her car. *I don't need this and yet...* Breena reclined the driver's seat and closed her eyes. When she arrived in the clearing, she was furious. *Apparently the calming effects of the pills don't transfer to my astral self.*

"Get out here, Atlas."

He padded from beneath a heavily shadowed tree. "Bossy, aren't we? You're like your mother." He unfolded his arms and cocked his head to one side as if he were expecting something from her. She had no intention of giving him anything. "I hope you're ready, because I will expect you here every night from now on until I say you're ready."

"Ready for what?" *Don't give in to his prompting so easily, Breena. You really are weak, aren't you?*

"I suppose I should tell you my plan."

Breena waited for what seemed like five minutes for him to continue his thought, expecting that there was more than just his supposition, but he stood stoically and stared at her. Tired of waiting, she turned to walk away. Breena was about to wake herself up when he caught her shoulder and spun her back around. Her breath caught in her throat. She couldn't deny that he was beautiful, but the new side of him still repulsed her. She fixed her eyes on the tree beside him and took in every detail of it. It was the only thing she could do to keep herself from admitting to still having feelings for him. Breena was well aware that he could sense her struggle because he began to chuckle low in his throat. She made the mistake of glancing up to his eyes. *Poor Breena; you're done for.*

"Now that I have your full attention, I will let you in on a bit of my plan. How's that sound?"

Breena nodded.

"My training has led me to a startling conclusion." He paused expectantly, but Breena was no longer in a conversational state. "Oh? What did you discover?" Atlas mocked in Breena's voice. "Well, Breena, thanks for asking. I found that no one is happy. Just the same thing I found in you." He waited, but Breena still said nothing. "But, I made you happy. Remember that? Back in London? When you and I went to your white-walled fortress and we danced together all night?"

He put her back in that moment through an illusion contained in her mind. Breena's pupils dilated. Atlas had gotten much stronger since London, Tabitha's doing, and he was using the full force of his capabilities against Breena. He kept the scene playing in her mind a few more minutes, watching her involuntary reactions.

Don't smile.

"Well, as I was saying. I made you happy with my illusions. *I* want to be happy with my illusions—no more nightmares; you know about that, don't you—and, I can do that for other people, too. So, I'm going to eliminate peoples' worries and guide them toward a life where they can have everything they want. No more gods, no more leaders and corrupt people in positions of power, just people guiding themselves. I will, well, actually *you* will, create an illusion that everyone will see simultaneously. They will start to think their God has turned against them, the governments will be overthrown when people realize they can't handle the chaos, and then, everyone will come with me, searching for more. 'Oh, Atlas, what a brilliant plan. I can't wait to help.' Thanks, for the compliment, Breena, but really, it's Tabitha's plan. You're here to carry out her legacy."

Rather than giving Breena a chance to recover from the state he'd put her in, Atlas sent her out of his illusion and back into the waking world to recover. "We'll start tomorrow."

****

"Wake up, Atlas!" Tabitha threw a bucket of ice water over him, and he thrashed into consciousness, yanked to a halt by the gouging restraints on his wrists and ankles. "Stop playing around with her and get to work. You know I can see the way you're indulging yourself, rehashing your old memories. Stop acting like you spent a lifetime together before she went back home."

"I *have* known her for a lifetime. We've dreamt together since we were children."

"Don't be silly. That time doesn't really count. You knew her for three months."

"If it doesn't count, why is our dream connection the thing that made me her chosen? If that time doesn't count, why can't you give her another guy? She hates me now, anyway, because of what you've made me into."

Tabitha cracked him in the ribs with a rod. Atlas' breath rushed out and he doubled over, gasping. "Sounds like your training is wearing off, Dear." She caressed his bruised cheek.

Atlas flinched away, continuing to hack for a moment before regaining enough breath to reply. "No, Mistress, I just, I don't think you know what it's like to be in my position, and it makes it very difficult to carry out your orders."

"Oh, I understand perfectly. How do you think I became Queen? And where is my king, now? Gone, turned mad, because he couldn't take the pressure. Is that going to be you?"

Atlas wanted to say yes, it was too much pressure; wanted to tell her that no one was playing with *her* from behind the scenes when her chosen came to find her; that when *she* came to power the previous Queen was content to let her take over and implement her own way of ruling, not force some new era of acephalous chaos onto the world. "No. I will carry your orders out nonetheless. Mistress."

"Let's hope so."

****

Jolted awake by the sudden casting out, Breena struggled to recall her conversation with Atlas. She always knew when she went outside of reality with him, but occasionally, their exchanges were blurry. *He's keeping this one from me on purpose. I can't stand who he's turned out to be. Sneaky. Rude. Threatening. Why'd he have to change? I miss my friend.* There was a knock on her back seat window. Normally, she would have jumped, but the mellowing effects of the pills hadn't worn off yet, and she calmly turned around to see who was there.

"Miss? Sorry to disturb you. The park is closing in fifteen minutes. We close at sundown in the winter."

"Oh, right. Sorry, Officer, I'll get going."

"Hey, Miss. You alright?" The park ranger touched his face.

Do I have something on my cheek? It was wet. *Oh. Well, I guess it's good I don't remember the conversation.* "Yeah. Yeah, of course. Allergies. Can't resist nature, though. I'll leave now so you can close up. Have a good night." She rolled up her window and the ranger strolled away. *I shouldn't be letting Atlas do this to me.*

The ride through the chilly night air sliced through the last of her drowsiness. She sped through the damp leaves covering the road. *Back-roads like these are never busy.* As Breena neared the edge of town, she began to dread going home. *I haven't been home in over twenty-four hours. Mom's going to want to talk. If she was worried she would have called, but she'll still have something to say about it. I hope dinner is ready at least.*

Breena was right about the questions. As she loped into the kitchen for supper, which was just coming out of the oven, the one-woman firing squad took aim.

"When do you get your homework done if you're out all afternoon?" Lexa questioned at the end of her spiel.

"Study hall mostly."

The TV was on in the living room and she could hear the news reporter over-articulating a story about a growing need for suicide hotline workers.

"—as many volunteers, unfortunately, burn out quickly from the emotional intensity of the task."

Breena leaned her chair back to get a view into the living room.

"Breena, do you want more water?"

"Consequently, one of the hotline's workers, Reid Case, is believed to be one of those who succumbed to the pressures of the job. Reid, one of the directors of the hotline shown in this previously recorded interview, has been missing for almost a year, now, with no evidence to suggest his whereabouts. Take a look at this previously recorded interview with Reid. Have you seen this man?"

Breena, still reclined, looked over to answer Lexa.

"Well, yes, Susan, our goal at its most basic is to prevent suicide—"

That's his *voice!* Breena reared back in the seat so hard that the legs slipped out from under her, sending the chair skidding across the floor. Ari hollered with laugher, but Breena was too shocked to fuss at him. She landed on her back, and immediately jumped up and ran into the living room in time to catch a glimpse of the reporter standing beside Atlas in front of the town's hotline center. Atlas was staring straight at the camera, like he was searching for Breena somewhere in the viewership.

But we hadn't met yet...

Lexa came running into the living room. "What has gotten into you, Breena? Are you Ok?" Breena ignored her.

The interview continued. "—but I believe in coaching our callers to find happiness, as well. It's not enough to tell them to keep living. That's what they're doing already, and they're tired of it. What they really need is some form of relief, a non-lethal escape, where they can find something fulfilling."

The clip of the old interview paused on a close-up of his face. In a voice-over, the newscaster implored the public once again to call the number on the screen with any information on Reid's location and signed off. An obnoxious detergent commercial came on, and Breena sank into the couch.

"Breena?"

Snap out of it! "Yeah?"

"Do you know him?"

"At first I thought I did."

"Well don't take it so hard. They'll find him."

"I was thinking psychology might be a good career path for me, you know, since I blew my chances at the cello thing." Bitter, Breena retreated to her room, taking only one loathing glimpse at the hulking instrument in the corner before getting on the internet to research Reid Case.

One day you need to read these emails. Her inbox was still full of get-well messages and concerned emails from distant relatives she wouldn't recognize if she saw them in a store. It was sweet, but she couldn't handle the task when she returned from London, and that hadn't changed.

A transcript of the interview will do. Probably better if I can't stare at him and hear his voice, the way he used to be, anyway. It makes me ache. So. Reid Case is his name. I wonder which one's the alias. This work at the hotline, he had to have lived here for a while to do it, and to be respected enough to be the one in the interview. Was London just a temp stay because he knew I'd be there?

She found the address and phone number of "Reid Case," and articles he had written about happiness. *From the look of it, this particular identity has a degree in social work and counseling. They've got to be fake. There's no way he's old enough for all that.* Breena bookmarked some of the web pages and copy-pasted the critical information into a blank document. She chuckled darkly. *The stalker becomes the stalked. I'll find out all about you, Atlas. See how it feels.*

****

"It's time for you to go back to the states, Atlas. She's not running from the truth anymore. She's digging. The truth would be better coming from you. You have to go take care of Reid. Do you understand what I'm saying?"

Atlas nodded, full of dread.

"Her trust is already fragile. Tie up your loose ends and remember who your Queen is. It will give you the strength to obey." Tabitha released Atlas, and he fell to the floor. "Oh, don't be dramatic. Go pack a bag. I'll book you a flight."

****

On top of all the web pages Breena had open, a box appeared with one large smiley face; Jordan was online. She replied with a smiley of her own—Japanese emoticon style. Her inner-debate on whether to tell Jordan about Atlas staying in town lasted merely seconds. *Nope. Keep it to yourself. Atlas' reactions are always worse after I've been around Jordan. If Jordan ran into Atlas, assuming Atlas actually lives here and not in London, Jordan might say something to him. It's scary that they've met. A recognizable face offers no protection.* She stuck with, "Hey," to start the chat.

"I finished my project. Wanna sleep over again? No one has come home yet." Jordan said this with what Breena imagined was cheerful enthusiasm, but she knew that it bothered him deep down that he was alone most of the time. He basically raised himself. Lexa was the biggest mother figure he had, and that was because she was Breena's mom, not because Lexa had any real mothering instinct or characteristics. *Jordan had to grow up really early, but it made him an attentive and responsible friend. He learned how to give wise advice from early on. Why have I never considered him a man before?*

"I don't know." She got up from the computer. *As much as I want to sleep over again, the last thing I need is another bad habit in our relationship. Too fast, too soon.* She paced a path into her carpet. Her thoughts bounced from jittery anticipation of training with Atlas to the lingering desire to use pills to buffer her sleep. She caved to Jordan's offer. *Jordan's safer than either of those other options.* "Yeah, I'll be over as soon as Mom's asleep."

Chapter 17

Breena scooched into Jordan's bed again. The warmth of his closeness, the calm of his even breath, the unspoken assurance of his protection gave the moment a heavy, important quality. She kept telling herself it was no different than it had ever been with them. *Childhood friends share beds. We're just lucky no one ever cared they we aren't both girls. But, I can't deny that things* have *changed.* She looked over at Jordan, who was lying on his back on the inside half of the bed, arms behind his head, eyes closed, and she gently shook her head. *This is not how I imagined my senior year.* Pangs of sadness about her time with Atlas interrupted her dumbfounded, yet thankful, reverie. *Maybe I do still love him.*

As soon as she thought it, Jordan turned to face her and asked, "Do you still care about him?"

She was silent for a while.

"You don't have to talk about it." Jordan pulled away and stared at the ceiling. Since summer, he had gotten used to being left in the dark. Breena felt like the same person lying beside him, but she wasn't. He liked to blame it on the drugs, but he didn't know how far back that problem went. Jordan considered the possibility that the Breena he knew *was* the Breena on drugs, and that this new Breena was a sober stranger he had a hard time cracking.

"No, it's not that. I'm just trying to decide my answer. I care about what we had in London and what I thought I'd continue to have with him back home, but he has demolished every bit of respect I had for him. But, even without respect, I still have memories, and memories are powerful. I still care about who he *was*, and I miss that version of him even though that person is gone." Breena turned to her side, facing away from Jordan, but she sensed another round of questions and peeked over her shoulder.

"If he's gone, what's left to miss?" Jordan threw an arm over his eyes.

"It's like someone died. You don't just stop caring because they aren't around anymore. Trust me, I know all about that. And wouldn't it hurt you? To think you fall in love with someone and find out they aren't who they told you they are, to be unable to escape his memory or presence, to see him in your dreams, inside your head, to know he can find you if he wants to. Yes, it hurts, and it's scary."

Jordan pursed his lips and stared. "How can I help you?"

"I'll have two cheeseburgers, a medium fry, and a chocolate shake, please."

Jordan shoved into Breena's shoulder with his. "Be serious. I know you're using again. That's not the right kind of help."

Breena's eyes popped open. *How'd he know? Just skip over that little statement. Acknowledging it is like admitting he's right.* "I don't know. Just having you helps. Can't that be enough?"

He turned on his side and pulled her close. "Sleep."

****

Atlas boarded his flight and reclined in the luxury of first class, the upgrade a reward and reparation from Tabitha for "being so hard on him the last few months." It was his first moment of comfort since Breena left London. He could feel the stares of the other passengers, all well-to-do people who would never think of flying coach, on his bruised face and lacerated wrists. He looked like he belonged under the plane, flattened on the tarmac, rather than inside the plane. He was used to stares, though. Years of fending for himself as a child had garnered a lot of concerned and disapproving looks from people wondering why a kid was out alone. As the plane ascended, he fell asleep to the lulling beat of his music. He didn't have the strength to contact Breena for training while awake.

****

Breena scooched into Jordan's grasp and closed her eyes hoping to trick herself into sleep. It worked. Despite dreading her meeting, she was in the clearing immediately, and Atlas was there waiting in plain view. When she approached him, her memories of their previous encounter became clear. *Godless world, chaos, 'happiness,' Tabitha's plan.* As the puzzle fit in her mind, her gut twisted. She covered her mouth, sickened. "Atlas, I have questions."

"I know."

"Reid Case? The suicide hotline, giving everyone lives where they get what they want? And my *mother.*" Her volume increased until she was yelling. "You're going to use his hotline callers as fodder for Tabitha's scheme. It's sick, giving hopeless people something to work toward, promising them better futures, positions of power or importance. What will they actually get in return? Pain?"

"Reid Case was my twin."

"Was?" Breena unclenched her fists.

"Was. It is customary in our culture to bear only one child, especially if the child is male. I was a twin. Of course, they couldn't get rid of one of us at birth because they had to wait to see if either was meant for you." Atlas reached to stroke Breena's hair. She pulled away. "Please. It's been so long."

"Keep talking."

"We were both sent out into the world, like you, so that we could learn about humanity and prepare for the possibility of being your chosen. After it became apparent that I was the stronger twin and had inherited all of the abilities of a child of Gehenna—Reid was brilliant, but ordinary—Tabitha decided to let Reid live his human life. If I hadn't been the chosen, maybe she would have continued to let him live. Right before your trip to London, once it was undoubtedly apparent that I was the only one connecting with you, she ordered him terminated."

"I'm sorry."

"I learned of him only after I met Tabitha. I didn't know him, so there is no brother to be mourned."

"You didn't grow up together?"

"No. There was to be no competition between us."

"Oh." *So he didn't lie about being alone growing up, and he didn't use an alias to get to me.* Breena sat on the grass. "You seem more like yourself today." *Don't let your guard down too much.*

Atlas sat across from her. "Tabitha said as much."

"Why are you hanging out with Tabitha? I thought you couldn't stand her."

"I wouldn't call it hanging out. Although, I guess in a literal way, I have been." Atlas continued, ignoring Breena's questioning look. "She's training me to carry out these plans. What you said about the call center is partially true. It was Reid's life's work. It also happened to be the perfect opportunity to sway new people into her service. And all the awful ways I've treated you have been because of her. I swear I didn't want to stand you up your last day in London."

Breena rolled her eyes.

"I wish you'd believe me. She had me kidnapped, tortured, conditioned to see her as the ultimate authority and to treat you a certain way. I was planning to have her killed. She found out. Now, if I want to live, if I want to have you, and I so desperately do, then I have to obey her. Unfortunately, that means you do, too."

"Why do I have anything to do with this? I wasn't plotting against her, and if she wanted to be my mother and to have me obey, she shouldn't have sent me into this world and abandoned me."

"She did it because that is the way of things and because you're next in line to lead. She has a very specific idea of how you should do that. You're not going to get out from under her until she's dead. That's how succession works."

"Stop pretending this is Ok!"

"Breena, this is life. If you want to change things, you have the power to do it, but for now, I have to follow orders. It's time to train."

"Fine. Just teach me."

"I'd like you to take me to the ocean, any coastline will do, and bring the tide in if you can."

Breena scowled at him. *He acts so nonchalant, like we're still an item.* It burned her up inside. She crossed her legs and slowed her breathing. The woodsy silence around her, the hollow hum of still trees, and the soft rustle of leaves would have been relaxing if Atlas hadn't been breathing eerily in time with her as if he were feeding off of her energy.

As her focus sharpened, it came to her, louder and louder, the hum of the world. She could feel the rhythm, too. When the vibrations individualized, she peeled the image of the ocean from her mind and wove it into the lines of the earth's vibrating waves. Soon enough, the thrumming subsided and she knew the image was complete. Bree opened her eyes greeted by the shores of Myrtle Beach stretching out on either side of them. She pulled from her memories of visiting as a child, the smell of boardwalk fries and the trill of children laughing. The waves crashed and the salt air filled their lungs. She turned to Atlas smiling as she had done months earlier, and reality struck. This time was not the same, and Breena could not allow herself to get sucked into his magnetism or her memories.

"Very nice." He sounded far away. "Now, if you'll slowly pull the tide in. I'll tell you when to stop."

Already in the illusion, she didn't have to close her eyes this time. Breena simply focused on the waves and pulled each one higher in the air, crashing them farther up-shore. She brought the tide about three feet from the board walk and stopped to question Atlas. Before she could ask if she could stop, he shook his head and motioned backward. He turned and started to walk up the block.

"No!"

Atlas stopped midway up the street and looked back at Breena. "Excuse me?"

"I said no. If the point of this is to teach me how to use my projections for destruction, I'm not doing that. I bring it further, and the boardwalk and all the shops will be demolished in reality, too. You haven't taught me anything about controlling these illusions."

"You *will* do as I say. Remember my terms. Think of Jordan, asleep beside you."

She crossed her arms. "Atlas, your Tabitha is showing. You owe me the truth."

"It's just an illusion in a dream. They cause no real damage. But, leave the tide. I've seen enough of what you can do for today. Dissolve this scenario, and we'll go back for a lesson."

"How much time passes in the waking world while I'm here?"

"You haven't missed your alarm, if that's your concern. You let me worry about logistics. You're here to learn."

"I'd learn something if you answered me, too," Breena mumbled under her breath. *I hate the way he always has everything under control. It stood out in London. Responsible, organized; he took good care of me. Pre-abandonment. Now, it just feels like my life is spiraling out of control. I have nothing to do with the when and where.*

When they returned, Atlas produced a notebook from somewhere. *I wonder if that's a real notebook. Can he actually write in it? Can I take it home to study? Don't say any of that out loud. Maintain your anger. It's your only protection against that face... and heart, and his fascinating mind.* Breena cringed at the satisfaction her practice brought, that *he* brought. There was no denying that it mollified the escapist need she had always tried to fulfill. In the moments where she wasn't furious at Tabitha, the practice was peaceful, even.

Breena studied Atlas as he drew out a complicated diagram that overlaid the illusory world with its waking world location.

"Ok. Look at this."

Breena squinted.

"Pretend that looks like a seashell. Certain objects produce small enough vibrations because they are either insignificant in size or importance and because they are non-living items. These things in the real world can actually be affected by the illusion if the illusion changes that same item within the image. So, that's stuff like seashells, *some* sand but not the whole beach, a trash can, etc. The range of what's considered a small or unimportant object is wide. Now, this is a building." Atlas used the trinket store on the boardwalk as an example.

Breena laughed. She couldn't help it.

"Humor me? Buildings, other large objects, and living things produce larger vibrations and are difficult or immovable by one person's illusion, no matter what happens within image. That is, except for your illusions and Tabitha's illusions. Dreaming can't impact anything. They're lucid creations of the mind which exist on another plane only accessible by the mind and soul. The building itself would not have been touched by the illusion at all. If you were awake and creating the image, the shop owner would have walked into his store to find many of the small items wet on the floor from the waves of your illusion. Had you done as I'd asked." He tacked on the last phrase with a rare grin, and Breena struggled not to swoon right there in front of him.

He is legitimately enjoying himself. Is it the talk of destruction or the joy of teaching? Sick bastard.

"Do you understand?"

Crap. He's expecting a reply. Breena nodded.

"Ok, well you need some real sleep before your alarm goes off. As much as I loathe sending you back into the arms of that limp noodle of a boyfriend, I guess I have to. Go, sleep, come back tomorrow." He tried to hug her with a final "Sleep sweet," but Breena shrugged out of his reach and backed away across the grassy expanse.

Good girl, Breena. Impressive resistance. "When you can act out of your own free will, maybe then you'll get a hug." Breena shouted from the far tree line.

"I look forward to that." He smiled, but it didn't take the torment out of his eyes, and sent her out of the lucid state back into the blackness of sleep.

Atlas stayed behind, certain that he had another couple hours left to sleep off his flight. He walked out of the clearing about fifty feet and found a cluster of trees that were heavily shaded from the moon. Atlas knelt, crunching the leaves that had fallen, and conjured another illusion. In it, his mother swung him around by his wrists in a meadow near his house. In the background, a door slammed loudly, and his mother looked behind her with startled eyes. She set young Atlas down and spread her hands over her dress like she was primping, but the way she wrung her fingers after gave away her nervousness. He didn't have to see his father walk into the image to know the story. Atlas let the illusion shatter before anything else happened. He sat there in the leaves for a long time. Worse than his memories of his abusive father was seeing them replayed in illusions so realistic one could live inside them indefinitely. "Tabitha wants more of this pain, more of this chaos. That *is* happiness to her. I want it to be real." He stood, brushing off his knees. "Breena is real."

Chapter 18

Breena crept into her quiet house at 5:00am and tiptoed up the stairs. In her drowsiness, she tripped over the cat, who had become one with a step, invisible in the darkness. "Shh." She froze in place waiting to be caught, but the only movement in the house was hers. Spud had already settled back in on the step below her. Finally reaching the top, she padded down the hall less carefully. As she passed Ari's room, he poked his head out. *So close.*

"Where were you?"

"In the bathroom."

"All night? You're a terrible liar."

"Go to bed."

"Same to you. Actually, I might be interested in telling Mom that you snuck out to go get a fix. You know, for your own good."

"Don't you dare. That's not what I was doing."

"Careful. If you raise your voice much more you'll wake her up, and then you can just tell her yourself."

"Ari, what do you want?"

"Maybe I want in."

"On..."

"A little pick-me-up."

"No."

"Oh, yes. Unless you want Mom to know."

"I'm not giving you anything. Go to bed." Breena stalked to her room, silently fuming. *I hate him sometimes. What's he got in his life that he needs to escape? I don't even care if he tells Mom. I'll just tell her he asked me for some.*

Her phone buzzed in her pocket. *Who the hell is calling so early?* Pulling it out, the screen lit up with a picture of Atlas, and her angry thoughts disappeared. All thought disappeared.

****

Atlas stood at baggage claim waiting for his leather garment bag to come around.

"Hey, it's Breena. I'm doing something else, so leave a message."

"Hi, Breena. It's Atlas. I know it's early. Sorry. And I haven't called since London, so I guess sorry for that, too. Look, I just wanted to tell you I'm in town—just got off the plane, actually—and I want to see you. Everything I told you earlier was true. Call me when you wake up. I've missed you."

His battered luggage chugged toward him, and he hauled it off the belt. "Well, by the end of the day everything I said will be true." Outside of the terminal, he flagged down a taxi. Flashbacks of his first arrival to the states after his mother died clouded his vision, and he swayed. "God, I hate it here."

"Where to?"

"The home of Reid Case. Here's the address."

****

Breena stared slack-jawed at the voice mail light blinking. *I can't listen to it. Can I? Don't listen to it.* She brought the phone up to her ear—*Don't*—and pressed play. Goosebumps rose on her arms and the back of her neck as his words filtered through. *Hearing him on the phone feels so much more real than when we're projecting. Like I can feel him in my chest. It aches, but it's kind of wonderful, too. Jordan doesn't make me feel like this.*

The message ended with electronic instructions on how to save and delete the voicemail. *I wasn't even listening to what he said.*

"Or press four to replay."

Pay attention this time.

Breena sat on the edge of her mattress and fell back into her pillows. The phone tumbled onto the bed beside her, the tinny electronic voice playing through once again. *I can't handle seeing him. The training is one thing. It feels real in the moment, but once I wake up it's shapeless, less than a dream. No, that's a lie. You're trying to escape it. It always feels real. Always sticks for the rest of the day. So, then, what's the problem? I'm not afraid of him. Ok, maybe a little bit, but that's not it.* Her alarm clock went off and Breena smacked at it. She glanced at the bottle of allergy pills beside it. *Not now. I want to be less anxious, not exhausted. That's it. It's my willpower. I just used all of it up. If I see him, I don't know what I'll do.*

****

The taxi slowed, stopping in front of Reid's mailbox. The little bungalow was dark, and the yard was unkempt.

"Looks like no one's home. You sure this is where you wanted to go?"

"Yes, certain. Thank you." Atlas handed the cabby a fifty and got out. The front door to the home was unlocked as expected, so Atlas pushed his way in and dropped his bag at the entrance. He went back into the cold, leaving the front door open. Crossing the front yard, Atlas let himself in to the neighboring house, to which Tabitha had given him a key before boarding his flight saying, "Make yourself at home. I own the place."

Rattling echoed through the empty house from the back room. "Reid, is that you back there, buddy?" The rattling stopped. In the master bedroom, Atlas found Reid locked in a steel cage that filled the room.

"What the hell? Who are you?"

"Nice to meet you, Brother. Or, I should say, 'Nice to *be* you.'"

"What's that supposed to mean? Why do you look like me? Where's the guy who usually brings dinner?"

Atlas examined the cage and its prisoner silently.

"Hey, man. Are you here to let me out? I gotta take a piss." Reid paced.

"You could say that." Atlas fished for Tabitha's keyring in his pocket, the second key's use apparent. He unlocked the bolt and swung the door open. Reid rushed to exit, but Atlas blocked the way.

"Move, man. It's like I told the other guy. I'm not going to run. I learned my lesson last time." He turned his head and pointed to the space an ear should have been.

Atlas stayed. His hands sweat. All the thoughts he would have had if he hadn't slept on the plane flooded him: *it isn't right, Breena won't understand, it's necessary to sacrifice one person to keep up appearances with Tabitha, and, in the end, I still owe Tabitha my life.*

"Come on!"

Atlas stepped aside, letting Reid get just past him before throwing an arm across Reid's neck from behind. He locked Reid in the hold using the crook of his elbow to secure the other arm against Reid's throat.

Reid thrashed about, throwing his arms to the sides, trying to punch at Atlas, and attempting to bite, but Atlas' grip was too tight for Reid to open his mouth, much less lower his chin enough to get a mouthful. Reid gasped and gurgled a revolting death symphony, and Atlas closed his eyes, pulling tighter. Atlas pictured Breena's face, his reason for following orders, until Reid went limp. He dropped his twin on the floor and stumbled out into the yard just in time to throw up.

Wiping his mouth, he went back to Reid's house, texted Tabitha to send for clean-up, and got the hotline number off the fridge to leave a message in his best American accent.

"Hi, this is Reid Case. I'm calling to apologize for my sudden and prolonged absence. I feel terrible for worrying everyone. I'm ready to get involved with the mission again. I had to take some time to help myself, and I was embarrassed to tell anyone about it. Such a hypocrite, right? But, now I'm ready to help others again, if you'll have me. Please call me back. Same number. 'Night."

Atlas fell into Reid's shabby recliner. "I am *exactly* what my father thought."

****

Breena managed to resist calling Atlas for the next two days and, with Jordan's help, she was also two days sober. Jordan went to

Breena's after school on Thursday to help confiscate all of Breena's over-the-counter crutches—Benadryl, cough syrup, Dramamine, and the like. She knew it was a victory of sorts, but it didn't feel like it. Besides being exhausted, restless, and on edge, Friday was a *social* disaster, too.

At school, Lilly and Jordan bickered about the usual lunch-table topics—murder, sports, and parents—but when the discussion about boys arose, Jordan clammed up and Lilly got inquisitive. She pressed harder, looking back and forth between Breena and Jordan waiting for answers about what dates they had gone on and how the kissing was. Jordan slammed his fists down on the table, rattling the three plastic trays.

"Stop! Not everything is your business." He gathered his trash and left.

Lilly shouted over her shoulder at him. "Your secrets aren't that special anyway."

Breena wrinkled her nose at Lilly. "What's your problem today?"

"You asked him for help instead of me. You know I know more about that kind of stuff than him."

"You're jealous?"

"Maybe. Look, I know you two are, well, something, and, you know, it's whatever. I give up. But he was already your best friend before he was your whatever-he-is-now, and so it's like there's no relationship slots left for me to fill. You don't call me anymore. You don't tell me stuff. I got close to Jordan while you were off in London, but I always wished it was you I was hanging out with, and I was just a replacement of you to him."

"What are you saying? You don't want me to be his friend? To date?"

Lilly had turned red, and she was cutting up her salad into shreds.

"Lilly."

"I'm saying..." She fumbled with her packet of dressing, which didn't want to open, until the edge finally tore off and splashed ranch all over Lilly's tray. "I'm saying maybe he's not the only one who wanted to date you, Ok?" Lilly threw down the ruined packet and stomped out of the cafeteria.

Breena was too stunned to go after her. *I don't understand why they all like me so much.*

Bree caught up with Jordan in math class later and thanked him for resisting Lilly's tactics. She kept the confession to herself. They walked to the parking lot separately after class, each thinking the others would be there. In her car, Breena dug through her glove box looking for any last pills, but there was nothing. She dropped her head back against the headrest. A twinge at the back of her eyes made her curse under her breath. "Guess who's looking for me, now. Might as well get this over with." Most of the cars had already pulled out, so she reclined her seat and allowed her consciousness to slip to Atlas' level.

He sat on the edge of a pier overlooking a lake. "You didn't call. Why?" Atlas' voice was flat, and his eyes were empty.

"I couldn't handle it." *I've been here before. It was a nightmare.*

"I thought you would be excited to hear from me. Come here. Sit down with me."

Breena dangled her legs over the edge. "Maybe a little, but scared, too. It's easier to see you like this. So what are you doing here?"

He sighed. "Taking Reid's place. Preparing."

"What's that supposed to mean?"

"Meet me in person and I'll tell you."

"You're so manipulative."

Atlas agreed, but didn't say anything.

Breena stood to go, irritated.

"Your phone is ringing. Go answer it. I'll see you over the weekend, I hope."

Breena's phone rang at top volume, and she lifted her head with a start. *That was a weird exchange.* "Shit, shit, shit," she mumbled as she noted she had completely slept through her shift at work. "Hello? Hey, Jordan. Yeah, I'm Ok, just a little disoriented. I fell asleep before leaving school."

"You did *what?*" Jordan's concerned exclamation forced Breena to pull the phone from her ear a few inches.

"Yeah, I fell asleep in my car. I'm still in the school parking lot. No, I didn't go to work."

"How the hell—"

"Man, I gotta get over there. Thanks. Yeah, later." Breena and Jordan hung up and she drove maniacally to the supermarket.

Breena shot through the office door. "Hi, Mr. Forst. I'm so sorry I missed my shift."

"Do you know how irresponsible that is? And you wanted me to give you regular four-hour shifts. This just proves you're not ready to come back."

"Yes, I know it looks bad. I really am ready to come back to a regular schedule. It's been months since I got out of the hospital. This was just a mistake. It has nothing to do with my health."

"I don't mind being lenient when it comes to health. There's nothing more important. But when an employee just chooses not to come, that's something else."

"I didn't choose. I just forgot. I'm very sorry, sir. It won't happen again."

"Then you'd better be here on time Monday. Remember, that's the next day I scheduled you. That's three days from now, the day that comes after the weekend."

Alright, you condescending jerk. "Yes, from 4 to 6. I promise."

At home, she flung her shoes off on the landing, and tossed her bags beside them.

"Hi, honey. You're still in your school clothes. Did you forget to take your uniform with you?"

"Yeah, you could say that," Breena called as she rounded the banister. *Pajamas here I come.*

She put the phone on speaker while she changed. "Jordan, I'm back home, now."

"Good. Boss chew you out?"

"Not too bad. More of the snide nastiness than the yelling and anger-type reaction."

"Well, glad you didn't get fired. Why were you napping in the parking lot anyway?"

"Migraine. Like the other night. You think you could bring me some of my medicine?"

"No deal. If you need them that bad you can come over here, and I will give you the proper dose and nothing more."

"I knew I shouldn't have let you take it all."

"Is it really a migraine, or is there something else?"

"Both, I guess."

"You can tell me, even if it's about him. I'd rather hear about that than hear you've started popping prescriptions again."

"I know in theory I can tell you. In reality, though..." she shook her head and closed her eyes. Jordan didn't say anything else and, minutes later, she was asleep.

Chapter 19

By Saturday morning, Breena's phone was so overloaded with texts from Lilly apologizing that Breena couldn't even respond to them all. More debilitating than the sheer quantity of texts was the growing anxiety about meeting Atlas. He hadn't come to train her overnight, a ploy she knew was designed to lure her to him in person. She wanted relief, but Breena had begun *hoping* to see him at night.

I can't deny that I'd like to meet up with him in person. And I do need more information about Tabitha's intentions if I'm going to help Atlas. Big if. Suppose what he said really is true, that it's her plan and he's trying to fight the impulse to obey, but can't win without me. I could actually do something important, something that protects the people I care about. I could earn the praise they all give so freely. But I don't want to get suckered into helping Tabitha destroy life as we know it. She traced over a post-it note on her nightstand. In messy script, she had written a quote on it just after returning from London.

"We also live in our dreams. We do not live only by day; sometimes we accomplish our greatest deeds in dreams. –Jung"

As she mulled over this likelihood, another text beeped in from Lilly asking for a visit with some real girl-talk. Heavy guilt settled over Bree's shoulders. *Lilly is right, as usual. She was out of line with the questioning, but I haven't been supportive of her at all. She was brave to tell me how she feels.*

"DELETE SAVED MESSAGES TO RECEIVE NEW TEXT."

Unwilling to part with any conversations, she shoved the phone under the pillow. Immediately, it rang in a tone she hadn't assigned to anyone. The number was blocked. Breena wavered on whether to answer it, and since her life wasn't following its usual path, she decided to take a chance. There were three clicks on the other end and a definite hanging-up sound. She said hello into the dead line a few times, then ended the call. Rather than bothering with all the text messages, she called Lilly to see if she wanted to go to lunch.

"Sure! I'd love that. I've got nothing planned for the day. What time?"

"Um, 1:00? At Lowell's?"

"Sounds good."

"Alright, see you there."

When Breena set down the phone, she was smiling. Apparently, she *did* need this girl time. She and Lilly hadn't hung out over a meal, outside of school lunches, since before London. Even so, Bree had no intention of discussing Atlas with her. *Lilly doesn't need to feel like there's any additional competition for my attention or friendship.* Breena hopped in the shower at noon and was dressed in her favorite torn jeans, cable-knit sweater, and Converse sneakers forty minutes later.

****

Atlas stumbled down the main road parallel to Breena's street for two hours worrying over how to approach her. He had even called her cell, but couldn't work up the nerve to say anything when she picked up. He feared she'd know what he had done. Eventually, he wandered to a hotel and booked a room. Atlas couldn't stand to be in Reid's house. From the rented bed, Atlas went to the clearing to wait until Breena came that night. As he positioned himself against his favorite redwood tree just outside the grassiest area, he heard light footsteps approaching from behind. He could feel her before he turned to look. The hairs on his arms stood, waiting like the rest of his body, to see whether she was there on business or pleasure—her pleasure.

Atlas turned around to look at Tabitha. "I don't want to do this anymore."

She gave Atlas a tight smile.

"Why are you here? This is where I come to get away from you."

"Stop talking to me like that. If you value the task I've entrusted you, you will respect me."

"Then just tell me why you're here so you can leave, Your Highness," Atlas sneered.

At that, Tabitha moved silently and immediately within reach of Atlas and smacked him hard across the face. "You call me Mistress, and without a stitch of sarcasm."

"Yes, Your Highness."

Another smack. Atlas didn't even grab his cheek, which was bruised with a handprint already. "Insolent bastard. I came to reward you, but clearly that's not what you want. So, instead, I'll say this. You're inconsistent and you scare her. At times you're kind, and at times you're harsh. Students like her only learn from consistency. I prefer the fear method, myself, but that doesn't work on her. Works on you, though." Tabitha nudged him playfully. She wasn't the type to joke, but in her rare moments of levity, it was always at someone else's expense.

"She's warming to you again, which to follow you, to follow *me*, she must do. You have to win back her full affection. She will not follow this fate if she does not love you. She will not do what you ask of her. She *must* love you. But, do not allow yourself to warm to her. Your pathetic weakness for her, this *love* you think you feel, needs to end. *She* is not your queen yet. She will blind you, and you will fail."

"Yes, Your Highness," he said again, head bowed.

"I will not continue to indulge you with the self-inflicted punishment you're so clearly craving right now. Remember, you didn't want your reward."

She was gone a second later. Atlas crumpled in on himself and rolled onto his side. "It's too late, Tabitha. I already love her, and I'm going to go see her."

****

Lilly was already at Lowell's, early as usual, and had ordered both of them coffees in big mugs that looked more like bowls with handles. She waved Breena over to the cozy table in the corner.

Before Breena even sat down, Lilly began firing the questions at her. London, boys, coffee shops, clubs, hospital stay, coma, *Jordan?*

"FYI, one at a time."

Lilly smiled boldly, no sheepish grin of embarrassment remaining, only the proud look of a job well done.

"You really think you've accomplished something huge, don't you? I'm seriously not talking about half the stuff you just listed."

"Drink your coffee. You're grumpy."

"Not grumpy, just picky."

"Well, I guess we haven't done this in a while. Since before your trip, actually. Remember, I ask a question, you answer, and vice versa."

"I know how conversations work, thank you. Why don't you tell me more about what you mentioned Friday?"

"Why don't we go get food?"

Breena sighed. Neither of them was interested in divulging any kind of personal details. It was sad, really, that the two best friends had drifted so far over one summer. *I might as well be in London still.*

The line to place their orders was long and neither could see the menus or how many cashiers they had working over the stretch of people.

"Hold my place. I'm going to go look at the menu closer up. Then you can." When she shuffled far enough aside to see the boards, she also caught the eye of one very troubled-looking Atlas. He was in the line adjacent to hers, about seven people ahead. Their eyes locked, and instead of the hungry, possessive look that usually lit up at the sight of her, his green stare was grey, his mouth set into a hard line, and she could see the muscles in his jaw clenching and unclenching. Breena's slapped a hand over her mouth to keep from screaming or running to him or crying out for him. *Don't stare. Get back in line!* Breena turned her back on his morbidly slim frame, shaggy hair, and disheveled clothes to shove her way back into line with Lilly.

"Lilly," Breena said barely louder than a whisper.

Lilly didn't hear.

"Lilly," Breena said louder this time, almost whining. She tapped Lilly's shoulder.

"What happened? You're blood red." Lilly looked as horrified as she sounded. She grabbed both of Breena's shoulders.

"Can we please go?"

"Why?"

"Please." Breena cringed at the sound of her begging voice. Lilly nodded her head wildly, eyebrows to her hairline, and grabbed Breena's hand to lead them out of the crowd. *Almost there. Go home, no, to Jordan's, get some pills, stay awake. He'll come to me if I sleep. He's following us.* "Lilly, faster!" *Don't look back.* Lilly pulled her by the hand, their heavy coats swishing as they speed-walked away from Lowell's. Breena turned to look. Atlas chased after them looking as pained as he had inside. Breena stopped walking, which jerked her hand free of Lilly's. Lilly paused to find Breena, still like death, one arm outreached, the other clenched to her chest, hand knotted in the collar of her shirt. Tears silently rolled down Breena's face.

Breena took two unstable steps toward Atlas and froze again. Atlas, who looked like he had aged, opened his mouth to speak, but hung his head instead.

"Atlas," Breena whispered. *Oh, this is much worse than seeing him at night. I feel like there's fire inside me. Anger.*

He looked up at her, but said nothing.

"What happened?" Breena questioned him in a gentle, curious tone, not the demanding, angry one she thought was going to come out.

"I don't want you to hate me."

Here it comes. "Do you think," Breena hollered, "that I *want* to hate you? You, who I *loved?*"

"So you do hate me?" Atlas questioned, barely whispering.

"Think about what you're making me do. Think about what we had before I came back here. Think about how I told you I felt and all the fun we had together. Do you seriously believe that I would be able to hold onto all of that and ignore what you're trying to force me into? Plus, you disappeared on me. Oh, and you've tried to kill me. I bet I can make the list longer." Lilly tried to pull Breena's livid, shaking form away from her spot in front of Atlas. "Yes, I loved you in London. Yes, I hate you, now."

At those words, Atlas collapsed onto his knees, head in his hands. Breena had to wonder whether she really hurt him or if it was his flair for the dramatic, an attempt to reel her back in. She didn't trust anything about him anymore.

"I wanted us to be partners in everything I have planned," he pleaded.

"I've heard enough." She turned. "Lilly, please, take me home."

"But your car..."

"I'll come back with Jordan. Let's go."

It was Atlas' turn to beg. In the time since London, even since Breena's first lesson Wednesday night, he had changed into this smaller form of himself. He seemed shrunken in, needy, and desperate. Breena wondered what had happened to him since Wednesday. *Maybe his appearance was an illusion, too. Is he groveling? He's effing groveling.*

Breena and Lilly quickly shuffled into Lilly's silver Nissan and began backing out. Atlas ran around to the front of the vehicle and slammed his fist down on the hood. Lilly moved to slam on the brakes.

"Just keep driving." Breena caught a glimpse of Atlas walking after their car in the passenger side mirror. *I hope he gets tired of walking, but he's not going to stop until he has my undivided attention.*

Lilly parked in Breena's driveway fifteen minutes later. She cut the engine and glared at Breena.

Breena pulled on the door handle. "Unlock the doors, please."

"No. You're going to tell me what the hell is going on."

Breena groaned.

"Yes. Spill."

"I really gotta pee. Please just let me out of the car."

"Hold it. I want answers."

Breena turned toward Lilly and crossed her legs in the seat. *This is going to be such a long conversation.* "I thought I had a stalker in London," Breena began. She went over her first night in the apartment, the café, how Jordan came "by mail," which Lilly interjected that she had advised him against doing, and the girls Bree met over tea and coffee. Breena even admitted to how she met Atlas, and that he was the reason she got kicked out of the symphony program. Breena went into embarrassingly personal details about her time with Atlas from that point onward.

"And I'm not as worried to tell you this as I was to tell Jordan because you're cautious in the same way he is hasty. All good intentions and protective. You're not going to get mixed up with Atlas, but I'm terrified that if Jordan could do something to get rid of him, he would try, and without a plan. You'd at least have a plan."

Breena went on, apprising Lilly of Atlas' proclivities, and how she was training to become more proficient in the illusions. The secrets just tumbled out once she got going, and Bree concluded with the fact that Atlas was now using her in some scheme to bring "true happiness" to the world, and that he was living somewhere in town.

"And now, I guess he's stalking me again, too," Breena tacked on after she finally took a breath.

Lilly was bug-eyed and slack-jawed—a feat. She hadn't gotten a word in during the whole confession, and Breena didn't know if she had even tried.

"Lilly? Please, say something."

"Do you love him?"

Breena drew back a bit, caught off-guard by the question. Of all the things she thought Lilly would demand to know given her fascination with crime stories and handy warnings about safety, that was not the one.

"I saw how you looked at him today. Do you still love him?"

"I don't want to."

"But you do."

"No, I... the only time he ever treated me well was in London."

"You can't say it, though. You can't say that you don't love him."

"Well, I can't say that I *do*, either!"

"Good. He doesn't deserve that, and you deserve better." There was a loud click that made Breena jump after hearing only their voices in the stuffy car. Lilly had unlocked the doors and was moving to get out. "Come on. We need to do some research."

Chapter 20

Breena and Lilly scrolled hopefully through pages of results returned on every variation of the names Atlas Thorley and Reid Case, plus the jobs, organizations, and history he had told Breena, which really wasn't much. Only what she already knew appeared— the hotline news interview, the missing person's report, and some tip-line phone numbers.

"I hate to tell you this, Breena, but your boyfriend doesn't exist." Lilly pushed her glasses up her nose.

"He is *not* my boyfriend."

"He either has one really good agent to erase every public trace he leaves, or he is nonexistent. Oh, oh, or maybe *he's* the agent. CIA? You know, they can teach people accents."

"Atlas is not CIA, and I told you already, Reid was his twin, not an alias."

"I'm not convinced you should believe him."

"I understand the hesitation. I think he's been telling me the truth lately, though. Look at it this way. He wants me back, right? So, he's trying to do things that earn my trust. Plus, he's terrified of being like his father. So, if he has a chance to prove to himself to me that he's different, then I think he'd take it. Telling me Reid is, was, his twin, well, I don't know how that fits in to his redemption story, but if his actions are simply to prove to me he's not a liar, then there are more reasons to believe him than not."

"Or is that just more of his manipulation?"

"I'd like to think it isn't."

"Please, be careful. He seems clinically insane."

"I will."

****

"Jordan!"

He sat on the edge of a retaining wall staring into the Zen garden below him. Breena had snuck out of the bed the other morning before school and gone home without telling him. Between his fight with Lilly, Breena's parking lot sleeping spell, and keeping her sober, he hadn't gotten the chance to tell Breena her quick escape bothered him. Under normal "friends" circumstances, it wouldn't have, but since the changes in their relationship, he felt kind of used.

"Jordan! Yo! I'm not paying you to count grains of sand. Get off your ass and load the truck. We're done." Jordan's boss stomped through the shrubs and smacked him in the head. "Hey!"

"Ow, what the hell was that for?"

"We're leaving. What's wrong with you today?"

"Nothing."

"That girl, again?"

Jordan finally stood up and started toward the dually truck that hauled all of their landscaping equipment. "Always."

****

Atlas reached to shake his supervisor's hand. He had had to gather his wits and head straight to the call center after his parking lot encounter with Breena. The hotline's new manager wanted Reid to jump back in as soon as possible.

"We're all so glad to see you're Ok. You really had us worried. I don't want to make you feel guilty for your absence. You did what you needed to do in order to get better, so please don't take this the wrong way. Obviously, if we had known your 'disappearance' was intentional, we would have never had to get the police involved. So, next time, if there is ever a next time, please tell us you need a break. We will respect your request for no contact."

Atlas shook Rod's hand. "My apologies. Sincerely. Thanks for understanding." He swayed, the contact sending a fresh wave of nausea and memories of his crime.

"Let's get you set up." Rod turned down the hall, and Atlas followed, trying not to show that he didn't know his way around. "I was given your cubicle, so you'll need a new station."

"It's fine."

"Thanks again for coming back to us. It must be hard in a way, returning to what hurt you, people hurting themselves."

Atlas coughed.

"And you always hated the day shift, too, so we appreciate it even more. It's tough finding people that can be here in the middle of the day on a Saturday. No one wants to give up a weekend."

"Right. Well, here I am."

"Yes, and here *we* are. You can make yourself at home. No one else uses this one—" he gestured at the drab space, "—so feel free to decorate."

Atlas mentally rolled his eyes wondering what purpose decorating would serve him. He grabbed the script binder from the shelf and sat down.

"Ah, back to the script? You're out of practice."

"Yeah. Alright. Better get to work. I'll pop in your office and say bye before I leave."

"Yeah, not like last time you left."

"Ouch."

Rod looked immediately guilty and lumbered away. After two hours, the phone finally rang.

"Central Michigan Suicide Helpline, what's your problem?" Atlas strayed from the prescribed script thinking he'd sound more approachable. As soon as it left his mouth he shook his head, realizing how abrasive he came across. *I can't even* pretend *not to be bitter.*

A whispered voice said, "I really don't want to be here anymore."

"Tell me about it."

The caller didn't pick up on Atlas' sarcasm and took the prompt literally. She dove into a detailed account of paranoia that the person who looked like her lover wasn't really her lover. She got louder the more agitated she became. "I swear it's on purpose. They want me dead. I'm telling you, if I'm going to die, I'm going to do it myself!"

"Capgras Delusion."

"What?"

"That's what it's called, the things you're feeling." Atlas cringed when he realized he'd wanted to get a call, that figuring people out was thrilling. "You're going to be Ok. Ideally, no one would ever need to call. But, that's why I'm here, to start forming a world where that is true." As much as he hated Tabitha's intention to bring about that change through chaos, he couldn't deny that the end result was something he believed in, and that it was nearly impossible to resist her orders because of the sheer biological impulse, which was an even stronger motivator than the torture and conditioning, to serve his queen.

"I have a plan. It's not affiliated with this hotline, or any other counseling service. It's all mine. I want to bring you happiness. People don't have the lives they want. You're one of those people. Soon, I'm going to change that. Those closest to me are helping already. They will get the largest benefit from the change. When the world realizes their fates are easily adjusted, they will follow me. People will resent being kept in the dark by their God, kept in their places by the elite, by the farce of the status quo. If you think people are out to get you, even the one you love, why don't you join me in changing that? Be your own person. Live for happiness, not for other peoples' expectations."

After a silence, a timid voice asked, "Are you a terrorist?"

"No, I'm a savior."

Another long silence.

"Are you with me, or do you want to wallow in your delusions?"

There was a faint, "Yes."

"Yes to which part? No matter. Meet me at 4:00 tomorrow at the coffee shop beside the call center." Atlas grinned, pleased his first call of the day was a success. Going off of Breena's reaction, he had expected more of the same, and he didn't have time to bother with those too scared to join him and too scared to go through with their own plans. *Too fragile. I want the hardy ones and, if I can't have them, I don't much care if they go through with their deaths or not.* "If you can't fight for your happiness, you don't deserve to benefit from other peoples' fights for a happier world."

"Oh—Ok."

By the end of the day, five callers had agreed to join him. Tabitha would be glad for the progress, but underwhelmed at the number of recruits, especially since he still hadn't made up with Breena.

****

"No, a movie sounds great," Jordan said to Breena.

"I'll be over soon. Go online and get the movie times."

"What movie?"

"You choose. See you in a few."

What does my hair look like? Oh, boy, there's a whole situation going on back there. Where's my brush? She picked up three piles of somewhat folded laundry from the top of her dresser. *No brush. Screw it. Fingers will do. Ow, tangle.*

Breena ran her fingers across the wall as she descended into the living room where she found her mom lounging on the couch. The TV was on, volume low, and Lexa had her laptop propped on her belly and knees.

"Mom, I'm going out with Jordan tonight—don't know when I'm coming back. Oh, and I've got to use your car."

Lexa nodded approval, but she was clearly engrossed in whatever was on the laptop screen, and Breena wondered if Lexa really heard. Breena shrugged, slipped on her shoes, and grabbed her keys and purse off the peg by the door. "Bye, Mom."

Breena blared the music in the car on the way to Jordan's, her iPod on shuffle. She was using all means of media, including the book she had read after Lilly went home, to escape her thoughts about seeing Atlas earlier in the day, but it was futile. A song *he* had put on the gadget blasted through the speakers causing Breena to swerve as she reached too quickly to turn the radio off. *Has to be everywhere, doesn't he?*

Jordan sat on the first step of his porch. *Two other cars? His parents are home. This must be why he wanted to get out of the house so badly.* As soon as she put the car in park, he was across the lawn and at the passenger door, tugging on the handle.

"I'm driving?" Breena questioned.

"I can if you're against it. I'm just blocked in and I really don't want to talk to—"

"Enough said. Get in. So, what movie did you choose?"

"I didn't. Nothing good out right now."

"Ok, so where am I going, then?"

"You want dinner?"

"I've had my fill of restaurants today. We can get fast food, but I don't want to go in anywhere."

"Hey, we could get something from a drive-thru and take it to a park. We can eat in the car and look at the stars."

"Sounds nice, but all the parks close at sundown this time of year."

"You can make it look like they left the gates open, right? If anyone says anything, just tell them they were open and you didn't know we weren't supposed to be there."

"I guess I can. Hadn't thought to use the illusions like that."

"What, for fun? To get something you want? To break rules?"

"All of the above. Let's go." Breena swung the car around at the next stop light and drove to the nearest greasy spoon for burgers and fries. At the park, she stopped in a dark section away from the light on the supplies shed. They broke out the fat-laden deliciousness and ate in comfortable silence for at least five minutes. After Jordan shoved the last fry in his mouth and swallowed, he turned to look at Breena.

"What?" Breena said through full cheeks of burger. "You're makin' me nervous."

Jordan laughed, which crinkled up the bridge of his nose and the freckled skin around his eyes. "I just like you."

"Thanks?"

"Finish eating so I can kiss you, please."

Breena let out a hoot of a laugh, and then slapped her hand over her mouth. "I'm not laughing at you, or your wanting to kiss me. I swear. I was laughing because I've never heard you so forward with a girl. Oh, hell," she said as she smacked her forehead with her palm, "I'm a girl to you now. That means you're going to try to *woo me*." Breena rolled her shoulders as said this last part with mock-seductive qualities.

Jordan beamed. "Yes, I am. Is it working?"

"I didn't realize you'd already started."

"Cold."

Breena shoved Jordan in the shoulder, but Jordan caught her hand as she tried to withdraw it, and he pulled her into him. "Kiss me, burger lips," he whispered.

"You're terrible at this," Breena laughed, "but Ok."

At 9:00pm, they came up for air and agreed it was time to make their way back to Jordan's place. Breena pointed to her overnight bag in the back of the car.

"I can stay, right?"

"You don't have to ask."

"Just checking." *Because if not, I'll have to go to Lilly's. Can't imagine tonight going well with Atlas.* "I hope everyone's out of the house when we get back."

"For real."

"It's not that I don't like your family—"

He gave her a skeptical look.

"Ha, it totally is."

****

"Finally, she's asleep," Atlas said to no one. He had laid out a large picnic blanket, classic-looking with red and white squares. Leaving his shoes by the edge, he lay down, arms behind his head. Above, the clouds mimicked his mood, swirling and gloomy. Quiet footsteps approached from the right. At Breena's presence, the sky cleared. It wasn't a natural phenomenon, just an attempt on his part to create a more positive setting for her. Otherwise, Atlas was content to continue luxuriating in his guilt.

He didn't look at her right away. He didn't need to. The air was alive and it carried her emotions over him—the sinking feeling of a rock at the bottom of her gut. So was the confusion and anger that, no doubt, had her balling her fists at her sides. She stopped at the edge of the picnic blanket. Atlas waited for her to say the first words. He wanted to give her that, to show her she had the power this time. Breena was quiet for so long, though, that he had to open his eyes and sit up.

"I thought you'd yell or something," he said softly.

"Wanted to." Breena was staring at her toes.

"But?"

She sighed. "But I have no words," she said as she sat beside him on the blanket. Pulling her knees up to her chest, Breena crossed her arms over the tops of her legs and put her forehead down.

"Look at me, please."

Breena shook her head without looking back up. She spoke into her lap, muffled. "I don't want to see that desperate look on your face. What was wrong with you earlier? Did you follow me there? I told you I didn't want to see you in person."

"That was sheer coincidence."

"You taught me not to believe in that. You told me everything in life is orchestrated by good or evil. Which one are you?"

"I don't know. I used to be so sure that my choices were leading me well away from my father, but now I can't tell. Everything I do is for us."

"Atlas, there *is* no us. Not anymore. You made that quite clear when I had to leave London without saying goodbye to you, and I haven't decided if I believe what you've told me since."

"That's fair. I hate it, but it's fair."

"Are we going to train, or what?"

"You're still going to learn from me?"

"I didn't think I had a choice. I'd like to keep Jordan safe. If that means training with you—"

"You're just doing this for him? Not me?"

"Atlas, really? What happened to the guy I met in London? You were smart there. You were kind there. You understood love there. I'm surprised you haven't put it together. You threaten boyfriend, I do what you say. That's what blackmail *is*."

Atlas pulled at his hair. "I guess I thought it would take more time for you to let go of our days in London. I didn't actually think Jordan was a threat." Breena looked at him then. He looked wrecked. His voice dropped to a resigned whisper. "I thought you'd choose *me.*"

Breena didn't want to give in to Atlas' show of emotion, but he looked legitimately heartbroken. She began to question her view of his behavior. She was tempted to believe him.

"I didn't want to push you away."

"But you did!"

"I never wanted it to happen like that."

"Yeah, me either! I *always* wanted you. I *searched* for you. I missed weeks of my waking life looking for you. Do you know how much time that is in dreams?" Breena angled her body away from his, about to leave.

"I want to show you something. It can be part of your training, that way you don't have to decide if you should come with me. I'm ordering this. You come with me. You see this. Maybe then you'll understand."

Before waiting for her reply, Atlas reproduced a play-by-play of Reid's murder. Breena reeled back, trying to turn away from the struggle.

"I said watch." Atlas held her head forward to the scene. "Don't close your eyes." The moment was over so much quicker than it had felt when Atlas first committed the crime. The illusion dissolved leaving a sweet smell in the air despite the bitter memories it held. He let go of Breena and stumbled off the blanket to retch in the nearby brush.

"What was that? Why was I watching your death? Whose eyes was I looking through?"

Atlas coughed for a few seconds and turned around. "That wasn't me you saw. That was Reid. You were seeing through my eyes."

"You're lying. Why would you show me that?"

He stared at her, knowing she'd wake herself if he came any closer.

Breena smacked the ground in front of her. "Answer me, Atlas."

"Proof I'm not lying to you about anything."

"All that proves is you're a murderer."

"If I truly wanted to manipulate you, to keep you in the dark, trick you for some terrible purpose, don't you think I would have hidden that from you? All of my sins are yours to judge."

"Don't treat me like I'm your god."

"I will treat you like my queen."

"You told me you wanted to create happiness."

"It was for the big picture."

"One sin committed for the greater good is still a sin." *Now it's my turn to throw up.* She grit her teeth against the impulse. "I need. A real. Explanation."

"I have already given you the explanation, but you refused to believe me. Remember your reasons for following my instructions? Remember why you kept me around. You were trying to find something, something more than what you have when you're awake. Tabitha's plan has similar goals, and until you're Queen, she will continue to pursue them in her way. I killed Reid Case in order to take his place and use the hotline to gain recruits for her. Just as you suspected. And I obeyed because it is nearly impossible for me to deny her. Reid also provided a way to prove my loyalty so she does not suspect we are trying to stop her."

"And you really think I could love you again?"

"You must. I am your chosen."

"*Enough*! I am no damsel in distress, bound by fate to love her savior, which you are *not*, by the way. If I am a queen, then you are my servant at best. You will train me because I ask you to, and because I will not let Tabitha go on like this. But, I do not, *will* not, love you for it." The air warmed. As if her body finally came to life after seventeen years, Breena's gold eyes shimmered and roiled, the flames of her power asserting themselves for the first time. "You think you're better than her because you're fighting for good, for happiness? That there won't be chaos? Whether you plunge the world into self-satisfying anarchy for happiness or she does the same for terror, it's all hedonism. There's no balance between heaven and hell. Neither of you can win. I will stop her, but not to help you."

Atlas kneeled in the wilting grass and let her go.

Chapter 21

Breena thrashed in her sleep. With the last kick Jordan could tolerate, he moved onto the floor. As soon as he left the bed, Breena fell still.

"Great, she's still now that I'm awake." He watched for a moment. "What are you dreaming about?"

Breena squeezed her eyes hard and moaned something garbled. Jordan watch her troubled sleep until she woke up, eyes flying wide and mouth sucking in air like she hadn't breathed in minutes.

"Good morning?"

She looked around the room, frantic, talking between swallows of air. "Everything was on fire." Jordan assumed it was another nightmare from the night of her father's death and left it alone. Breena yawned and took in Jordan's bare chest, messy copper bed head, and Pink Floyd boxers. "Why are you up so early?"

"You're up, too..." Jordan avoided her question knowing she would feel bad if he said she kicked him awake at 4:00am.

"I had a dream and, for once, I think I got my way. Are you sure you're Ok? You're never up before me."

"For some reason, I couldn't sleep." He smacked playfully at her foot. "It's 5:15. Want to go to IHOP?"

What he's really saying is, 'I want to go to IHOP.' Look at the excitement in his eyes. I can't say no to that. I also don't think I can get out of bed yet. It's like I used up all my sleep while *I was sleeping.* She remembered Atlas kneeling for her. *He* did *say it was impossible to resist the will of a true queen. It takes a lot of energy to have that kind of power.* "Let's just lie around." To someone unfamiliar with Jordan, the fall of disappointment on his face would have been invisible. *Aww, look what I did. Salvage it.* "We can cook together. Naked."

Jordan's mouth fell open.

"Sorry, I'm just kidding. Bacon grease pops."

"Catch!" Breena threw an apron at Jordan and tied her own.

Jordan missed the toss, preoccupied with concerns that Atlas damaged Bree's brain rather than enhanced her consciousness. Breena's looming survivor's guilt, from a young age, made her a skeptic—resistant to authority, and an unwilling to rely on anyone but herself. Since her return from the hospital, though, her tendency to believe what she was told, to follow, or, more accurately, to be led, had grown. It didn't matter that Jordan didn't know exactly what took place during her dreams. The illusions Breena showed him upon her confession about Atlas was proof enough that her acceptance of and entry into Atlas' world of parallel planes of existence, of half-baked reality, changed her. As sure as he had always been of their relationship, he worried that their future was beginning to divert from his long-held view of it.

"Your face is a great catcher. Come on, put on the apron. There's bacon to fry."

"Right. Sorry." He pulled the apron over his head and turned on the stove.

"Are you upset I didn't want to go out?"

"It's not that."

"But you are upset?" Breena's anxiety showed in the pace of her egg whisking. Not much stayed in the bowl.

"Not at all. Worried, maybe, but not upset. Your dreams are getting worse."

"Actually, they're not. It's gotten better since meeting... Atlas." She didn't want to say it to Jordan, but it was the truth. *Might as well keep talking.* "The worst of them stopped after we met because I learned how to control when and where I saw him. He wasn't just lurking anymore."

"Then what was last night all about?"

"I stood up to him."

Jordan flipped a pancake and peered over his shoulder. "So it's over?"

"In a way." *Things will be different.* She lost herself in chopping.

"Right?" she heard Jordan say.

"Huh?" Breena questioned lamely.

"You use ketchup for your hash browns, right?"

"Uh, yeah. Thanks." *Stupid. Don't waste time thinking about Atlas while Jordan's around.* Jordan no doubt saw the tension on her face. All she could muster was a tight smile and forced "happy eyes."

"Do you want to eat in the bed? We can put on a movie."

"Yes!"

They piled their breakfast, the condiments, silverware, and napkins up on a big serving tray. Jordan headed out of the kitchen and up the stairs with the pile of foodstuffs. Breena followed, eyes trained on two very full glasses of juice—apple for Jordan, cranberry for Breena. In Jordan's room, the pair had to settle on gingerly balancing the tray at the end of the bed. There was no other space uncluttered enough for it.

While Jordan tried as carefully as he could to climb across the bed, Breena shuffled through his drawer of DVDs. "This alright? We've seen it before, so we don't have to pay real attention to it."

"It's fine."

Shouldn't have mentioned Atlas. Now he's annoyed.

Breakfast was gone in minutes. Breena licked her fingers happily, and Jordan tried to find a better place for the tray. He gave up quickly, putting it on the floor since it was empty. Jordan climbed on top of Breena on the way back up. Instead of moving to his side of the bed, he collapsed over her legs, groaning. "So full. And tired."

Breena shoved him out of her lap. "You sleep. I'm going to take a shower."

"I'll be right here if you need me." Jordan threw a pillow over his head.

Breena ditched her clothes and stepped into the shower. She loved showering at his house because there was never anyone else around. *No Mom to barge in on me, no Ari to flush the toilet on me, and virtually limitless hot water.* She grabbed a fancy bar of soap off of one of the built-in shelves. She held the cube in front of her, pinky out, imagining for just a second that she was a wealthy chateau owner, that she was someone else. *And the Savon de Marseille Jordan's mom brings back from France doesn't hurt, either.*

As Breena scrubbed, an idea came to mind. *I wonder if I can use my new powers while I'm awake, whatever they are.* She snorted after she thought it. *Powers. Sounds ridiculous. Did Atlas kneel because he wanted to or because he had to? Even the grass wilted. Was that from heat or some sort of psychic compulsion?* Figuring it was worth a try, Breena stood out of the water and turned the cold knob all the way up. *Can I heat it? Hard to replicate when I don't really know what I did the first time.*

I was angry when I did it, so maybe that's why. She thought about how fed up she was with Atlas acting like he could save everyone, with how he pretended to be a mastermind yet still had to have other people to do his work, how he lamely took orders. *If you want it done right, you do it yourself. I can do it myself. To hell with them.* She chuckled. *Literally.*

Breena's body heated up like a warm current traveled through the soles of her feet, through her extremities, and into her head. She stepped back into the water. It sizzled when it hit her, but not because she had heated it. She heated herself to the degree that the icy water evaporated as it hit her skin. Before her shock could register, the moment was lost as Jordan came into the bathroom grumbling.

"It seems we forgot something when we cleaned up after breakfast. The bed is full of syrup, and so am I."

Breena poked her head out from the curtain.

"Look! It's all in my leg hair." He stuck a leg out in her direction. "Hurry up and finish so I can get in there. I had finally fallen asleep."

Breena stuck her arm out and reached toward him. She leaned forward and kissed him. "Just get in." She popped back in the shower. *What? That just came out.*

Jordan pulled the curtain back and inch and peaked in. Breena was perched on the corner seat, out of the water. "Are you sure?"

"It's no big deal. We did it all the time when we were younger."

"And now we're older."

"And now we're older, which means we can be mature about it. Right, Jordan? No giggling?"

His face reddened. "Definitely not."

Jordan climbed in front of her, his eyes locked on hers. Only Atlas had looked her in the eyes like that, and she couldn't decide if it was a good replacement for his gaze, or a painful reminder.

Suddenly, after an uncounted amount of time staring, Jordan remembered why he had gotten in in the first place. He stuck a leg into the falling water then immediately jumped back from it. "Fu—*dge*. Why do you have it so cold?"

"I was just trying something. It didn't work."

Jordan side-shuffled down the wall, out of the water's spray, to the faucet to turn the cold water off. Once it warmed, he stood in the downpour and shivered, the heat making him realize how cold he'd been. "What were you trying?"

"Not important. I'd rather try this." Breena's shot up from her seat and grabbed Jordan's face. She was immediately on his lips. They kissed fiercely and without restraint. Water ran into their frequently opening mouths. *My chest is on his chest. I can feel his hip bones. There's... other stuff.*

Their previous experiences making out had been fun, and quick, and passionate, but clumsy and clothed. *This. This burns inside.* Every place his flesh touched hers burned on the outside, too. It was like one of them might be leaving, like they were trying to brand their imprints on the skin of the other as a sign that they had truly been together—that it was not a dream. *This isn't like any of my memories.*

They found their ways down the tiled wall of the shower and onto the bottom of the tub. Jordan straddled Breena's legs. She didn't take her eyes off of his. He traced her jaw line with his thumb and leaned in for another kiss.

Quite a while later, Jordan looked up at Breena's elated face from his own sated slump at the other end of the tub. He turned the water off and threw a towel at her. Giggling, she wrapped up in it and climbed out of the shower.

"Hey, you said no giggling."

As they scrounged for clothes not syrupy or otherwise dirty, Jordan mentioned that his skin hurt. "My back and my face feel like I got a sunburn."

"Let me see. Turn around."

Jordan faced the wall.

"Well, you do have a few red spots here and here." She poked at them and Jordan winced away from her.

"Don't touch them, geez."

"They're starting to welt. The water wasn't that hot." He turned back to face her and Breena gasped. Jordan had an angry pink handprint forming on the side of his face and another on the side of his neck.

"What? What is it?"

"You know that thing I was trying? I think it burnt you. *I* burnt you."

Jordan went to the mirror. "How?" He traced the mark.

"You know how I told you that Lexa isn't my real mom?"

"I've known that since we met."

"I didn't tell you everything at the park that day, but the parents I had before Lexa weren't my real parents either. Atlas told me. My real mom's name is Tabitha, and she's... you're never going to believe me."

"She's what?"

"She's the queen of hell."

"She can't be that bad. When'd you meet her?"

"No. I mean literally. So, all this stuff I can do is because of that."

"So—"

"I'm, apparently, capable of harnessing hellfire or something. I burned you."

Jordan breathed out a "huh" before Breena's phone started to ring. She let it go to voicemail.

"I have a question."

"*You* have a question? Bree, I think I should be the one with questions."

"Does this have any effect on you?" She tried to use the energy she'd felt with Atlas to have some sway over Jordan's next action.

"What you just told me?"

"No, what I'm doing."

"You're not doing anything."

"Nope. Nothing." *Ok, so a queen's influence only works on her subjects? That means he kissed me because he wanted to. Good. Unless I just wasn't doing it right...* Pulling on her jeans, Breena played Lilly's voice message on speaker. She let Lilly know they'd meet her at the mall in twenty and stuffed her phone in her pocket. A loud noise and a shout rang out behind her, and she spun around to see Jordan hopping around holding his foot. His entire jar of coins was on the floor. There was money everywhere.

"Looks like it wants to get spent at the mall today."

"Nice try. That's beach week all over my floor. I go as far as that money takes me."

So I really can't sway him.

Jordan lived like his family wasn't rich. He paid for everything himself. One day, he had explained it to Breena as a no-brainer. His family had never supported him emotionally, so he wanted nothing to do with their financial support. Sadly, it was the only support they really offered him.

"I should start saving, too. We could go together. Pooling our money would get us twice as far." Breena always respected his financial choices. She didn't have the same home life as he did, but she could understand not wanting to be bought. She would definitely pay her way on their trip.

"That would be great!"

"Well, then, don't let me buy anything at the mall today, please." Her family was *not* rich, and they weren't giving her any handouts after she squandered her symphony opportunity. *I still don't know how Mom afforded that trip for me.* Breena walked over to where Jordan was still scooping coins back into the jar. Stooping down to help, their hands touched on the same quarter.

Jordan snatched his hand back and shouted again.

"Oh, my gosh, Jordan. Are you Ok? I'm so sorry. Let me see!" Tears were waiting at the edge of her lashes.

"Aw, Breena. I was just joking. Don't cry."

"That was mean!" She pulled away from his reaching hand.

"Sorry. Not ready to joke about it I guess?"

"No, and I'm surprised you are. I burned your face!"

"It's no big deal."

"How can it be 'no big deal?' I'm having a hard time accepting it. I don't know how you can."

"Accepting and understanding are two different steps. Come on, babe, let's go." Jordan stood and smoothed his pants. "I'm sorry."

Breena took the opportunity to really look him over. His muscular thighs filled out the black corduroys in just the right places, and the grey Fender t-shirt hugged Jordan's strong shoulders and skimmed lightly over his flat stomach. Jordan had taken out his contacts, too, which was rare. He was wearing black Ray-Ban glasses and a chocolate brown beanie.

"Toss me those white Converse, please?"

"Sure."

He stared.

"What?"

"You haven't gotten dressed yet? All you got on was pants in that time?"

"I was admiring."

"And pouting."

"Give me two minutes." Breena pulled on the purple t-shirt she'd packed and a faded hoodie. She threw her wet hair into a clip. "Tada."

Chapter 22

At the mall, Jordan and Breena walked hand-in-hand through the food court until they found Lilly. Lilly greeted them both with a big hug. Unfortunately, the first thing out of her mouth after, "Hey," was, "What's wrong with your face, Jordan?"

Breena shot knives at Lilly with her eyes. Lilly just muttered, "Oh," and played with her fingers. "Sorry. That was rude. But it looks like you got smacked."

"Yeah, my boss runs a tight ship." He nudged Breena.

"Oh my gosh! Your boss hit you? Have you told anyone? I saw this 20/20 story one time about this guy who was—"

"Stop, stop. I was joking. Breena's the boss."

Lilly gasped. "So Bree smacked you?"

He sighed. "No, no one hit me. It's a long story." Jordan rolled his eyes. Even for him, there was no escaping Atlas. His existence seeped into the lives of everyone involved with Breena. Jordan couldn't fully comprehend the whole "Queen of Hell" thing, but it was easy to understand that Breena was fully entrenched in Atlas' lies. The worst part of understanding her involvement was realizing that Atlas' outrageous claims might actually be the truth. He touched the burn on his neck.

Lilly glared at Breena. This was code for, "We need to talk."

"Hey, let's walk around," Jordan shouted into what had become an awkward lull in the equally awkward conversation. "Maybe find me some cream. Face cream. Ice cream. Something."

Breena, standing between Lilly and Jordan, grabbed Jordan's hand and looped her other arm through Lilly's and began to walk.

"Let's stop here. This is one of the only stores I know of that carries bathing suits in the winter." Lilly beelined for the clearance rack.

"I like this one," Jordan said, holding up a truly hideous mustard yellow one-piece with an oversized bow across the rear, "But which side's the front?"

"Neither side is the front because I am *not* wearing that. Here, what about this one, Bree?" She held up a turquoise blue bikini.

"I like it. You should try it on."

"Come with me. I want your opinion."

The girls went back to the fitting rooms leaving Jordan to his obsession with trying on every pair of sunglasses in the store. Breena followed Lilly into the cubicle and locked the door behind them. Lilly immediately started whispering questions and accusations about Breena's night with Jordan and her visit with Atlas. Breena faced the wall while Lilly changed. She could feel Lilly's pointed questions on the back of her head.

"Are you going to let me answer any of those questions, or do you have more fun just listing the things you want to know?" Breena bit out through her teeth.

"Well, I want to know what happened with Atlas first. Then, you can tell me all the gory details about your night with Jordan."

Jordan would hate them later for the world's longest bathing suit try-on. Breena went into the full account of her trip to the clearing and, Lilly, being the intelligent investigator she was, put together the origin of Jordan's pink handprints.

Bree wound down after a good five minutes trying to defend Atlas. "I want to help him."

"Oh, like spy on Tabitha for him? That's a great idea!"

"No. Let me rephrase that. I want to *rule* him."

"What would Tabby do without her precious servant? Buh-bye Tabitha." Lilly was elated. They left the fitting room. "What about Jordan? Wasn't last night... aren't you guys serious?"

Jordan walked across the store to meet them.

"There is no rule out there that says I can't love one and boss around the other. Atlas can have his happiness, but he's getting it my way."

Just as Jordan got within earshot, Lilly caught Breena's nuanced meaning and shouted, "You love Jordan?"

He paused momentarily but, seeing Breena elbow Lilly in the side as her face turned to a beet, Jordan decided to act like he hadn't heard. He was used to Lilly spilling secrets, so it was equally common to act surprised or clueless or gracious the next time the truth came out. Jordan grabbed Breena's hand and asked Lilly if the bathing suit was alright.

"Meh. It gave me a uni-boob."

"I bet Lilly thought we were ditching her to go home and make out," Breena mused once in Jordan's car.

"So why are we *really* ditching her?"

"To go home and make out."

"And?"

"And because I think I should teach you how to project and, at the very least, give you some lessons on energy exchange."

"Really? You think I can learn to alter reality?"

"I don't know. You're fully human, so that might be an obstacle."

Jordan pulled into his driveway cautiously. There was a thin sheet of ice covering the whole thing.

"Hitting Dad's prized convertible is the last thing I need."

"Why doesn't he put it in the garage if it's so important?"

"Because it's less important than the two he's already got in there." Jordan snorted.

"Oh. Hey, let's make hot chocolate," Breena suggested as they gingerly stepped out of the car.

"Mmm, yes."

They grabbed mugs, spoons, and marshmallows while waiting for the water to boil. The timer on the stove beeped and Jordan bumped Breena playfully aside from the drawer that held the potholders. He insisted on pouring the water. Hot water splashed up on his thumb as he poured. "Crap on a cracker! That's why I wanted to pour it."

"If I had poured, it might not have splashed at all." Breena grabbed his hand after Jordan put down the pot and popped his thumb in her mouth. From around it she said, "All better?"

He nodded, a hungry look suddenly in his eyes.

"Alright. Put your drink down." Jordan smiled until his eyes were narrow, assuming she was going to kiss him. His face fell when she started lecturing him.

"The most important part of doing the things Atlas taught me is that you are able to get in touch with the world. You have to find calmness inside. Strong emotions will prevent you from creating an illusion when you're a beginner, and they can break apart an illusion you've already created, too. This problem goes away with practice, but everyone has their weaknesses."

Jordan looked interested enough, even amused, but it was obvious that he wasn't going to truly understand until Breena showed him what she was talking about.

"The first thing I want you to do," Breena guided, "is center yourself. I know it sounds cheesy, but it's necessary. You have to get down to the very you-est you. Then, reach out with that part of you and feel the life around you. When you get good at this, it can get overwhelming. You'll feel the whole world thriving around you. It's a busy place."

Jordan stared at Breena, already overwhelmed. He wasn't a natural. It would take smaller steps to train him.

"Ok, so close your eyes and breathe deeply. This is just normal meditation at this point. I'm going to watch. Don't talk when you get to your center—I'll know. Then, I'll guide you into the next part."

Jordan sat on the kitchen floor and closed his eyes. *His deepest breathing isn't deep enough. This will take a while.* Eventually, his breathing slowed and expanded. He was almost in a sleep-state. Breena recognized this as the perfect moment to guide him in reaching out around him.

In the softest voice she could muster she said, "Now, take this most inner part of you and feel around with it. Feel the thrumming vibrations of my energy right next to you."

Jordan sucked in a breath, and Breena knew he had felt her there. From what Atlas had told her, she had "an all-encompassing, languid vibration of pure goodness." *This must have been the one true thing he had said judging by Jordan's reaction to her.*

"Now, feel the trees and plants outside. Feel the small animals that live in them. Each time you reach out, reach for bigger things at a farther distance." She let Jordan try this on his own for about five minutes then asked him to come to. "As a beginner, just this will exhaust you. If you overdo it in one sitting, you won't be able to even connect with yourself in the next attempt. That's all you're going to learn for tonight. Practice only that for the next week or so, then I'll teach you more."

"I didn't expect this to be such a slow and tiring process. I'm beat."

"You're not used to using that part of yourself. Atlas found me because I was doing it involuntarily during my sleep. To learn it when it doesn't come as second nature, so Atlas says, is like teaching yourself to write with your feet."

"Do you think you'll ever be better at it than him? That way you can stop quoting him?" Jordan scowled.

Breena hadn't even realized she was bringing Atlas up repeatedly. In truth, she already far surpassed Atlas in natural ability, strength, and stamina. Bringing him up was just a bad habit—like loving him. "I already am," was the only reply she could think of.

Recovering from the unpleasant realization that she was holding on to Atlas even after everything that had happened, Breena told Jordan that she would demonstrate the next step he would learn. "So you have an end-goal in mind." Breena didn't bother explaining that illusions were created by interrupting the natural vibrations with ones created by the meditator because she didn't want Jordan to try it before he was ready.

"If you look over at that wall, you'll see it warp or shimmer. That's me picking the waves like a guitar." Breena humored Jordan's over-eager requests for amusement for a few minutes by turning the oven into a fire place, changing the color of her hair, and bringing some snow inside. "I'm getting another migraine. You know what that means." Breena lied, not feeling the pull into another place by Atlas' desperate searching, but the pull of excitement to plan against Tabitha before the next time she met with Atlas. *I can stop Tabitha.*

Jordan bought her story and had her to her front door in fifteen minutes. "Want me to come in, make you soup or get you a cold rag?"

"You're sweet. I just want to take a nap. I'm sure you're tired, too. Your nap got interrupted earlier. I'll call you when I wake up." Letting Jordan down easily only made Breena feel guiltier for what she planned on doing when she got to her room.

"I hope you feel better." He leaned in and kissed her sweetly on the lips.

"Thank you. Thank you for everything. Sorry about your face." Breena tried her hardest not to think about earlier that morning, or she would lose her nerve to send him home. "I'm glad you told me how you felt that day in the parking lot. None of this would have ever happened if you hadn't."

"I'm glad I have you, finally."

Tabitha lay on her chaise lounge with cucumbers on her eyes. "Vos, has Atlas reported back today?"

"No, Ma'am."

"Then do something about it."

"Can't you just watch with the dove, Ma'am?"

Tabitha sat bolt upright and threw a cucumber at Vos. "If I wanted to do that, don't you think I already would have?" She ate the other cucumber off her chest. Between coordinating safe houses and putting underlings in key locations to help dismantle governments from the inside, she was too exhausted to continue watching over Atlas through the bird's eyes.

"Yes, Ma'am. What would you like me to do, Ma'am?"

"Oh, I wonder. What could a gorilla like you possibly do? Get me a progress report! Atlas is not strong enough to create the storm without Breena. If she's not on board, I'll have to force her. And that would include things a mother should never have to do to her daughter."

Chapter 23

Breena shouldered through the door to her room and squinted, the sun streaming through the window and the extra squish of freshly vacuumed carpet evidence her mom had gone on a cleaning spree. Lexa always threw the curtains wide to let the light in. Breena peeled off her clothes on the way to her bed where there was a note on the pillow. Since she was a toddler, her mom had left her sticky notes in her room after cleaning up. It had started as a game of "Hotel," complete with pillow mint and fluffy slippers. Now, it was a less elaborate affair that let her know that not everything had changed since she was young. *But everything feels different.*

Breena slipped into her baggiest t-shirt and climbed onto her bed. *If I'm going to take Tabitha down, I need to learn how to use the powers I've inherited from her. If I gain her confidence, maybe she'll let Atlas off the hook. She doesn't need to depend on him to get me on board with her plan if I go straight to the source and make like I'm all for it. Besides, there are things he just can't teach me.* Breena pulled the light-blocking shade down over her window and fished out her iPod from the drawer of her nightstand. Before she popped in the earbuds and put the playlist on shuffle, Breena sent a quick text to Tabitha.

"Sorry I was rude to you at our little get together. Atlas has taught me a lot since then, and I guess you're the one to thank for all of it. I heard you came to see me in the hospital. That was thoughtful. I have some questions, if you're willing."

Now, an epic nap. I have a feeling I'm going to have another exhausting night. She pulled the covers up to her neck, rolled onto her belly, and tucked the blankets under her sides, feet, and shoulders to cocoon herself. *Nap now, Atlas later.*

Breena's hot breath dampened her pillow as she struggled to find a comfortable position where her face wasn't at least partially buried. Kicking the blanket off of one leg, and then the other, rolling over, and then wrapping into a burrito once again, she shuffled around in this fitful attempt at rest for thirty minutes.

When sleep finally stole her anxious thoughts, Breena drifted into her typical dreams. Gaining lucidity, she rolled her eyes. *Of course I end up here. Like muscle memory.* Her habit of joining Atlas while she slept made the transition to the small glade they used involuntary. *Well, since I'm here I might as well fill Atlas in.* Breena paced a path into the ankle-length grass then decided to check for him lounging in the woods. She knew his spots by the trace vibrations of his energy. Flowering patches of moss, fern, and other underbrush surrounded the places Atlas liked to sit, as if signaling to her that he couldn't be all bad, or there would be death and rot. *Like that.* The space across the opening remained wilted from their last encounter. *I can't believe I had a permanent effect.*

The grove rustled with small animals and a gentle breeze. Bree picked carefully through a thickening path of forest. The isolation allowed her to take fuller breaths, ones she hadn't noticed she was holding when she'd first arrived. *Maybe he's not here.* A strong sensation of desire and belonging pulled her toward the chapel, which had been recreated. *Go check in there.*

A new plaque stood in front. "Rebuilt for My Love, NEVER to be destroyed again." *How touching.* Remaining animosity rose up her spine. *Don't hold a grudge. Just go inside. He's not around to turn this into a nightmare.*

Breena knew that the air of peace and holiness she felt in presence of the building was something her mind had filled in. Illusions didn't have any inherent qualities, and those were two characteristics Atlas wouldn't have supplied. She wanted to believe, though, that she could walk inside and find the answers and relief she'd arrived without.

The white doors were unlocked, but it took a lot of effort to pull the solid masses open. Once she got the doors wide, they stayed that way as if sentient and wishing to air out the tiny church.

The wooden floor boards creaked as Breena walked between the two aisles of pews. At the front of the chapel, the stained glass window depicted a large, detailed image of a man standing, arms raised, in a field of flowing grain. The night sky twinkled with white stars—dots less literally represented than the rest of the image. The colors were rich like jewels. She sat on the floor and stared up at it.

What am I even doing here? These trips have no purpose without Atlas. No, no. There's no more finding my reason in him. I am the reason. He's just a guide. A servant. Breena pinched the bridge of her nose then yawned. *This was supposed to be a restful nap, not an astral journey. I should be getting better at controlling when and where I go during sleep, not floating away involuntarily. I'm afraid one day I won't go back to my body, and then everyone will have to watch me sleep in a hospital bed again, soulless, forever. Even now, I can't feel my body. I can't move it. Why can't I wake myself up?*

As Breena began drowning in her anxieties, a dove flew in and landed on the back of the first pew. It cooed, getting Breena's attention. The dove cocked its head to the left and to the right, and Breena expected it to fly back out of the chapel. It stayed.

"Hmm. You don't belong here, do you? Your energy is different. Are you a spirit? Well, at least I'm not talking to myself, now, right?" she chuckled. *Although talking to a bird isn't much better, but whatever.* "I miss him. I really, really miss him. I miss when things were simple. I miss the short time between being stalked and abandoned where I fully trusted him. Listen to that. That sounds so unhealthy. But, that's why he can't be anything more than a pawn, now. A player in Tabitha's game, someone to occupy the right spaces at the right times, to keep the others safe. I'm only doing any of this to keep the others safe. Even so, it doesn't make me miss our time in London any less."

The sun shifted around the chapel and baked a warm spot on her arm. She gazed back up at the stained glass through her eyelashes. In the new light, the field was on fire, amber grains now oranges, yellows, and reds blazing under a jet sky. "That's how I felt when I stood up to him—alive, on fire, in the night. Like *I* was what lit the sky." Guilt washed through her for being like Tabitha, for subjugating him. "No, it's fine. He's my chosen, created specifically for me to... to use. I'm the fire, he's the field."

The dove watched, regarding her with avian amusement. Breena held out her hand toward the bird, offering it a perch on her finger. The bird stared back. "You know, if I had better control, you'd be an obedient illusion and come land on my finger." The dove shot into the air and flew toward Breena. It stopped just out of her reach and froze. Breena looked around quickly. *Did I break time?* In the same second, the bird transformed, leaving Breena staring up at her mother for the first time since finding out the truth about her lineage.

"I got your text."

"I should have known you brought me here."

"You wanted to talk. Well, you've already told me a lot—"

"I wouldn't have said anything if I'd known you were listening."

"Oh, come. You can always talk to me. I'm your mother."

"Maybe so, but I don't think of you that way."

"Then why did you want to meet?"

"I need you to train me to be a queen."

"Atlas isn't pulling his weight, it seems. I'll have to do something about that."

"No! No, don't punish him. He's doing fine. But I've started to think certain lessons have to come from you. Like the other day, I swayed him to my will. I wasn't trying to, but it happened. When I tried to do it again, I couldn't tell if my friend was resistant to it because he's a normal human or if I was doing it wrong."

"Ah. You're right. These are things you need to know. Your human friend can only be swayed in human ways. Greed, fear, lust, these are scenarios we can set up for a human to react to, but we can't sway them by skipping straight to the reaction. Our people, though, are wired to obey those in our special position of power."

Breena nodded, distance in her eyes. "I don't even know what I really am. Who are our people?"

"We're the ones everyone fears. You think God is the reason people choose good over evil?" Tabitha shook her head wearing a prideful smirk. "They don't obey God for the sake of doing the right thing. They do it to avoid *us.* Don't be mistaken. We're not only in the punishment game. We make messes for the fun of it, too. For the sake of 'the balance'—" Tabitha made air quotes and screwed up her face, mocking. "—sometimes things just have to go wrong. Personally, I don't think it happens often enough."

Of course she does.

"But, that's an argument about your decrepit grandfather for another time."

Bree shifted. "My grandfather?"

"Satan."

A wry laugh rushed out of Breena at the matter-of-fact way Tabitha clarified her lineage. "Right, of course. So that makes me—"

"The first granddaughter to take over. I'm the last daughter of Satan. My sisters have already reigned. After me, a new generation begins. I want to leave you with something magnificent to rule."

I always wanted to be someone else. This is not what I had in mind.

A harsh breeze cut through the chapel and both doors slammed shut. Breena jumped to her feet at the sound. In the rear of the chapel, Atlas stood wearing all black.

"I asked him to join us."

He looked like a mourner, or maybe the corpse. Breena walked down the aisle toward him. A thought briefly entered her mind with a little pop like a dish soap bubble. It seemed somehow symbolic that she was walking the wrong way down the aisle toward him. She acknowledged the idea then let the bubble float away. Atlas stared at Tabitha and suddenly dropped to his knees. He hit the floor repeating something Breena couldn't understand. His face contorted, and he curled in on himself.

"Is this what you meant, Breena?"

"Stop hurting him!"

"You wanted to control him, so try. Let him have it."

"This isn't what I wanted."

"You said it yourself. He's the field. Consume him."

Vos waited outside the church trying his best not to hear the agonized noises coming from Atlas. He considered him a friend even though Atlas was the reason he had been captured, tortured, and conditioned to serve Tabitha. It was times like these where the strain between obedience and conscience ripped at his insides. Still, Vos remained rooted to the spot, close enough to hear Tabitha coaching a resistant Breena through her first brutal exercise of power, but too far, too scared, to do anything about it.

"Breena, if you keep wincing every time I strike him he will never fear you the way he fears me. I told him once, and now I'll tell you, that fear is one of the surefire ways to create a faithful servant."

It's also a foolproof way to make a resentful servant.

"Now's your chance to cast off all that anger and pay him back for his unhelpful behavior. Your turn."

She thinks she can use his cruelty to her advantage, pretending it wasn't her who ordered him to act that way. I have to play along. Tabitha still thinks I'm angry about how he treated me after London, and she knows I've only been training with him to protect Jordan. Breena approached.

Rather than staring up at her with defiance, Atlas bowed his head. There was no doubt in his mind that this meeting played into a larger plan he couldn't know about. He trusted Breena. *She is a queen worth taking a beating for.*

Breena stood over him trying to work up the nerve to hit him or kick him, something that would look fearsome in Tabitha's eyes. *This isn't what I wanted to learn, and this isn't who I wanted to practice on. If her only strength as queen is intimidation and physical abuse, there's nothing to learn from her. If it's only biology and brutality compelling people to obey her, then I must be stronger.*

"We're all waiting."

Breena tried to focus in on the abundance of emotional moments before Atlas had started to mend their relationship. Since sobering up, it wasn't hard for Breena to go dark. There was no false relaxation to block her from dwelling on the negativity. *It's never far under the surface. I guess I'm really not over it.* Her hands shook, and heat rose inside her. *Here goes.*

"How could you leave me in my dreams? I loved you! You told me I was beautiful; you told me we were the *same*, but you left me. Where was I supposed to find you? You never told me. You *wanted* me to get lost in that dream-hell of a coma. You never cared, hateful bastard. You never *cared!* You haunt me in my sleep, threaten the people I love, and then demand my attention and obedience in return. Power is all you're after, and you don't fucking deserve all this power you have over me. I'm nothing like you, and you can't treat me like that. *I'm* the one with the power." To punctuate her rage, she landed a searing smack across Atlas' face.

His skin immediately bubbled with welts, boiling from contact with her hand. The smell of seared flesh and Tabitha's pleased expression sickened her. Breena's pulse thumped in her ears, and the heat sweltering beneath her ribs awoke a panicked, choking sensation. She stumbled outside and swallowed down the cool air just in time to stave off her heaving.

Vos watched her with pity. He liked her already, and it was hard to see her struggle. Before he and Atlas were taken, he learned a lot about Breena, or at least a lot about what Atlas thought Breena would be like in person. Atlas' dreams and fantasies about her ended up being true. She was everything Atlas had predicted. Since working for Tabitha, Vos knew as much about Breena and her importance to Gehenna as Tabitha did. Tabitha thought of him as a raven, an extension of herself she could send into the world to do her bidding, mostly relaying information. She never guarded her conversations around him, thinking him only smart enough to pass on the material, not comprehend it. And, despite his conditioning, he recognized another queen when he saw one. Tabitha hadn't erased his desire to overthrow her, only his capacity to carry it out alone.

Breena heard Tabitha inspecting Atlas' face.

Tabitha clicked her tongue. "She needs to learn to control her fire. Quite the burn, Atlas. What a shame. You were a pretty one."

"It will heal."

I burned him, too. Breena threw herself out of the dream and woke, still nauseated. *Tabitha's so wrong about the world that she managed to make three left turns and get something right. Atlas is a pawn, and he's not the only one.* Breena made two phone calls and went outside to wait for one to deliver.

Chapter 24

Vos held the door for Tabitha. She pushed past him, large gator skin bag swinging from her elbow, cellphone to her ear.

"Things are changing. She's reaching out to me for training, and she's already stronger than I expected." The bag landed on the table with a clunk. "I know." Vos helped her out of her coat. "Well it's not like I saw it coming, Daddy. I'll use him however I need to in order to prepare her. And I know what you're going to say, 'She needs to love her chosen. It's the way of things,' but let me tell you. The way is changing."

Vos couldn't help but listen in. He wasn't permitted to go about his own doings unless Tabitha ordered him to give her privacy—a rare occurrence. He waited on her hand and foot. She pointed at the curtains mouthing to Vos. He flung them wide not trying to ignore her conversation any longer. He could hear her father yelling in her ear. She held the phone away from her face and rolled her eyes.

"Maybe it's not the *way* that is changing, Tabitha. Maybe it's *you*. You're losing your sight."

"Am not."

"Your predictions aren't realizing."

"My predictions are fine. It's Breena. She's not normal."

"Of course not, Darling. She's *your* daughter."

Tabitha screeched in frustration and hung up, catching Vos' stare across the room. "What?"

"Nothing, Mistress. I was just thinking that I might meet with Breena and Atlas. Help make sure nothing else changes."

"And why would I want you to do that?"

"I heard what your father said about your sight. I can be your eyes."

"I'm not losing my sight, you idiot. It's my father who's losing sight. Eons of existence have made him predictable."

"Of course."

The phone rang, buzzing across the marble countertop. Tabitha answered without looking. "Did you forget already, Daddy? We just talked."

"I-it's Linda. I was just calling to tell you I scheduled your flight."

"Fine. Thanks."

"Wait!"

"Hmm?"

"How old are you, really? When were you going to tell me Breena is your daughter?"

****

"Ari." Breena put her ear to his door. Something rustled from inside the bedroom, and it fell quiet again. She knocked with a knuckle. "Ari, let me in."

The door drifted open as Ari shuffled back to his bed in the dark.

"Why's it so dark in here?"

"Watchin' a movie."

"The TV's off..."

"Yeah, because you interrupted."

"I have a good reason." Breena threw a bag at his back. When he picked it off the floor, a smug smile spread across his face. "I already told Mom. It's too late to bribe me."

"Like I said, I don't care if she knows since it wasn't true. And this isn't a bribe. It's payment. I need a favor."

"It might cost more than this." He thumbed through the bag of pills. "Only five here."

"Remember Linda who came to the hospital before I woke up? You said you were attracted to her, right? I believe she's recently become single."

Ari turned on the lamp by his bed.

His hair looks like he stuck a finger in the lamp.

"I thought she was a lesbian. And doesn't she live in London?"

"Just because she was with a woman doesn't mean she's a lesbian. Besides, I know you're still into her."

"If I remember correctly, you told me she was too old for me and to stay away." Ari eyed Breena. "Why do you want me to do this?"

"She needs better friends." *And Tabitha needs fewer.* "Long story short, her girlfriend, Tabitha, not who she thought."

"So she's on the rebound. Perfect."

"Hey, I didn't ask you to date her. Just... offer her some long-distance companionship."

"The friend zone experience costs extra."

Breena shoved Ari. "Don't be a jerk."

"If you don't want to pay more, what else do I get in return?"

Safety. A world that won't fall into chaos. "A date. Maybe."

"You *just* said you didn't want me to date her."

"I said I wouldn't *pay* you to date her. But, if you're a good friend to her, and if she ends up liking you, you might get a real date out of it." Breena stood. "Or, just think of it as doing something nice for someone."

"I'll think about it."

"No time. I already gave her your number." Breena smirked and went back to her room. *If I can isolate Tabitha while appearing to want her company, I'll have the advantage.*

****

"Central Michigan Suicide Helpline."

"Hi, is this Atlas' extension?"

Atlas blanched. "There's no one here by that name. This is Reid. How can I help?"

"I actually don't need any help. I'm not calling about suicide or anything. A friend gave me the number. She said I should talk to Atlas."

"Who gave you my number?"

"A girl named Breena."

Atlas exhaled. "Oh, I see."

"So are you him or not?"

"I am. And what's your name?"

"I'm Linda. I actually think we may have met once or twice around London. You used to work for Tabitha."

"Still do."

"Oh? I'm surprised she sent you to Michigan."

"So why are you calling?"

"Right. Sorry. I'm, *was*, her girlfriend. Tabitha's been lying to me for... a while, apparently. I don't even know how she's old enough to have a daughter. I thought she was my age. Apparently she dated you in the past as well—"

"She tried. Nothing happened."

"Oh, that's good. Anyway, I want to help you. Breena explained everything, and, although I can't say I fully believe her either, I still want some sort of justice."

Atlas tried to break in and clarify his role in Tabitha's plans, knowing that Breena couldn't have painted him in the best light, but Linda went on.

"I wasted six years of my life with that woman thinking she loved me, thinking she was my age, that she was working in the property investment field, but no. She's something else from somewhere else. She was using me to sure up her fake life. I should have known. She's always been kind of awful. I don't know why I stuck around. She's such a control freak—doesn't want anyone else to have the power, but she doesn't really want to take responsibility, either." Linda took a breath. "Breena's just as furious with her. Said she wants to get back at her for abandoning her when she was born. Sounds like Tabitha was just cycling through a bunch of identities, casting them off each time someone got in the way. I don't know how someone could do that to a baby. Anyway, Breena told me I could help her ruin Tabitha's career and to call you. So what's the plan? Breena said there is one."

"The strategy is to act like we're still on Tabitha's side. I have to go on as I have been. I have to keep working for Tabitha, following her orders, the usual. None of this will work if she thinks I'm not under her control anymore."

"I have a question. Why does Tabitha have you working a suicide hotline? If she's not in real estate—"

"Surprisingly, that part is true. She does own a lot of properties."

"Ok, well, even if she is in real estate, I don't understand."

Breena clearly didn't tell her everything. Make something up. "She wants me to find people that need a new outlook on life and offer them positions working under her." *More like recruit people to be anarchists and rioters...*

"And Breena?"

Breena has to play along, too, unless she thinks of a way to get rid of Tabitha before the storms come. "Most of the plan is in Breena's hands. She's unpredictable to Tabitha, and Tabitha's overconfidence in her ability to see how things will turn out is going to cripple her. We just have to let Breena be Breena. Besides, if I knew exactly what Breena was planning, that would put us all at risk. Tabitha monitors me closely. She's even starting to send Vos to check on me."

"Who's Vos?"

"A friend. I won't go into the gory details, but you know how persuasive Tabitha can be, and she convinced him to be her little watchdog. I'm hoping he can break free from her control and help us, but so far it hasn't happened."

"What can I do to help?"

"I want you to do anything Breena asks. I realize you're only human, and it might be hard to take orders from someone you don't know well, especially on the heels of being in a controlling relationship, but—"

"But Breena is nothing like Tabitha. She asked me to make friends with her brother."

"Then do it."

"I don't know how that will help get back at Tab."

"Aren't you angry at her?"

"Furious."

"Then it doesn't matter how, does it? Do it anyway."

After they hung up, Atlas put his head on the desk. He was relieved at how much Breena got done within a night. He touched his cheek. The remnants of the burn stung, but Atlas enjoyed his reminder of Breena's immense power. He had never gotten an injury in the astral plane that remained once returning to his body. It was a good sign. If Breena hoped to take Tabitha down, she could do it in person or otherwise.

****

"Oh, Lilly. Hi. I thought you and Breena went out earlier."

"We did. I just wanted to see how she was feeling."

"Was she feeling bad? She didn't say. Bree, Lilly's here."

"She can come up."

Lilly kicked her shoes off and ran upstairs. "Are you feeling better?"

"Much. You didn't have to come all the way over here to ask me that, though."

"I know that, but I figured why not. You're not away from Jordan often, so this was my chance."

Her chance to make a move on me? She blushed.

"You're so red! Do you have a fever?"

"Ha, no. It's nothing. Thanks for stopping by. That was sweet of you."

"So what's going on?" Lilly glanced around the room. Breena was surrounded by clothes she never wore. Shoving a pile aside, Lilly plopped on the bed next to Breena.

"Just trying to decide what to wear when I take out Tabitha. It's a special occasion."

"Oh? A mother-daughter dinner. I'm surprised. Where are you taking her?"

"No, not take out, like to dinner. I mean *take out* take out. Permanently."

"You're going to kill her?" Lilly knew she should look shocked or appalled, but she couldn't fight the thrilled expression from her face.

Breena sighed. "That's the part I can't decide on. It would be easier if she's truly gone, but does that make me as bad as she is?"

"Of course not. Motive is everything."

"Typically, the only way I would be able to ascend the throne—ugh, I still can't get used to the sound of that—is if the current queen dies. Of natural causes. That was always their intention for me and, because I'm the heir, I'm supposed to work with her on whatever she wants to do with the last years of her rule."

"And that's where the crazy comes in." Lilly bounced on the edge of the bed.

"Right. Helping her get all biblical on the world and then plunging it into anarchy doesn't interest me in the least. She's not honoring the balance with heaven. Our job is to regulate God's goodness with, well, evil. She's going way overboard, though. Thinks toppling the balance would be better for everyone, that each person can make their own happiness if they don't have to follow heaven's rule or anyone else's. She shouldn't be allowed to rule. I can't believe her father is allowing this."

"Wait, who's her father?"

"The devil himself. Literally."

"If he's her father, and she's the queen, is she married to her dad? Gross!"

"No, no, no. According to Atlas, his daughters rule, and then when all of his daughters have moved on, the granddaughters. That's where I come in. He takes more of an advisory role. He's like the figurehead everyone is taught to fear."

"Typical chauvinism. Fear the big man, don't worry about the little lady that's actually running things while he gets all the credit."

"Right? So anyway, that's where I am so far."

"I'd kill her. I can tell you how, too. Saw it on one of my shows last night." Lilly elaborated until Breena made her stop, waving her hands around like she was directing a plane to taxi.

"Ok, Ok, that is disgusting. Why do watch those unsolved murder shows?"

"Morbid curiosity mixed with raging anxiety." Her tone was sardonic, but it was the truth.

"As one does."

They nodded.

"Lilly, I need you to promise me that you'll try and get my family safe if things go wrong. I'm going to train with Tabitha for as long as I can keep my opinions to myself, and after that, I think I'll be ready. I didn't tell Jordan because he'll worry, and I can't tell Atlas because Tabitha is watching him too closely. Linda already knows what I need her to do. She's going to get Ari out of here just in case, and have Vos finish off Tabitha's physical body. From now on, you're my voice. Feed everyone the necessary information to keep my plan a secret. Tell them only what they must know."

She made a face.

"I thought this would excite you. It's just in case, Lil. Are you staying the night?"

"Hadn't planned on it. Why?"

"Because I'm ready for bed. I've got to meet with Atlas."

Chapter 25

The spongy, pale-green grass in the dell transformed into a stretch of warm sand with a dusty flourish. Breena called up the Myrtle Beach illusion once again and shifted the scene from night to day in an endless loop. At once, the hot sun warmed the sand to an uncomfortable temperature for their bare feet, and the waves crashed loudly over giggling children. In another instant, the full moon and stars made the ocean into glitter. The sand was cool. The rhythmic strike of waves upon the shore settled Breena's nerves. Creating wet arcs and ripple patterns in the sand after each wave moved back to sea was an artistic endeavor for her. Atlas marveled at Bree's ability to pack the little details so quickly into her illusion, which she changed from day to night every few seconds.

Breena, standing at the water's edge, looked back at Atlas with a gleaming grin. Her attention drifted from the waves, and the ocean stilled for a moment as she thought. *Don't get sucked back in. He is a means to an end.* She threw herself into the training exercise wholly and with abandon. *I'm going to beat her.*

Atlas called. "What made you change your mind?"

"You."

He grinned.

"Don't be flattered. I was tired of being a cog in a plan. *You* made me tired of it. The plan is mine, now." Leaving the visionary world in the navy blue of night, Breena went to Atlas. "I want you to get what you deserve. Our desires for the future aren't so different, but I couldn't keep playing into Tabitha's hands, and you shouldn't either, so I'm going to help you."

"But you don't trust me."

"No, I don't. But I miss you, anyway. I want to be here with you."

Atlas scooped her up in a hug and whirled around. Breena giggled. "I'm so proud of the person you're becoming. You're so talented." He set her down and brushed a strand of hair out of her eyes.

Breena stilled. It was like every cliché scene from every romantic movie. *Back away, change the subject, wake up.* He kissed her and she kissed him back. The illusion of the beach played on. *He doesn't make me lose concentration anymore.* She smiled into the kiss.

"Let's get a hotel room," Atlas suggested lowly in her ear.

"Here?"

"It's free."

Keep a healthy distance so he doesn't get the wrong idea about us, or risk it and stay here to keep up appearances? It's more dangerous to blow our cover than it is to disappoint him. "That one."

They rode the elevator to the penthouse on top. Breena hadn't bothered populating the insides of each building with people, so they had the entire hotel to themselves. *How much time has passed? I'll have to wake up for school soon.* She surveyed the room. *Not bad, Breena. Things are falling into place. I have Atlas at my disposal, a solid plan in mind to deal with Tabitha, and, even if the only reason Atlas is acting his old self is because I'm compelling him to, it's nice to feel comfortable around him again.*

She pushed open a heavy pocket door into the palatial bathroom. *Oh, a whirlpool tub. I think I can hear it talking. 'Breena, get in! Hurry!'* She turned it on without hesitation, calling Atlas in as it filled. *You shouldn't do this to Jordan. Even if it's to save the world? Who are you kidding, Breena? Keeping up appearances doesn't require all this. You're doing it because you want to.* Guilt got her in the stomach, but it didn't make her push Atlas' hands away from the waistband of her jeans, and it didn't make her withdraw her hand from his hair.

In the frothing, hot water, Breena relaxed dramatically. Tension she hadn't realized she held melted off her shoulders and back, sliding into the water and out of existence. Atlas scooted around the seats in the wall of the tub to sit beside her. She reached around underwater for his hand. She accidentally grabbed something else and jerked her hand back with a yelp of embarrassment.

"Don't act like we're strangers, Bree."

****

Jordan dropped his bag on the cafeteria table beside Lilly. "Was she Ok last night when you went to visit?"

"Seemed fine. She's struggling with how to handle the whole 'Tabitha is her mother' thing, but she said her headache had gone away. She didn't get more pills did she?"

"Not that I know of."

Ari overheard as he passed and doubled back to them. "I wouldn't be so sure of that. She gave me some yesterday afternoon."

"What? Where did she get them? I took all of it home with me."

"Well maybe she snuck some back from you. She's always over there."

"No way. She'd never find them. She must have called someone."

Lilly broke in. "And why did she give them to *you*? I know you guys don't really get along, but she cares about you too much to get you hooked."

"It was a bribe. Wants to me to get friendly with Linda. Going well so far. Breena owes me more pills, though. Calling London isn't cheap, and making friends with a girl like that without trying to date her is even more expensive."

"You're terrible. So where's Breena, then? We can't get a hold of her this morning."

"Mom had a hard time getting her to wake up, so she let her stay home and sleep. She's probably just smacked. I wouldn't worry." Lilly and Jordan shared a startled glance, revisiting the fear of Breena's overdose.

****

Across town, Tabitha's plane disembarked. Vos lugged her designer carry-ons behind him, doubling his already cumbersome width in the crowded terminal. Atlas was waiting at pick-up for them.

"Hurry, I'm supposed to be at the hotline right now."

"What a warm greeting. I almost thought you didn't miss me."

"Sorry, Mistress. Just in a hurry." He popped the trunk and took a bag. "Vos. Good to see you. How are you?"

"Can't complain." The strained look in his eyes said he physically couldn't regardless of his true feelings.

Atlas shook his head. "What a shame."

"What's that, Atlas?"

"It's a shame that Vos can't come help out at the hotline. We're short-staffed, and it might be good to have another one in on the plan, but I see how much help he is to you already." Atlas took another bag and stuffed it into the trunk.

"Be careful with those. They're couture. As for Vos, he can go. He's not as useful as he looks." She gave him a pouting once-over. "Can't seem to entice him as easily as you."

Vos looked at his feet.

"Drop me off at the house and get on with your recruiting. You've already wasted ten minutes chatting me up. Get back to Breena after you've returned Vos to me."

"Apologies, Mistress. I certainly never wanted to chat you up."

Tabitha narrowed her eyes at Atlas. "We'll work on that mouth later."

Atlas shivered.

****

Breena let the sun cycle through each day on the beach more rapidly than they would in reality. True time stood still in that plane, but Breena was utterly blissful, and hopelessly oblivious to the flaw. She trained constantly, but the time-passage defect went unfixed. Atlas never raised concern that it was still mid-winter there, and Breena hadn't noticed in the first place. Tabitha met her daily, focusing the lessons on things like thought manipulation and remote viewing, things only queens could do, rather than illusion and construct basics. Breena had so excelled at astral and real-time projections that everyone assumed the stasis of her beach world was purposeful.

While Tabitha, still having visions of a successfully achieved acephalous world and thoroughly convinced of Breena's devotion, trained Breena, Atlas worked at the hotline. He recruited over fifty people to pose as Tabitha's feet on the ground. After giving each caller his spiel about a new world, he referred them to Linda to undo what he had done. On the surface, he was still carrying out Tabitha's orders and, without knowing exactly what Linda told them, he was safe from any suspicion of sedition. Linda needed only to convince them to stay safely away from the coming riots and to be ready to serve Breena once the chaos died down. Neither Linda nor Atlas knew that the storms would never come.

One cookie-cutter morning with no time or date, Breena rose early to walk to a park she scrounged up during a practice. Atlas was at the hotline already, so she made quick work of a breakfast and a hairdo. With more motivation than usual, she jogged to her favorite training spot. It was sunlit but cool from the breeze of surrounding trees. There was plush grass perfect for sleeping and big boulders Breena sat atop when she needed a new perspective. To the left of the boulders grew a thick cluster of trees.

Breena started her training with a sun salutation before Tabitha arrived. As she got into position, she noticed a figure dressed in deep purple within the accumulation of trees near the boulders. The one in purple reached out, as if someone else was there. Breena scooted to the side. *There is someone else, but I can't tell who. Totally obscured by a pine tree.* She squinted in the glaring sunrays. The people embraced, kissing with eagerness.

That's so romantic. I shouldn't watch. Why am I moving closer? I can't help it. It's weird, though. I don't think I released any population into the park this morning. Just one more look. When she reached the tree-line, she caught a clear, horrible shot. Breena gasped loudly and the pair looked over with total indifference.

"I told you we should have gone back to the waking world for a while," Tabitha said with apathy.

"And I told *you* her stupid friends have been watching me too closely when they aren't at the hospital," Atlas replied.

Breena shook her head, but it didn't add clarity. *What is this? Should I be angry? He's just playing his role. It's nothing.* She began to back away. *This is my illusion. It's not real.* It was the first time in many sun-ups that Breena had readily acknowledged the false nature of the world she'd been living in with Atlas. Atlas closed the space between them, Tabitha following. Breena was about to run, close the illusion, and wake up when Atlas grabbed her wrist. A wicked grin spread across his face, and every ounce of love, compassion, and gentleness he had displayed vanished in their fantasy land. *Or she's overpowered my influence on him...*

"Breena, your mom's here."

Through gritted teeth Breena spat, "What are you doing with her?"

Tabitha chuckled. "Oh, look how mad she's getting. This is fun. Jealous of your old lady?"

Bree winced, taking in Atlas' indifferent stare. "I never should have..." Breena moaned. "I've done so much for you here." Her burning eyes nailed Tabitha. "And you! I don't even want to talk to you. He's *my* chosen." Breena jerked her wrist from Atlas' grasp and began to run. His speeding footfalls pounded close behind her.

Breena made it out of the park and was running down the sidewalk when a dove landed in front of her. She tried to dodge, but it transformed into Tabitha, who stood directly in Breena's path. Bree tripped, falling onto the sidewalk. Tabitha reached for Breena, seizing her without effort. Breena attempted to roll away, to use the burning heat she carried inside against her mother, but Bree's vision turned red and hazy around the edges, and blackness engulfed her.

When Breena came to, she was sitting in the attic of Atlas' cabin hideout. Tabitha and Atlas leaned against the wall. Tabitha's deceptively young face was stone, and Atlas' hard features rested in less sinister angles. His head lay on Tabitha's shoulder. Bree heated with jealousy at the sight. Breena scanned her surroundings though she knew every inch of the room. Nothing had changed. Taking advantage of the sleeping captors, she moved to uncross her legs and found they were bound to her wrists, which lay in her lap.

Atlas and Tabitha snapped awake at Breena's movement. He crawled toward Breena and got right in her face. "You sit there and listen to me," he growled. Breena stared back at him because fear took her voice. *He's not acting.* "You're going to help me even if it means I have to keep you tied up here until it's over. You *will* choose me, and you *will* make this illusion. I've got fifty people back home waiting to ensure you follow through."

"Atlas, you're acting crazy. What has Tabitha turned you into?"

"She has made me stronger, smarter, and she has shown me how weak my love for you made me."

"Apparently you never loved me," Breena yelled. A hurt look flashed across Atlas' face and Tabitha laughed in the background.

"Don't be silly. It was never about love. The distance had made his loyalty to me fade. My influence is much stronger in person, don't you think? He was simply starting to succumb to you. Can you believe that? You, not even a fully realized queen. Unfortunately for him, he did genuinely love you. Isn't that right, Atlas? I didn't realize when I first sent him to you in person that he would be unable of making you love him without himself falling in love. Hard to believe he was your chosen. What a weakling."

Keep playing into her hands and this will end exactly how it's supposed to. "Don't talk about him like that! Can't you see how hard he's working to please both of us at once?"

"Oh, I very much can see. He was working to please you very hard. Ultimately, though, his duty is to me until I'm gone, your chosen or not, so he offered up all sorts of details about your opinion of my plan. It only took a kiss to convince him to tell. Is he that easy with you?"

He's just a pawn. Don't lose it.

Atlas battled the emotion off his face. Inside, he fought the compulsion to lash out at Breena, a side-effect of Tabitha's control, but the drive to obey didn't reach his heart, and he felt like drowning in his guilt for betraying Breena.

Tabitha reclined in the tight space. "Ah, it was a weak kiss on his part, though. I wasn't able to break him of his attachment to you. Now, because of his feelings for you, he's not strong enough to accomplish his part after all this is over."

Breena couldn't keep the inquisitive look off her face.

"Surely you didn't think you were his only responsibility. As a chosen, it's his job to help you produce an heir and then complete the crossing ceremony. He didn't tell you about it because he's too weak with love to go through with it. He doesn't want to leave you."

Atlas wore a miserable expression. His eyes begged Tabitha not to say any more even though his mouth would never allow him to say as much.

"The crossing ceremony is completed after he has given you an heir. On the day of birth, he must descend into the pit of Gehenna to allow his body to die."

"I don't want him to die. Why can't he stay with me?"

"Queens do not permit chosen to interfere in the ruling of Gehenna, and that includes family affairs. Remember, he's not family. I'm surprised that you're surprised. You must have known at least instinctually. You even said he was to be consumed, that he's a means, a pawn."

"That is *not* what I meant." *But it does help.* Breena tried to wipe at the tears rolling down her cheeks with her shoulder.

"But, enough about that. Back to the plan. On the Summer Solstice, I will show the world a great Eye-Opener. With your help, your illusion, we will flood the coasts of the world. Minimal damage will come to pass in reality. But—" at this Tabitha grinned widely, "—witnesses will see their homes destroyed, their countries in crisis, and no end in sight. Millions of people will begin to believe that their God has forsaken them and gone back on his word. After all, it was promised that a global flood would never happen again. The world will see their beliefs contradicted before their eyes. Imagine. Washington, D.C., Moscow, Dubai, the Sahara Desert, all under water. How beautiful."

Atlas cut in unable to resist Tabitha's prompting glare. "With the help of those I've been recruiting from the hotline, I will usher the heartbroken, religiously displaced into a time of chaos. Things often get messier before they get better. The recruits will find their happiness by stripping away the constructs that have governed them and held them back for so long. Those who come willingly will find favorable places in her ranks. Those who fight will be the toilers; they'll struggle for happiness they might never find. It's not much different from how things are now. So, you may think I'm upsetting the balance, but really, I'm just maintaining the status quo with some flair. When the change has been made and the world is headless, the flood waters will recede and the illusion will dissolve."

"I know all of that! That has been the plan from the beginning. What do you think I've been here practicing for? But what happens when the illusion breaks and everyone sees that it was fake? No one will follow you after a deception like that." Breena was going to gesture violently toward Tabitha, but she was still bound, and the ropes bit into her skin. The pain kept her mind clear. *Breena, you have to be more convincing.*

"Finally letting me hear your criticisms, now? See? This is nice, open mother-daughter dialogue."

Breena bit her tongue. *Tabitha doesn't know about my plan, only that I dislike hers. She's trying to get me to slip up.*

Atlas continued to explain. "This will not be a quick process. By the time you drop the illusion and let the waters go back to sea, the change will be complete."

Tabitha butted in. "Everyone will expect the waters to recede by that point. The illusion is meant to seem real. It's for our own consciences, well, yours and your fragile little chosen, that we don't kill millions of people, that we are creating the *image* of floods rather than real ones."

"You two act like you're invincible. You're fading. You couldn't make real floods if you wanted to—not if you need me to make these illusions, and definitely not if you've been recruiting others to help. What, are you cobbling together a replacement for yourself out of a bunch of inferior pieces?"

Atlas spat at her. "You have no clue what I'm capable of. I could destroy this world with the things she has taught me. But I'm after happiness, not more death and pain."

"Then why bring in this happiness with what *appears* to be death and loss and pain?"

"Because these things motivate people."

"Like you?"

"I suppose. Perfection can be messy."

"And what's wrong with my friends? You said they were spending a lot of time at the hospital."

Atlas drew back from Breena and leaned against the wall. He folded his arms behind his head and lounged there like everything occurring was absolutely normal. "*You're* the one in the hospital, my love."

Breena flinched.

"You've been in another one of your fantastic sleep comas for almost four months."

"*Four months?* Why didn't you tell me so much time had passed? Why didn't you tell me?"

"I thought it was intentional."

Breena gaped.

"You didn't want to go back. You found *your* happiness. I wasn't going to stop you."

"My happiness? You and this wicked bitch are holding me hostage in an illusion within another plane, and you let me stay so long I can't feel my way back to my body. What about this is happy?"

"Admit it, Breena. You followed me into that illusion and you had everything you wanted. Better yet, you buried yourself in that illusion. You came to *me* and told me you wanted to help. Back home, you're lying in a hospital bed, pissing through a tube, wasting away your senior year of high school, and worrying everyone who loves you because *you chose to help me.*"

Breena shook her head frantically. *I wasn't supposed to be gone so long. How do I wake up?*

Tabitha had gone downstairs, which Breena considered an advantage. She could take Atlas, who was apparently weak with love.

Shuffling her wrists back and forth, Breena loosened the ties. Atlas looked ready to call Tabitha for back-up, but Breena put on her best "I'm sorry" pout and scooched over to him.

"You're right. I just wanted to be with you. I'm sorry. I'll help you, okay? Just make Tabitha leave, please."

Atlas relaxed into Breena's body, smelling her hair deeply. "I knew you'd come around. I can't do this without you. I hate serving Tabitha, but I physically cannot resist with her present. It's like there's a trampoline in my mind and both of you are jumping, and sometimes I roll to one side and sometimes to the other, but either way I can't stand unless you're both still. And she will never still. I'm sorry about how I yelled at you earlier. That was her talking. I'm not willing to give you up. Tabitha... she wants me for herself, but I just can't stomach that forked tongue of hers."

Breena reared back, appalled. "What?"

"Jokes, jokes."

"Are they?"

There's one thing Tabitha got right; Atlas is mush. I can't believe how easily his guard comes down when she's out of the room. Breena leaned in for a kiss and could see the illusion wavering in her peripheral vision. Tracing Atlas' jawline, it shook more. The vibrations Atlas trained her to look for were obvious, now, and she reached out with her mind and grabbed them. Bending with everything she had, she heard the tell-tale splitting sound. Cold air poured over them as the cottage illusion, and her restraints, broke apart. Soon enough, she was back on the sidewalk at the beach.

Tabitha, dropping out of the image of the cottage, hit the concrete and jogged toward them. Atlas looked between both women, their compelling natures tearing at him. He dropped to his knees, holding his head.

Breena grabbed Atlas by the collar. "Play along." *He'll have no choice once Tabitha's beside him.* With all the strength she could muster, she shoved Atlas back onto the cement with both palms to his chest. He hit the ground, head bouncing off of it, clutching at his shirt. Two scorched handprints sizzled against his skin. Breena stood up and ran.

In the lavish hotel room, the eerie calm caused her ears to ring. She palmed the fancy letter-opener from the desk and slipped off her shoes. *Not as sharp as it looks like it should be.* She gripped the handle in proper form for knife fighting, just in case, and soundlessly tiptoed to the bathroom. A hot flash of adrenaline took her breath as she rounded the corner of the door jamb. In Breena's intense state, the robe hanging on its hook might as well have been Tabitha. Bree's hands tingled. As the fighting instinct of her adrenaline wore off, her stomach cramped. *Breathe.*

No one's here. Good. Breena opened one of the cabinets in the excessive kitchen and grabbed a crystal champagne flute. After living in her own creation so long, she couldn't find the vibrations of the image needed to break it apart. Because of the unity she had gained with the scenery, Bree's only option to go back, to snap out of her comatose sleep, was to bring her created body near death. She smashed the glass on the floor, grabbed a piece, and sat on the edge of the bed with it. *This was always the plan. You knew you would have to do this to get Atlas to break. Now, you need to do it to escape, too. It's necessary. It won't hurt. No, it doesn't matter if it does. Do it!* Holding her breath, Breena slid the shard swiftly from wrist to elbow on both arms.

Breena sat on the edge of her bed, arms in her lap, watching her jeans and the bedspread darken. *Don't scream.* Despite the blood loss, Bree knew the process wasn't moving fast enough. *They're coming.* She tugged her shirt over her head, smearing red across it and her face in the process. Laying back, glass fragment still in hand, she sliced an angry diagonal from shoulder to hip. This time, she screamed. The physical trauma finally sent her soul frantically seeking out her physical form to shield itself from the death of her second self. *Perfection is messy.*

"Jordan?" *I can hear his voice.* An inky void engulfed Breena, but a faint glow in the distance illuminated her hands enough to see the somewhat translucent grey gel that coated them. She stepped in the direction of the light. The substance wasn't just on her hands. It completely surrounded her. She swam through the void, through something like gelatin two hours shy of setting or sunburn aloe.

"Jordan, where are you?"

The sound of his laugh crept toward her from the glowing end of the dark world. She pushed toward it, swimming her arms in front of her like a frog. Breena knew she was moving, though the light never got closer.

"Breena, I'm not ready for you to go."

She heard those words as if they were said directly into her ear. She was about to call out for Jordan another time when the viscous world transformed. Bree watched from above as Atlas cradled her bloody body on the hotel bed, forehead to forehead. *See? Perfection.* Immediately after registering the sight, it morphed another time, Jordan replacing Atlas in the scene. Jordan looked up at the ceiling, then, directly at Breena's spying presence. His eyes were missing, just two black holes in his head, but they saw her. He hissed, revealing a thin snake's tongue.

Breena tried to scream, but her soul rocketed back into her body before the sound escaped. Once more, she heard Jordan talking into her ear.

Chapter 26

Jordan sat on Breena's hospital bed, stroking her hair. The others were in the cafeteria. He couldn't eat. "Breena, you've been asleep so long. Are you going to wake up? You have to wake up. I know I haven't been very understanding, but who could be? People don't just break reality every day. Here you are, sleeping away your hurt and you've left me here, all of us here, to feel it for you."

He stood, moving to pace around the room. The familiar dread of an impending emotional purge pressed out from inside his chest. "You're selfish. And I love you anyway. You make me feel like I'm crazy. When you live one way, with one belief about the world, for so long, it's hard to immediately come to terms with this notion that we can recreate what we see, that we can shape the world around us to fit our whims. You're playing God, and you're playing *with* the devil. You think you know Atlas. Do you really?" He screwed his fist up in his hair.

"If you did, how would he be able to hurt us so many times? Do you even try to protect yourself? He says a couple charismatic words to you in a grocery store and boom, you're his? I wish you'd grow up. I hope you can hear me in there. I kind of don't, too. But you should know how hard it's been to stay around, believe you, trust you when all you say and do somehow revolves around him. Do you even realize you're doing it? I see it when that look washes over your face, that vacant way your eyes start looking at something that's not there. Are you watching the memories play out right in front of you, between us, over me?"

His voice rose among the steady beeping of the pulse ox machine. "Stop wearing your pain like some kind of veil that keeps the world just out of reach. You can still see all of us out here. We're here. Live among us. I could make you smile again. But you have to wake up, first."

At the knock on the door, Jordan bit down on his anger and opened it. Letting the group in, he turned back to Breena. "Bree, the doctor's here. If you won't wake up for me, wake up for him this time." *You're good at doing things for other guys.*

Lexa wrapped an arm around Jordan's shoulder. "You Ok? We heard you yelling."

If there had been any color left in Jordan's face, it would have drained then.

"Don't worry. I couldn't tell what you were saying."

All he could do was nod at her. Lexa, Jordan, and Lilly mirrored the tableau from months earlier, standing around Breena's hospital bed with concern. Ari, too infatuated with Linda to pry the phone from his hands, texted in the hall.

The doctor stood with his back toward Breena, arms crossed. "As I've mentioned many times before, this was not an overdose, either. In all likelihood, her first episode in London was not an overdose. Looking at her charts from St. Barts, it's apparent that there were drugs in her system at the time. It's completely possible that what looked like an overdose was truly the drugs, a large amount, but not enough to OD, serving their purposes in making her sleep, and in turn waking her disorder from dormancy."

Lexa cracked her knuckles. "If it's not drug related, what is it?"

"She's still in a deep sleep. Her sleep cycles are still normal. It's as if she's sleeping for the evening. A very long evening. I've got a diagnosis, but I'm sorry to report that it does not come with a cure. Sleeping Beauty Syndrome."

"What?" The expression on Lexa's face changed for the first time in days from depressed to unimpressed.

"That's not a real thing." Jordan didn't bother moving away from Breena's ear as he yelled. He turned to Breena. "I wish you could hear this."

"I assure you it is real."

"Is that like narcolepsy?" Lilly interceded on the group's behalf, keeping her typical investigative wits about her.

"Well, yes, in that is also a sleep disorder, but that is the only relation. We don't know what causes this or how to fix it. The good news is most patients grow out of it in eight to twelve years."

Lilly squeezed her head between her hands.

****

"Dammit, dammit, dammit!" Atlas shouted over Breena's body. He stooped to check her breathing, but he already knew what she had done. He yelled again—the tiny slivers of glass on the floor vibrated and danced at the sound.

Tabitha swooped in and landed in her human form beside Atlas. She clicked her tongue. "Look what you've done." Atlas looked over at Tabitha with stricken eyes. Tabitha examined her cuticles with blasé scrutiny. She gave even less attention to the blood that meandered nearer to her feet.

As if on Breena's cue, Atlas erupted. "This is your fault!" Inches away from Tabitha's face, he raised his hand to her, knowing he couldn't actually strike her, and she calmly brought it back to his side. She knew, too.

"Don't forget that you're in a contract with me, I am your superior, your *queen*, and you must respect me. Think very carefully before you act."

Desperation overtook Atlas. In the sudden, jerky movements of a man who had just lost everything, he turned his back on Tabitha, scooped bloody Breena up in his arms, and shattered the illusion to arrive back in the clearing.

He dropped to his knees and held Breena close to his chest. His attempts at resurrecting her started with a low chant of unintelligible syllables, desperate magic he didn't even believe in. Unsuccessful, he rocked forward and back, still holding her. His eyes squeezed shut, but it didn't block out the knowledge that her death in the illusory world meant she could never return to the illusions, and he would never find her in her dreams again.

"I will take Tabitha down. She owes me a life and she owes me my happiness." He fulminated through gritted teeth. "'Don't push her away,' she said. 'Breena won't help unless she loves you,' she said. The price was too high. I can't make her love me without loving her back. Tabitha! Do you see this? I tried being vicious to her. My love never changed. This is what vicious gets me. Are you happy, now?"

It was the ideal moment of rage Breena had hoped for. The last of her awareness slipped away.

Tabitha watched him from her perch on top of a pine tree. Hours later, Atlas simmered down. He stopped his ranting and gazed at Breena's now-blue illusory body, his rage the only power keeping her vacant image there. With one last kiss and a tight squeeze, Atlas stood up, letting Breena's hollow replica shatter into sweet-smelling dust. The instant he no longer held her in his heart, the space was filled with bone-splitting energy that transformed his illusory image into the hell-filled monster he always believed he was.

He grew in height and bulk, skin darkening to a ruddy clay color. Atlas' fingernails sharpened into talons, and his eyes blackened. Tabitha materialized in front of him and smiled.

"Why are you smiling, Tabitha? Your sight is really going." Atlas swiped at her face with his massive hand, gouging at her eyes. She screamed.

"I'm not serving you anymore." Using the energy he had transferred from Breena's dying projection into himself, Atlas hoisted the flailing Tabitha into the air. She kicked and beat at his arm. "There's no use in struggling. Don't forget. I've done this before." He knew he couldn't kill her physical body from the astral plane, not even with some of Breena's strength coursing through him, but he could disable her long enough for Vos to take care of the rest of her, the end-game Atlas' only intel on Breena's plan.

While at the hotline with Vos on the day of Tabitha's arrival, Vos had expressed his desire to be free of her. Atlas put him in touch with Linda, who sent him to Lilly. Breena had insured that Lilly was the only person who knew the whole plan. All Atlas knew was that Vos would be the one to finish things. He hadn't realized how soon it would end.

****

The blood and life drained slowly from one Breena and flowed into the other. After the jolt of horror, a whirlwind of colors flew past her in the darkness of that first, wet world, and Breena's waking body greedily pulled its soul home. A sucking sound whooshed past her ears, then, with a jolt, everything stilled.

She heard Lilly grilling the doctor. Warm air brushed across her neck. Someone was on the bed beside her. *Jordan.*

"Well if she's not in danger, can't we take her home to sleep there?"

Breena fluttered her eyes open on the fifth try; they were crusty with sleep and blurry from nonuse. Jordan didn't see her blink at him. He was staring knives at the doctor, who had ignored his question.

Knowing Jordan was by her side, she scanned the room for Atlas. *Wait, why would he be here?* To her horror, she saw Tabitha instead. Tabitha noticed the look of terror on Breena's face for what it was and smirked. *Don't react. Tabitha wouldn't put her abilities on display.*

Breena, arm to arm with Jordan in the small bed, brushed her fingers lightly over his wrist. He glanced over casually—there had been a lot of false alarms—but was inconsolable with relief as she looked clearly back at him. No one noticed Breena's drawn face of panic at Tabitha's presence.

Lexa cried openly, Lilly gripped Breena's leg from her perch on the side of the bed, and the doctor stared on in disbelief. To let Lexa in, Jordan moved to the corner of the room. He wrapped around himself. Breena looked over her mom's shoulder to where he stood, flashing panic and fear about Tabitha in her expression, but Jordan wouldn't look at her.

"Come back over here."

He shook his head. Seeing him for the first time in months, in that condition, demolished the small amount of composure Breena had left. Guilt, fear, and love were a heavy combination to bear.

"Jordan, come here."

He shook his head again. Jordan tried so hard to lock down his anger and sadness. He'd done well the whole time Breena was out. Too well. His coping mechanism was not to cope. Between the extra shifts, the back-breaking workouts, and the meditation practice, he hadn't dealt with any of his fears. Tasks kept his mind busy. With it occupied, his full focus went toward keeping his heart as quiet.

"Why won't you?" Breena lost it when Jordan locked eyes with her. "I'd like to be alone."

Lexa stared at her daughter for a moment, tears flowing. "But we've missed you, honey."

"This is overwhelming. I just need a minute. Please." Breena meant to look at her mother as she pleaded her case, but she found her eyes wandering over to Jordan's bewildered stare.

"Ok, but not long. You've had months to yourself already." Lexa blew her nose.

Mom's right, and I'm sure it was hard on her, but she doesn't realize how traumatic this was for me, that my list of horrible thoughts is growing.

The group made their way through the door. Tabitha sauntered out in front of everyone, walking like her hips would cast a spell and a hospital was an appropriate place to do it. Jordan was last in line. Breena called out quietly for him to stay. He paused for a moment, not looking back, considering leaving her. *He doesn't want to stay.* The idea seemed outrageous to Breena even though she had just asked to be alone. Still not prepared to face his feelings, he turned back into the room and pulled the door behind him.

At Bree's bedside, Jordan was silent, his face, ashen.

"I thought—" and, "I have something—" hung in the sterile-smelling air at the same time. The pair stopped, each waiting for the other to finish their sentences.

Jordan tried again, barely audible. "I thought you were dead." Breena recoiled. "When your mom called me after she found you... you looked dead."

She grabbed his hand. "There's something I have to tell you," Breena managed.

"Shh, I know. I love you, too."

"Jordan, no. I mean, yes. I do love you, but that's not what I have to tell you. Please, don't hate me."

"How could I hate you?"

"I cheated on you with Atlas." Breena paused to allow Jordan's reaction. He closed his eyes. "I should've realized sooner that I missed him and that I *was* trying to replace him with you. Really, it was just the escape that I was missing, but I can only see that now, after everything that's happened."

Jordan stood. "Keep talking, or I'm leaving."

"After the mall the other day, well I guess it wasn't the other day, after I taught you how to project, I went home to take a nap. That part was true, but I didn't get a migraine. I was just excited to start taking down Tabitha, so I made a plan, then tried to sleep. It wasn't my intention to go see Atlas or anyone else, but I ended up there anyway. I thought it was muscle memory, but it could have been Tabitha dragging me in. I don't know. Anyway, she showed up with Atlas and her body guard, and I ended up training with her. I hurt Atlas pretty bad. I tried not to care. I tried to look at him as just a pawn, another way to take Tabitha down, but afterwards, I felt so guilty."

Jordan clenched his jaw.

"When I woke up, I called Linda to help distract Ari, and I filled Lilly in on the plan. I didn't feel like I could tell you because I knew you'd worry."

"Well, I worried anyway."

"I know. I'm sorry. It wasn't my intention to be gone so long. When I went back that night, my goal was to train with Tabitha for as long as I could tolerate it and then come back. But, it was good for a while. Atlas was acting like his old self, and I wanted to be near him. I wanted the diversion and the challenge. The fantasy drew me in and, after a while, wore away at my connection to reality. Whatever made me happy, I could create."

"You're so selfish! Why would you run back to the people who keep hurting you? I just wanted to make you happy, but you keep asking for more pain."

"Because I know I deserve it. I shouldn't be here, and I don't earn any of the love I'm given. Especially yours. Maybe I just wanted to prove that to everyone. I got what I deserved, though. Atlas betrayed me, again, even if it was all Tabitha's doing. He couldn't disobey her orders. I had to kill myself in order to provoke him into going against her. I hope it worked."

Tabitha knocked on the door. "Why is she here?" Breena felt Tabitha watching through the window in the hall. "If everything went as planned, she should be dead."

"She called your cell this morning. Your mom answered and told her we were here. Tabitha felt bad for how she acted in London. Said she wanted to make a better impression and get to know the family."

"How convenient. Vos must not have been able to resist her command."

"I think she knows you started teaching me. She kept staring. I tried to put a protective bubble around you, but you never finished that lesson, and I don't know what the hell I'm doing. I've been practicing, but it's hard to practice when you're just making up what you think comes next."

Tabitha poked her head in. "Everything Ok?"

Breena noticed the black bruise around Tabitha's neck and smiled. "Everything's perfect."

A week later, Breena left the hospital with no restrictions on her activity. All of her tests were consistently normal, and the doctor was pleased to see she hadn't fallen back into a deep sleep. He warned that Sleeping Beauty Syndrome could result in months or years without incident, leading patients to feel they had outgrown the condition, only to be suddenly floored by a week or longer sleep. Lexa nodded diligently as the doctor explained his thoughts on the disorder, while Breena sat in her mandatory hospital discharge wheelchair wondering whether it was her talents that allowed her to sleep and dream for so long or if she really had a syndrome. *What if none of it's real? What if it's always been the disease?*

Since her confession, Jordan flipped between relief and rage at the drop of a hat. It made him mad that he had allowed anything between them to progress, and it made him mad that he was mad. In one moment, he felt guilty for being unable to just be thankful she was awake again, and in the next, he felt stupid for caring about her well-being at all. The meditation didn't help like he read it was supposed to. Instead of finding peace, or relaxation, or a blissful moment of silence and emptiness, finding his center meant stewing on his frustrations. In the week since her release, they had practiced every day at her house. Lexa was still in a stage of hyper-vigilance and didn't want Breena going too many places.

Breena tried her best to power through Jordan's resistance toward her, arguing the necessity of the exercises now that Tabitha was in town. He did his best, but it wasn't enough, and, for a moment, he understood how Breena viewed herself. Then, he got angry again, not fully ready to empathize with her. On Friday night, Jordan, despite himself, picked Breena up for dinner and a movie.

While she primped, if the one stroke of a brush and hole-less jeans could be considered primping, Ari knocked on her bedroom door. She finished dressing and let him in. True to custom, he made himself right at home on her bed.

"I got a date with Linda. Finally sealed the deal."

She exhaled. Breena hadn't been in touch with Linda since the night she gave her Ari's and Atlas' numbers. *I'm so glad something is going as planned.* "Congrats. See, I told you if you were kind and supportive she might genuinely like you."

"Yeah, I'm infectious like that."

"So, a date, huh? How are you going to make that happen? Is she still in London?"

"Promise you won't rat me out? You keep my secret and I'll forgive your pill debt."

Wasn't going to give you more anyway. "Sure."

"We're going to go on a cruise together."

"A what? No way."

"You can't stop us. Just because you slept through my birthday doesn't mean it didn't happen. I'm a free man. You still owe me a present, by the way."

"I don't care that you're running off with her. I care that you chose a cruise!" *Of all things to choose, Linda.* "You know, I heard cruises are really dangerous this time of year. Rough waters. Maybe you should go somewhere else."

"Whatevs." Ari left before she could think of anything more convincing to say to him.

"Well, what if you get in a fight? I mean, you don't really know her. You'll be stuck out there in the middle of the ocean with her."

Lexa called from the kitchen. "Jordan's here!"

Outside, he held Breena's hand as she descended the steps, then handed her a bouquet of grocery store roses. They kissed and walked to the car.

"Jordan, thank you for all this." *He's so tense.*

"Of course. Only the best."

"But I haven't given you the best." Tears welled up in Breena's eyes. "I haven't treated you well at all. You deserve so much better."

"Don't do this tonight, Bree. I've told you, your past and your mistakes are your business. Plus, Atlas is a manipulator. I don't totally blame you for what happened. I just want to help you."

"Let's stay at your house after the movie."

"Sure. I don't sleep well anymore either."

The movie was a dud, and neither could focus, so they snuck out forty-five minutes in. Breena's mind wandered on their drive home. *I'm surprised Atlas hasn't come looking for me. He's probably playing lap dog to Tabitha now that she's in town. It's weird that neither of them has come to see me since the hospital, not in person or in sleep. Fine by me. I'll go back to finish her off, and that will be the end of it.* "That's surprising."

"What?"

"That your parents are home."

"Oh, actually, that's the new trend. They were here a lot while you were in the hospital. Whoever Mom was seeing in Chicago must have dumped her. She hasn't traveled in a while. Dad's company is trying to reduce travel expenses, so they've been doing a lot more teleconferences."

"Your mom was cheating on your dad?" *Is that why he's so tolerant of me? He thinks it's normal?*

"I don't know for sure, but it would make sense. It doesn't matter, though. My parents are more like a business arrangement than a couple."

"How romantic." *Don't judge.*

In his room together for the first time in nearly five months, Breena looked stiff and uncomfortable, her last memory of being there with him playing on repeat. *I'm not here for that.*

"Ok. Show me what you've mastered."

"How about you show me what you've mastered first. You said you learned things only queens can do."

"I can't. They're too dangerous. I don't want to burn you again, and truthfully, I didn't learn anything from her that wasn't meant to be harmful in some way. She's the worst. Likes to rule through fear and pain."

"I can take it."

"No. But, I suppose I do owe you something, so I'll show you what I was working on in my own time, before the episode. It has nothing to do with Tabitha—I don't even know if it's something she can do—so I hope to use it against her." Breena called an image of herself in full armor to mind. Jordan stared in anticipation. Breena struggled to hold the picture in the forefront of her consciousness, and fought even more to find its energy. *I can't even find my own energy.*

Jordan couldn't tell that she was having difficulty creating the illusion, and he was too unskilled to notice that it took her much longer than usual to focus. Breena, however, was succumbing to her panic as she struggled unsuccessfully to project her vibrations into the room around her. *It's just nerves. Focus.* It didn't matter how many positive ways she mentally cheered herself on. Breena couldn't do it anymore.

"Jordan, it's gone." Her hands shook and she held her breath to keep back sobs. Living in the illusion for so many months had made that world a second home, a great escape from normal life, a place to find her true happiness. She hated to admit that Atlas had been right about her happiness. Breena couldn't stand that Tabitha's plan might actually, in some twisted way, offer that same relief to everyone. The realization that she, for some reason, couldn't go back there terrified her.

"Calm down, Bree. It's probably just nerves. So much happened to you last time you... crossed over? Illuded? What do you call it, exactly?"

"I don't have a fancy name for it. Can we focus on the problem right now?"

"Sorry, just curious. Why don't we sleep? You can try again tomorrow."

"I don't think I should stay. Sorry. Will you take me home?" Her eyes spoke the fear and loss her mouth didn't.

Jordan nodded. He wasn't surprised that Breena couldn't execute the shift since it had been months since she had done anything new, but it didn't feel so momentary to her. There had been a wall around her vibrations. She couldn't reach out at all to the world around her. As she buckled her seatbelt, Bree wondered if she could even dream anymore.

For the next two weeks, Jordan progressed to shifting appearances of objects already present and creating energy barriers that Breena, lacking any of her own energy exchange abilities, couldn't breech. Breena's failure became Jordan's success. Her weakness spurred him on to work harder, concentrate better, and to surpass her expectations. *This is what he's like when he's out of my shadow.* Breena tried to break through the big black wall around her psyche, but grew despondent. The block remained. With increasing certainty, she believed it was permanent.

Chapter 27

"May I have a restroom pass, please?"

"En Francais."

"Est-ce que je peux aller aux WC, s'il vous plaît?"

"Oui. Tu as dix minutes."

Running out of French class, Breena barged into the bathroom.

"Breena! Fancy meeting you here!"

"Get out, Kelly."

"I'm not done washing. Thirty seconds to get the nasty doody particles—"

"Kelly! Out!" Breena's hands curled into tight fists, her knuckles popping under the pressure. "Go. Before I say something mean."

Kelly flicked the water from her hands, spattering the mirror. She did a little dance in front of the door, debating whether to take the time to get a paper towel as a barrier for the door handle or to hurry up and get out. Breena glared, and Kelly pulled violently on the heavy door with just her pinky finger until it opened wide enough for her to slip out.

"Finally." Bree locked herself in the restroom, turning the deadbolt on the main door so no classmates or hall monitors would interrupt. Out of ideas to solve her projection paralysis, and too distracted by the missing part of her, Breena got desperate and called Atlas.

"Hello?"

Breena was silent for a second. Her breath caught, her heart skipped a beat, and her belly flopped at his gentle tone. "Hi," she muttered. "It's me."

Breena heard a clamber of papers and what she imagined was a jar of pens fall to the ground amidst a low mutter of curses from Atlas' end. "Why did you call me?"

"You know exactly why," Breena fumed.

"You miss me?" he chuckled in a low voice.

"Why can't I project anymore, Atlas?" Breena screamed through the phone. The attack echoed in the empty restroom. Atlas laughed. "You don't want anything to do with me. I was just a pawn in your plan."

"Now you know how I felt."

"You're a lot like your mother," he sneered. "Why should I answer you?" Atlas had no affection left for Breena. His power was complete without her. Had he believed that accepting his solitary position in the world would give him all he needed, he would have never searched so long for someone to fulfill him, to help him, to share his dreams and goals.

"Because I need it." Breena played at meekness hoping to stir some concern.

Silence issued for a moment. Breena almost hung up.

"You died."

"Excuse me?" *That's what Jordan said.*

"At the beach when you slit your wrists, you died there. You severed your tie with that world. That's why you can't get back."

But that means Tabitha is in the same boat judging by those bruises. If she's no better off than me, she can't go forward with the storms. She put Atlas on speaker and texted Linda:

"No need to go on that cruise. Stay put for now."

Atlas continued. "And when you severed that tie, I severed my tie with you—I let you go. Do you know what happened when I did that? I got stronger, just like Tabitha said I would, and I suppose also thanks to the energy I took from your lifeless image. It was thrilling, strangling her. But, unlike you, I'm done with the pain and fighting. Happiness is all I was ever after. I wonder though, why would you want to go back?"

Play to his ego. "That's none of your business. How can I reconnect with that part of myself?"

"If you'd like to know how to get back, I'd like to know why you want to."

"I miss it. You were right about my happiness. I love the freedom, the belonging." *He loves to be right.*

Atlas chuckled. "I expected more obstinacy from you. What would you do to have your connection back?"

Tabitha's still alive. "Anything," Breena breathed into the phone barely audible.

They met at a coffee shop just outside of town. Breena had canceled plans with Jordan to meet Atlas, but there was no guilt gnawing at her gut. Her desperation was full-fledged, a replacement for the pills, as if it hadn't been when she went back to help Atlas months ago. He waited for her in a cozy booth far from the door. She regretted to acknowledge that his form-fitting black shirt and low-slung jeans still did it for her, but her heart skipped a beat despite her reticence. She slid into the banquette; he smiled at her. It seemed genuine on the surface, but she knew nothing about him was. His coldness on the phone gave her no hope for the impending conversation. Breena wondered what he wanted out of this meeting.

Each said a polite hello, but Breena was the first to cut through the niceties. "What do I do to get through the wall?"

"Go to hell."

"Already there, thank you. Now, tell me."

"I just did. You'll have to go. To. Hell."

Breena stared, slack-jawed, her pulse rushing in her ears. *He's serious.* "How am I supposed to do that?"

"Finish what you started. Kill Tabitha and ascend the throne. But, you're on your own. I'm finished, as I've said."

"I don't *need* your help. I'm stronger than I ever was before all of your drama dragged me down."

Atlas coughed a laugh into his coffee. "Stronger than ever? You can't even project."

"I don't need to. I have Jordan for that."

"You're kidding. He's less trained than a puppy. That will never work."

"It has to, and if Vos is any indication, it's a good thing Jordan's not like us, or he'd be susceptible to Tabitha just like you two. Besides. I heard from Linda that Tabitha can't return either. You served your purpose well. I only need to kill her here. It should be easy. She's lost her sight and her astral self."

"Good luck getting past Vos."

****

The guilt of blowing Jordan off for Atlas hit her as Jordan bounded down the stairs.

"I'm so glad you're here."

"Sorry about earlier. Had some homework I didn't realize I hadn't done."

"You want some cake?"

"Um, sure." Breena relied on Jordan's ability to let go of disappointments easily. Even so, he hadn't fully forgiven Breena for cheating. They hadn't spent the night with one another since.

"Sit; I'll bring you a slice," Jordan ordered.

Breena took her favorite corner seat at the end of the couch and waited.

A few minutes later, Jordan walked in with a cake stand covered in a mound of crumbs. "So, it kind of fell apart when I tried to cut off a piece." He thrust the cake pedestal in front of Breena along with a fork. "We'll share."

Breena laughed at the mess. "Did you try to cut it with a chain saw?"

"Ha. Ha. I used a fork."

"Clearly, that's not any better." Breena took a bite. "Mmm, but it doesn't change the taste." They ate in silence chewing happily and, when the cake was gone, Jordan pulled Breena off the couch.

"Come upstairs with me. I've got something to show you." Jordan flopped down on his bed. Breena followed.

"So show me what it is." She scanned the room for a large box like he'd used in London.

Jordan closed his eyes and, immediately, Breena could feel the vibrations in the room sway around her. Breena clenched her fists. Their conversation on the topic three days earlier had turned into an argument. Jordan was eager to learn, and it flattered her that he valued her insight so much, but admitting to him that, after two weeks, she still couldn't connect to her astral self was embarrassing. Breena yelled at Jordan to back off and stop bugging her about learning the next step. "It's too dangerous, and I don't have the energy to deal with you," she'd hollered. He'd yelled back, releasing the anger and resentment he had been holding since her confession in the hospital. The words "selfish" and "cheater" banged around in Bree's head as she reconsidered his request.

Jordan reached to their surroundings, reading his energy very closely. When he could distinguish himself within his environment's energy, he tried to copy those waves into the more calm space on the other side of the room. The busy waves of his liveliness buzzed and lit up brightly within his mind as he pressed the identical pattern of vibrations into the corner of the room. When he felt the thrumming in that corner give way, he opened his eyes to stare at a mirror image of himself.

Breena jumped off the bed. "Jordan!"

The image flickered.

Both Jordans answered. "I learned something new."

She shook Jordan's shoulders, but her excitement compromised the illusion, so she reigned in her exhilaration.

The Jordans stared at her with looks of awe and adoration that made her squirm. Another pang of guilt lanced through Breena at her betrayal, but she brushed it off as best as she could. *I haven't earned that look.*

"That's incredible," she whispered.

Jordan could only nod. His perfectly formed illusion stared sweetly at the two of them.

"Does he work?"

"If you mean does he act like a person versus just stand wherever I put him, I hope so."

"How did you learn to do this?"

Jordan blushed. "It's lame."

"No, tell me. We can use this to our advantage." *I'm such a user.*

"Well, I was meditating like you taught me, and for once I had pretty good focus, until a thought drifted in. I tried to ignore it, but I kept coming back to it."

"And that thought was?"

"That I wished there were two of me." He didn't mention the part about having one self to love her and one self to hate her so that he wouldn't feel so conflicted all the time. Even when angry, he was considerate.

"Huh."

"Yeah. I guess that desire was the truest version of me that night, and the energy just kind of peeled off of me. There he was."

"I'm really proud of you."

"Thanks." Breena shook her head. *I will never doubt him again.*

Jordan dropped the double and went to the window. "You hear all that? Must've been a massive accident on the highway. Never heard that many sirens at once."

****

Vos swished the water and spit the pink mess into the sink. Tabitha's violence toward him increased daily since she lost her astral body. The TV blared in the living room. Reports of riots across the world broke into the nightly news she usually watched. He wondered for a moment if she only watched the news in hopes of seeing her malice played out on screen. Most major crimes on TV were due to her influence on the world.

"Vos, get out here! It's starting."

Miserable, but obedient, he trudged down the hall. On the screen, hundreds of people rushed a government building. Some waved flags with the anarchy symbol on it, while others held posters depicting the headless horseman. Those not part of the vicious pep-squad set fire to the huge wooden doors and smashed windows with Molotov cocktails.

The footage shifted to another part of the world where masked demonstrators had a row of men, council members according to the ticker at the bottom of the screen, hog-tied in the street.

"Look, Vos. We did it. People are so willing to flock to a cause they know nothing about that they join in on the chaos just because others are. It's times like these I'm thankful for the simple-minded nature of humans. All I had to do was get my recruits to start making a scene and look. Entire cities are falling." She whirled around and kissed Vos. He flinched away, his split lip opening up again, but she held his face to hers until she was satisfied.

"Vos, go make sure the doors are locked. It won't be safe out tonight."

****

Breena and Jordan clicked on the TV after devouring the entire cake. Using so much energy made Jordan ravenous, and coping with her perceived inadequacies made Breena hungry for distraction.

"We're bringing you live footage from Detroit right now that shows the massive rioting that broke out about three hours ago, just as the sun was beginning to set. It's not clear what brought about the fights and chaos, but it is certain to get worse, as nighttime will make it more difficult for authorities to locate key suspects and get the situation under control. Currently, there are fires across the city, many of which seem purposefully targeted at government and religious facilities. Here in Grayling, additional incidents have been reported, and though not to the scale of Detroit, the damage is already costly. Authorities advise everyone to stay indoors tonight and into tomorrow as they work to assess the situation. We'll bring you more information as details come in."

Breena grabbed Jordan's arm. "That's Tabitha's doing. She failed at the first step of her plan, so she just dove right in with the next one."

"Isn't that a good thing? Or at least better than it could have been?"

"I guess, but this is still going to get very ugly unless we can stop her soon."

****

As Tabitha reveled in the sight of the Statue of Liberty in flames, Parliament surrounded by the furious masses, and the Sacre Coeur pummeled with cannon fire, the last she was particularly proud of, as it meant the French Navy itself had succumbed to her suggestion, Jordan and Breena snuck around to the back of Tabitha's house.

"What are we doing when we get in there? This was rash. We don't have a plan!"

"Shh. It's fine. I'll go in and you'll send your double after me. You stay out here where it's safe. I'll get to Vos and see if I can't persuade him to help." *I probably don't have any of that power left.* "We'll tie her up somewhere and burn the place down. It will look like riot damage."

Please, God, let this work. I have no energy, no weapons, and no combat training. I guess that leaves me with a death-wish. I know it's not my place to ask you for help, but it's in your best interest to help me since I'm only doing this to preserve the balance. You couldn't possibly allow this to continue, could you? Oh, and if Atlas is in there, spare him.

Breena kissed Jordan and broke the window on the back door. She reached in and unlocked it with ease. *So far so good.* The back entrance opened into the laundry room. Thankful to find that the door into the rest of the house was closed, Breena took a moment to search for a weapon. There was a tool box on the floor beside the dryer. She seized a long wrench and a hammer. *Keep the hammer.* She shoved a box cutter into her pocket.

Creeping into the kitchen from the laundry room, she froze at the sight of Vos' enormous back at the refrigerator. He closed the door and saw her as he turned around. Breena put a finger to her lips and prayed she was queen enough for him to at least stay quiet. Vos exhaled heavily. *He looks relieved to see me. This is good.* Pushing her luck a little more, Bree motioned for him to come over to her. She pulled him back into the laundry room. Tabitha's pleased laughter peeled in the other room. Breena's skin crawled.

"Vos. I need your help." *Don't ask for his help, demand it.* "Vos, you're going to help me kill Tabitha. This disorder can't continue. I need to kill her so I can become queen. *Your* queen. Do you understand?"

"You *are* my queen."

No time to be emotional. Thank him later. "I need you to tie her up or something."

"There's a cage in the bedroom."

"What?"

Vos nodded.

"Well that's convenient. Lock her up, then. I'll do the rest."

Breena stayed behind as Vos went into the living room with the hammer.

"Vos, what are you doing with that?"

"The picture behind you is crooked. I thought I'd fix it for you." He scooted the couch from the wall with Tabitha still on it and walked behind. Vos fiddled with the picture frame until Tabitha resumed her entertainment. Then, he struck her over the head with the hammer. She slumped to the side, and he scooped her up.

Breena walked into the living room, a bit disappointed. "That was too easy."

When Tabitha came to, Vos, the Jordans, and Breena were gathered around the cage. Tabitha grinned, knowing exactly what was going on.

"Should've gone back to London."

Breena smiled. "I'm so glad you didn't. Your sight is gone. It's my turn."

"What are you going to do about it?"

"I'm going to burn this place to the ground with you in it."

Tabitha howled with laughter. "Burn? You're going to burn it? Me, the queen of hell? You do know there's fire there, right? We're not susceptible to fire, daughter."

Breena tried to appear nonplussed, but she was furious with herself for not knowing such a simple fact about her true nature. *It makes sense, too, that I survived and Dad died.* A new realization rocked her. *Unless he was Tabitha's chosen and isn't dead dead, but has crossed into the pit. Of course he was. The same will happen to my heirs, to Atlas. I can't...* Tabitha chuckled darkly in the corner. *Not now, Breena.* Thinking on her feet, Breena snatched the key from Vos and let herself into the cage, pulling the door behind her.

"Breena, no!" Jordan dashed forward.

"Stop, Jordan. It's fine." She flung the key out of the enclosure. "Hold on to that. Let me out when I'm done. Not before, or she'll get out, too." She turned to Tabitha. "I'll just have to do this myself. Face to face."

"You won't survive."

"As long as you don't, that's fine." She looked back at Vos. "Whether I die or not, she does not get out. Understand?"

He nodded, and Jordan threw himself at the cage.

"Hold him back."

Vos hauled Jordan away from the enclosure and pinned his arms behind his back.

Breena approached Tabitha. "First one dead loses." She shot forward, grabbing Tabitha around her already-battered throat and shoving her into the metal bars. "You know, I always wondered if I could out-queen you, make you bend to my will." She looked Tabitha in the eyes. Breena recognized the fire roiling beneath the surface.

Having no defense without Vos, Tabitha tried a new tactic. "Oh, please, Breena. You wouldn't do this to your mother. It's the filthiest way of ascending the throne. The whole court will look down on you. Don't embarrass the family like this."

"Embarrass the family? You're not my family. I don't know those people. I don't care if they think I'm shameful. They're probably more ashamed of you, too self-indulgent to realize you've gone overboard. What does God do to his counterparts when they break their promises to him? You think it's as simple as going through the crossing and giving up your body to live in the pit? I highly doubt it. He would never send you home as punishment.

That's no lesson." Breena laughed as an image crossed her mind. "I bet he'd make you an angel, bound to serve good for the rest of your existence. You know what they say about keeping enemies closest. He'd have an eye on you for eternity."

Tabitha's eyes screamed even though Breena was choking her too hard for sound to escape.

"And, while that sounds like a just punishment, I guess I am a little like you after all. I'd rather just have you out of my way." Breena pulled on the energy of the others in the room to access the fire in her hands. "Now, I know you said fire was ineffective, but, I wonder if that's all fire, or just ones burning in the physical world." She heated her hands like so many times before with a fire that came from something other than rapid oxidation and the physics of Earth. It was ancient, fluid, and satisfying. Instead of letting it spread across the skin and engulf her, Breena pushed flaming energy into Tabitha's body. Tabitha hung on to Breena's wrists, trying to pry her away. "This is what you like, right, Tabitha? Evil and chaos. Pain. Here. You can have all of my evil. *You* are the field. Die knowing you were consumed by what you loved so much. Your dear daughter."

Tabitha didn't scream like Jordan expected she would. It was a different kind of burning, he supposed. One more like drowning. Jordan watched in shock as the smile on Tabitha's face faded, her hands fell from Breena's wrists, and she slumped to the ground. Beside him, Vos kneeled for Breena, and Breena fell with her mother, drained of all energy, wrists peeling from burns. Breena looked up as she stood, letting Tabitha roll onto the floor with a thud, and saw a man outside the window staring in at them, grinning.

Epilogue

The first two weeks following Tabitha's death wore on as if she was still pulling the strings. The riots had taken on independent lives. She would have loved that, but most developed nations were under martial law, a far cry from Tabitha's vision of an acephalous world. Hundreds of the world's most treasured historical landmarks were gone.

In Grayling, parts of town looked as if a devastating storm had come through after all, assuming a storm smashed cars and windows, destroyed buildings, and downed power lines without any evidence of wind damage. The rioters took care of all of that. After giving up on step one, Tabitha had loosed her recruits on the world anyway.

Those that Linda intercepted were a small fraction of the force, and most of them did as she originally instructed by staying inside and away from the violence. The rest followed Atlas' original instructions even though he was nowhere, leading nothing. Breena was thankful Atlas' recruiting had merely been a farce to keep Tabitha satisfied because they hadn't received any legitimate training to fight, only a message: don't follow that woman; whatever she asks, do the opposite.

In more densely populated parts of the world, the riots raged on. China and India were particularly bad off. Mob mentality prospered everywhere, but especially in those countries with large populations of poor people. Everyone placed their own intentions and meanings on the protests, resulting in factions of rebels asking for different things. The groups brought anarchy as a whole, but even within groups, there was mayhem, people fighting one another for the power to decide what to trash and who to kill next. It wasn't the type of unrest Tabitha had hoped for, but her impact was visible nonetheless. Breena smiled every time she thought about how Tabitha would never get to see what she had done.

Atlas went back to London after the fourth week of rioting. He didn't say goodbye. There was nothing for him to part with.

Tabitha was gone and Breena was a new person, still without her astral connection, but a fully realized queen. The elders wanted both of them, her to ascend, and him to make an heir and cross over. Despite their shaky relationship, Breena was his queen. If she demanded it, he would go, but she'd have to find him first.

****

"Is everything Ok?" Jordan let the flames fall and splash into water around him, then crack into millions of pieces as the illusion faded completely.

"Yeah, but I need to make an appearance at home every now and then. Mom acts like I don't live there anymore."

"Well you don't, really, except that all your stuff is still there."

"That's my point, Jordan. I either need to go home sometimes, or we should move in together for real." Breena said the statement casually, not meant as an actual suggestion, but Jordan practically levitated at the suggestion.

"Yes! Let's get an apartment. How great would that be?"

"Woah, I was just making a point. I don't know if we should do that. I love you and all but..." Breena trailed off. "I should go."

They agreed to postpone the moving in talk, but it wasn't enough to keep Breena there for the night. Since Tabitha's death, Breena kept odd hours. Sleep was even harder to come by without the dreams and without Atlas than it had been with.

Saying goodbye, Breena held on to Jordan tighter than usual and kissed him deeper as well. "In case I don't see you tomorrow." Jordan didn't question her unusually strong display of affection. *Thanks, Jordan.*

When Breena arrived home, her mother was pouring over credit card statements and cell phone bills trying to determine where Ari and Linda were. They had already jumped town by the time Breena sent the text to Linda cancelling her escape orders. Ari left a note on the refrigerator saying he had gone to South Africa with Linda to do humanitarian work, but no evidence suggested that's where they actually went. Breena figured the cruise story was a diversion, too. *Linda's too good at this, but I guess I chose the right person. I'm sure she learned from all that time with Tabitha.* Lexa's tears warped the paper. Bree consoled her as much as she could without letting on that she knew more about the run-away. *Not that I know much at this point. I'm sure they have new phones by now.*

Upstairs, Breena cleared a space on the floor and sat down in her meditation position. Crossing her ankles up over her knees, she tried to focus. Nerves made her breath quake, but she pressed on for hours. After a few hours, she gave up. *I hate when Atlas is right.* While soaking in the tub, she called Atlas. "Ok, I'm ready. What do I need to do to get to hell?"

He chuckled. "Lying, check. Murder, check. Have you coveted your neighbor's wife, yet?"

"Atlas, be serious. It's time I get my connection repaired."

"I thought you didn't want to rule."

"I don't."

"You're so selfish."

"I know."

After a complicated conversation, it came down to a simple answer. All she needed to do was make a call to someone he called R. *A task for tomorrow.*

Breena stayed home from school. She hadn't slept, and her energy was completely gone from trying to repair her connection. *It's not like anything happens during the last two weeks of school anyway.* Jordan called, but she didn't answer. She knew her silence would only worry him more, but there was nothing she could say. *Maybe this time will teach him to stop trusting me.* Instead, she dialed a different number.

"Vos? Come get me."

About the Author

Amanda Marsico is the tea-sipping, cat-cuddling, chocolate-sneaking author of the *Humans In My House* series (middle-grade fiction, book 2 coming Winter 2017); owner of Red Ink Enthusiast, a writing services company; and professor of English and Composition. When she's not swimming in post-it notes, she's crafting, baking, or enjoying the beach.

www.redinkenthusiast.com

Look for book 2 of the *Acephalous* series, Winter 2018.

www.ingramcontent.com/pod-product-compliance
Lightning Source LLC
Chambersburg PA
CBHW020747250626
47155CB00003B/958